Heir in a Year

—

ELIZABETH BEVARLY

HARLEQUIN
SPECIAL
EDITION

HARLEQUIN®
SPECIAL
EDITION™

Recycling programs
for this product may
not exist in your area.

ISBN-13: 978-1-335-72476-2

Heir in a Year

Copyright © 2023 by Elizabeth Bevarly

For questions and comments about the quality of this book,
please contact us at CustomerService@Harlequin.com.

Harlequin Enterprises ULC
22 Adelaide St. West, 41st Floor
Toronto, Ontario M5H 4E3, Canada
www.Harlequin.com

Printed in U.S.A.

Elizabeth Bevarly is the award-winning *New York Times* bestselling author of more than seventy books, novellas and screenplays. Although she has called places like San Juan, Puerto Rico, and Haddonfield, New Jersey, home, she's now happily settled back in her native Kentucky with her husband and son. When she's not writing, she's binge-watching documentaries on Netflix, spending too much time on Reddit or making soup out of whatever she finds in the freezer. Visit her at elizabethbevarly.com for news about current and upcoming projects; book, music and film recommendations; recipes; and lots of other fun stuff.

Books by Elizabeth Bevarly

Harlequin Special Edition

Seasons in Sudbury

Heir in a Year

Lucky Stars

Be Careful What You Wish For
Her Good-Luck Charm
Secret under the Stars

Harlequin Desire

Taming the Prince
Taming the Beastly M.D.
Married to His Business
The Billionaire Gets His Way
My Fair Billionaire
Caught in the Billionaire's Embrace

Visit the Author Profile page
at Harlequin.com for more titles.

For David.

Again.

On account of home renovation never ends.

Can we do the kitchen next?

Chapter One

Haven Moreau sat in the waiting room of the Fifth Avenue office of probate attorney Sterling Crittenden and wondered, not for the first time, why she was there. Although she'd certainly had more than her fair share of legal woes over the years—or, at least, her family had—she'd never heard of Sterling Crittenden. And she certainly never had any business on Fifth Avenue. She barely ever made it off Staten Island these days. But here she sat, in the nicest outfit she'd been able to pull from her closet—a black-and-white houndstooth pencil skirt paired with a sapphire turtleneck and black Eton jacket, all from her favorite thrift store—and she'd been doing it for going on... She quickly checked her phone. Twenty-five minutes? A Fifth Avenue attorney named Sterling Crittenden was running that late? Even the most recent personal injury lawyer her uncle Cecil had retained for his most recent insurance scam was more punctual than that. Anyway, here Haven sat, in her nicest outfit, waiting for…something. She had no idea what.

Outside the windows, a bright blue sky dotted with puffy white clouds belied the fact that it was an unseasonably chilly early October morning. New York City was gradually easing its way into autumn. Already, the trees in her neighborhood were kissed with gold and orange and scarlet—well, as much as they could be, gasping for life as most of them were, thanks to the urban environment to which none of them was suited. Mrs. Bandara at the Sri Lankan bakery up the street had already trotted out her pumpkin spice *helapa*. The return of hockey season was imminent. Let's go, Rangers. Best of all, though, the alley behind her tiny studio apartment had stopped smelling like *Eau de Dumpster de la Ville*. All in all, life was—reasonably—good. Except for the waiting here in confusion and missing a half day of work to do it, she meant.

An efficient-looking young man sitting behind the receptionist's desk, whose nameplate identified him as Mateo Colón, smiled at her reassuringly. "I'm sorry for the delay, Ms. Moreau," he said. "Mr. Crittenden is waiting, too. There's another party we're expecting for your meeting with him who seems to be running a bit late. If that party isn't here by nine thirty, we'll reschedule."

Great. And then she'd have to lose another half day of work. Not that there was a lot of work out there anyway for a Jill-of-all-trades handywoman who was too often dismissed from any home improvement jobs she solicited the minute the potential client saw that she was a "girl"—all twenty-seven years of her—who couldn't possibly know the difference between a hand plane and a mole grip. This despite her having those tools and dozens more in the collection she'd inherited from her father after his death when she was twelve. And in spite of having used them all for years before that, because she'd started tagging along with him on his handyman jobs on the days when she wasn't in school as soon as she was old enough to wield a socket wrench.

Even so, she'd managed to eke out a living since graduating from college, doing something she loved and at which she was very good, thanks to her father's teachings. Maybe the profits for Right at Home, her rehab and renovation business, weren't massive, but at least there were profits these days. Still, the loss of even a half day of work meant skipping lunch for a week. Losing two half days would mean biking it all over Staten Island instead of even taking the bus.

She was staring at her phone, willing the numbers to not turn over from 9:29 to 9:30, when the door to the law office opened and the presumed third party bustled in. The first thing Haven thought when she saw him was of course he would be late. She should be surprised he showed up at all, since abandoning people was the thing Bennett Hadden did best. The second thing she thought was...

Well, she never had the chance to have a second thought, because he turned so that she could see him almost full face, and whatever thoughts she might have had dried up completely because he was even more handsome now than he was the last time she saw him this close up—during her sophomore year in high school. This would have been right around the time he and his cadre of elitist friends and family had a good laugh at her audacity in thinking that Bennett would give her the time of day.

The last person she ever wanted to see again in her life, up close *or* at a distance, was Bennett Hadden, even if family history—both hers and his—would make that impossible. The feud between the Haddens and the Moreaus spanned more than a century, with each generation spewing more vitriol about the other family than any that came before. The Haddens were thieves who stole the Moreaus' fortune. No, the Moreaus were criminals who lost their fortune through a scandal of their own making. The Haddens had no morals. The Moreaus had no souls. The Haddens cheated on their taxes. The Moreaus kited checks. The Haddens kicked puppies. The Moreaus cut in lines. The charges each family had leveled against the other went from the ridiculous to the slanderous, ad nauseum.

And there was no end for it in sight, since the most recent generation of both families, some not even teenagers yet, were being brought up the same way Haven and Bennett had—to loathe and despise everything about each other. Never turn your back on a Hadden, her cousin Dexter once told her, because they'll stick a knife right into it. Never trust a word that comes out of a Hadden's mouth, her aunt Rose added, because it's an outright lie. The only good Hadden, her uncle Desmond always said, was a... Well, there were no good

Haddens. Period. If Haven couldn't keep her distance from a Hadden, her cousin Claudia once told her, then she better keep herself armed.

With Haven, though, where the Haddens were concerned—where Bennett Hadden in particular was concerned—it was personal. Because Bennett Hadden, damn him, had broken her heart.

He turned to close the door behind himself, and when he finally glanced up, it was at the receptionist, not at Haven. He ran a hand roughly through his overly long dark hair, then smoothed it over the jacket of his trendy dark blue suit. Then he shifted, from one hand to the other, the kind of messenger bag that was meant to look fashionably battered and casual but probably had cost him more than her monthly rent and grocery budget combined.

How could he be the third party they had been waiting on? What could she and Bennett possibly have to be party to together? Sure, their families had been embroiled in a bitter legal battle for generations, but they'd never used the services of Fifth Avenue attorney Sterling Crittenden. Certainly, the Haddens could afford him, but last Haven had heard, they'd been employing the services of someone her uncle Desmond called a "frump-battle-axe-witch-harridan," as if it were all one word, so probably not Sterling Crittenden.

"Mr. Hadden, I presume," Mateo Colón said as he stood. "Mr. Crittenden is expecting you. If you and Ms. Moreau will follow me?"

At the *Ms. Moreau*, Bennett snapped around to look at Haven, and for a solid nanosecond, he had the decency to look embarrassed and possibly even ashamed. Nah, just kidding. Haddens didn't know embarrassment *or* shame. They were the most arrogant, most callous, most heartless people to ever exist. It hadn't taken Haven's cousin Nanette to tell her that—even though Nanette had told her that. It was something Haven had witnessed for herself where Bennett was concerned.

As she rose from her seat, she suddenly felt compelled to lift a hand to smooth back her own hair, to ensure it was still neatly tucked into the short, dark blond ponytail she'd bound at her nape that morning. Naturally, it wasn't, because her hair never behaved itself. Hastily, she did her best to stuff a few strands back into the elastic, though why she would bother was beyond her. She didn't care what Bennett thought of her appearance. She didn't. She just wanted to present as professional an image as possible to the first Fifth Avenue attorney she'd ever met, that was all.

Instead of greeting her—why would he?—Bennett just gazed at her in that arrogant, callous, heartless way the Haddens had perfected probably even before Bertie Hadden swindled Winston Moreau out of a fortune in the late nineteenth century. So Haven did her best to gaze back with the grace, dignity and self-respect her mother had always told her was the best revenge where the Haddens were concerned. Then she made sure she cut in front of Bennett to follow Mateo Colón down the hall first, to a big room bisected by a big table and lined with wall-to-wall windows that looked out onto the Flatiron Building across the street.

When Mateo asked them to take a seat, Haven

grabbed the one at the head of the table, just to spite Bennett. Not to be outdone, however, he covered the half-dozen strides it took to fold himself into the chair at the other end. When Sterling Crittenden, a kind-looking man with white hair and dark eyes, dressed in a dazzling double-breasted pinstripe suit, entered a few seconds later, he assessed their positions, shook his head almost imperceptibly and took a seat at the table exactly halfway between them. Mateo, ever the attentive associate, moved to stand to his right, looking supremely comfortable in the position. As Mr. Crittenden sat down, he placed a stack of three navy blue folders on the table in front of himself. They were the kind of folders Haven remembered her mother always stocking up on during back-to-school sales, when she could buy packets of ten at the dollar store. Though Haven was pretty sure that wasn't where Mr. Crittenden had gotten his.

"Good morning," he said to them both, nodding first at Haven, then at Bennett. "I think each of you are familiar with who the other is, but have you ever actually met in person before now?"

At this, it was all Haven could do to stifle the wave of indignation that roared up inside her. Oh yes. They'd met many times. Most of which had ended very badly indeed. Bennett, too, was clearly battling some rancor at his own memories, because when his gaze met hers, even with a mile-long table separating them, it was hot and relentless.

"Oh, Moreau and I have met a time or two," he said crisply.

"Hadden and I went to high school together," Haven

clarified just as coolly. Unable to help herself, she added, "Among other things."

Whereas that last comment seemed to multiply Bennett's animosity, the first part clearly surprised Mr. Crittenden. "Indeed?" he asked. "I knew Mr. Hadden and his family were all Barnaby Prep alumni. He graduated with my grandson, in fact. But I didn't realize you were an alumna, as well, Ms. Moreau. It's an excellent school."

Haven bit back another ripple of resentment at the not-quite-hidden astonishment in the attorney's voice, even though she was sure he meant no ill will toward her. Yeah, nobody realized she was a Barnaby alum, because illiterate blue-collar scum from Staten Island never received full scholarships to tony private academies such as Barnaby. She knew that, because virtually all her classmates had told her so while she was attending, pretty much every day, and all of them had always wondered how she'd *really* managed to gain admission and stay there, always insinuating it must be because of skills her mother—or even she herself—had used with expert knowledge under the headmaster's desk. Evidently, a 4.0 grade point average, twenty hours a week of community service, publishing a critical essay about *His Dark Materials* in a national student publication when she was in sixth grade and captaining her middle-school intramural volleyball team to a state title wasn't enough to qualify her for something like that.

Before she could reply to the attorney, however, Bennett said, "Moreau here could have been one of Barnaby's biggest success stories, Mr. Crittenden. They took a girl from the wrong side of the tracks, gave her every opportunity to become a working-class hero, then she ran back to the wrong side of the tracks and became a... What is it you are now, Moreau? A plumber or something?"

Haven bristled, not just at the misguided comment and his condescending tone of voice but because of his conviction that anyone who didn't live and work the way he did was somehow less than him. Sitting up even straighter in her chair—no small feat, since she'd been as stiff as a board since seeing Bennett—she replied, "And many other things, as well. Thanks for the recommendation, Hadden. Coming from someone like you—a privileged, pampered kid from the Upper East Side who was only able to land a place at Barnaby because his parents paid twice the tuition they normally would have since he only had half the requirements needed for admission—it means a lot."

The smug grin twisting his features fell. But instead of feeling vindicated, Haven felt sick. There was nothing like reverting to an anxious, out-of-place teenager without warning. But that was exactly how she was suddenly feeling. Sure, she could retort with zingers now when someone dismissed her, instead of slinking off to the girls' bathroom to cry, but she still hated confrontation.

So what if she hadn't accepted any of the full-ride scholarship offers she'd received from top-tier colleges after graduation and had attended The City of New York's College of Staten Island instead? So, sue her. She'd been tired of being bullied for her perfectly acceptable background and had been reasonably certain she would have been just as badly targeted and unhappy at some tony Ivy League school. Maybe the rest of her family still felt like they belonged in the one-percent class, a designation that had been stripped away from their ancestor by the Haddens nearly a century and a half ago. Haven was perfectly content wearing her blue collar, thanks. Or would be, if she could just land enough work to keep a roof over her head and food on her table.

Sterling Crittenden looked first at Haven, then at Bennett, then evidently decided there was no reason to further that particular discussion. Instead, he turned his attention to the trio of folders he'd placed in front of himself on the table. "Well, then" he said. "Let's just get right to the heart of the matter, shall we?"

He handed two folders to Mateo, who strode over to deliver one to Haven, then traveled to the other end of the table to give the second to Bennett. To his credit, Bennett seemed to be as confused about their purpose as Haven was. Neither opened them up to see what was inside.

So Sterling Crittenden told them. "What you each have is a copy of the last will and testament of Aurelia Hadden. The original is on file."

Now Bennett looked even more confused. Aurelia Hadden was his great-aunt who had died earlier this month. She'd lived upstate in the Finger Lakes Region, in a massive Gilded Age mansion called Summerlight, which overlooked a small town called Sudbury on one side and Cayuga Lake on the other. The Haddens and Moreaus had been bickering and hurling accusations—and suing each other—over ownership of that house since the 1880s. Because that was when robber baron

Winston Moreau was forced to sign its ownership over to notorious con man and swindler Bertie Hadden, who'd cheated Winston out of it during a rigged poker game after slipping him a Mickey.

At least, that was how the Moreaus knew the story actually unfolded. The Haddens would have had others believe some nonsense about how Winston was a notorious profligate who legally deeded the place—and everything inside it—to his chauffeur, Bertie, as a bribe in exchange for Bertie's silence after witnessing Winston's contribution to the ruination and ensuing death of an innocent Park Avenue socialite. The Haddens had made up and perpetuated the other story for more than a century, because they just didn't want to admit that their ancestor was, at best, a villain and, at worst, a criminal.

Anyway, it was weird that Haven and Bennett would be sitting here for the reading of Aurelia's will. As had always been the case with Summerlight, it was a matter of concern for the older generations of both their families. Bennett's grandfather was still alive, and he was not only of sound mind and body but also Aurelia's brother-in-law and a direct descendant of Bertie. And although Haven's father, a direct descendant of Winston, had died when she was twelve, his younger brothers and sister—her uncles Cecil and Desmond and her aunt Rose—were all still around. And so was her paternal grandfather, for that matter. Even if he was in a memory care facility, it seemed like he would figure into the equation somewhere. Certainly more than Haven would.

Summerlight, everyone in both families knew, had always been passed to the eldest son of the eldest son in each ensuing generation of Haddens, ever since Bertie stole it from the Moreaus. Bennett's aunt Aurelia and uncle Nathaniel, though, never had children. Everyone in both families had assumed she was only living there after her husband's death as a courtesy, and that the house would go to Bennett's grandfather after she died. Then to Bennett's father, then, someday, to Bennett. Well, unless Haven's uncles and aunt won their most recent lawsuit against the family to have ownership of Summerlight restored to the Moreaus. But that wasn't likely, considering how similar lawsuits dating back more than a hundred years hadn't changed anything. Evidently, hope sprang eternal in a family who kept it watered with bitterness and resentment for generations.

Mr. Crittenden turned to his associate. "Thank you, Mateo. That will be all for now."

With a nod to his employer and a quick farewell to Haven and Bennett, Mateo dismissed himself, leaving just the three of them in the big meeting room. Haven halfway expected the attorney to say something like "I guess you're all wondering why I've called you here today."

Instead, he told them, "Although both the Haddens and the Moreaus think the tradition of bequeathing ownership of the Summerlight estate to the eldest son of each Hadden's eldest son is an ironclad aspect of the original deed transfer, that isn't the case at all. It is simply a tradition. Each owner of Summerlight has had the freedom and power to will the property to whomever they wished. It was simply an aspect of the times that the eldest son generally inherited. Aurelia's husband could have left the house to his brother, Bennett's grandfather, upon his death, but he didn't. He left it, and all of its furnishings, to his wife instead."

This clearly surprised Bennett. "My father always said Aunt Aurelia had the right to live out her life at Summerlight, but that after her death, it would go to my grandfather. Then to my father. Then to me."

"Traditionally, that might have been the case," Mr. Crittenden said. "But your aunt and uncle were very much in love and not especially traditional. Nathaniel Hadden wanted to make sure his wife was cared for in every way possible. He left his entire estate to her, including Summerlight. Until her death, she was the sole owner. And it was within her rights to bequeath the house and the rest of her estate to whomever she saw fit."

"But—" Bennett halted after that single word and seemed to not know what to say next.

Haven didn't blame him. She didn't have any words, either. She still wasn't sure why she was here.

"And as to whom Aurelia saw fit to bequeath her house and all of its contents—" Here, Mr. Crittenden opened his folder. "If the two of you will open your dossiers to page three, please."

Haven and Bennett did as the attorney asked in an almost identical manner. But neither of them looked at the folder in front of them. Instead, for some reason, they looked at each other. And Haven was pretty sure her own expression probably mirrored Bennett's in its bewilderment, turbulence and...panic? Yeah, *panic* was a good word for what she was feeling at the moment, even if she had no idea why.

"Aurelia Hadden saw fit to bequeath Summerlight and all of its contents," Mr. Crittenden continued, "to the youngest member of each family—one on the Hadden side and one on the Moreau side—who has reached the age of majority." He looked up again at Haven and Bennett. "That would be the two of you. She wished for you each to have equal ownership of Summerlight and all of its furnishings."

Now Haven and Bennett turned to look at Sterling Crittenden. He offered a reassuring smile to each in turn.

"There are a few conditions, however. Principal among them is that the two of you must live in the house together for one year. Exclusively and continuously, never missing a full night away, effective date…" With that, he dropped an even bigger bombshell. Mr. Crittenden glanced down at the folder in front of him, but Haven was pretty sure he was only doing it for dramatic effect, since he must know Aurelia's will backward and forward.

"Well, look at that," he said with feigned astonishment. He returned his attention to Haven and Bennett. "The effective date is upon announcement of Summerlight's new ownership to its inheritors. That would make the conditions effective beginning today."

Bennett Hadden looked at Sterling Crittenden sitting halfway down the table and wondered how such an already crappy week could have gotten so much crappier. First, Greenback Directive, the green consulting firm he'd started right after earning his MBA, had lost what could have been a billion-dollar client because said potential client had misunderstood the play on words and thought Greenback referred to, well, greenbacks—as in money—and not backing green solutions that made businesses and corporations more environmentally friendly. Then, a woman he'd been interacting with online—one he'd thought was gradually becoming a romantic interest—had instead asked him if he could house-sit her place in Scarsdale while she and her husband and their girlfriend spent a month overseas.

And as if neither of those had been bad enough, he'd had to suffer through his thirtieth birthday two days ago, complete with the traditional Hadden surprise party—which was never a surprise, because his mother spent the year leading up to each of her three children's turn-of-the-decade milestones planning a major gala that included everyone who would fit into their Park Avenue brownstone. Though he supposed he should count himself lucky. His two older sisters had had to endure parties even more extravagant than his because his parents always felt like they had to show them favoritism, since their only son would someday inherit the house their daughters would be denied, thanks to something as capricious as gender. Or so they'd all thought. Now it looked as though Bennett would be coming into that bequest a lot sooner than any of them had realized.

And he was going to have to share it with a Moreau.

He looked at Haven again. She'd grown into quite the beauty since high school, he had to admit, so the view at the other end of the table, at least, improved the state of his week a bit. And she'd found her spine since those days, too, considering the way she'd stood up to him a minute ago. The last time he saw her, she was all bony limbs and graceless posture, in an ill-fitting school uniform she'd always accessorized with a billion weird bracelets and ridiculous high-top sneakers. She'd been a working-class dork who literally tripped over her own feet, bobbing frantically in an ocean of rich, cotillion-classed peers. Not that anyone at Barnaby Prep had really been a peer of Haven Moreau's. Then again, it wasn't such a bad thing to be an outcast among ingrates.

Even so, as improvements to his week went, the one with Haven becoming such a beauty was pretty pointless. She hated his guts. And he hated hers. Hell, thanks to her grudges and overreactions, his dream of attending the college of his choice in a city he loved had been ripped right out from under him. And only days before he'd planned to leave, too, with his bags already packed and half his belongings already shipped across the country. He'd been forced to start college a semester late because of her, at a school right here in New York that he'd only gained entry to because his mother practically blackmailed someone on the admissions committee. Even if he had ultimately landed on his feet, no way did he have to show Haven Moreau even an ounce of tolerance.

He pushed thoughts of the past away to focus on Mr. Crittenden's announcement that he had just inherited his aunt Aurelia's house—something that could ensure once and for all that it would remain in Hadden hands for good. Why the gargantuan French Renaissance Revival mansion was so important to his family, though, he had no idea. It was just a pile of brick and wood and mortar—and, okay, twenty thousand square feet filled with antiques, jewelry and art, not to mention that it sat on sixty-four acres of exquisite lakefront land, two of which were gardens, along with riding stables, a carriage house, and not one, but two turrets. Though now that his family would have to share all that with one of their most hated enemies...

"There are a few other stipulations to Aurelia's bequest, as well," Mr. Crittenden said, bringing Bennett's thoughts back to the present.

Of course there were stipulations. Why leave the place to both him and Haven—neither of whom deserved or had earned it—unless there were lots of conditions? His great aunt probably expected them to battle to the death to see which family would win the place once and for all, like some kind of upper-class Thunderdome.

The attorney continued, "Should one of you decline to live in the house, exclusively and continuously for one year, then Aurelia's estate will revert in its entirety to the other. If both of you decline to live in the house, exclusively and continuously for one year—"

Why did he keep reiterating that part? Jeez, they got it. They had to live together in a gigantic house for a year. Not a great development, but not impossible. He could work remotely as well as at the office and just fly into Manhattan for a day every now and then to stay abreast of things. He had good people working for him. Half of them could probably run the business as well as he did. And Summerlight was so big, he and Haven would barely have to see each other.

"—then Aurelia's entire estate," Mr. Crittenden continued, "will go to the community of Sudbury, to be used as its town council sees fit."

Yeah, that isn't going to happen, Bennett thought. If he let Summerlight get away from the Hadden family that easily, they'd excommunicate him. Not that there hadn't been times in his life, even today, when he'd wished they would do that anyway. He was still going to do whatever he had to to keep the place in the Hadden hold.

"Excuse me, Mr. Crittenden?" Haven asked.

"Yes, Ms. Moreau?"

She hesitated, as if trying to frame her words carefully. "I don't want to sound ungrateful or anything, but why would Aurelia Hadden want me to own half of Summerlight?" She looked down the table at Bennett as she continued, "I mean, I know my family are the *true* rightful owners—"

Ha. That's a good one.

"—but it's been, like, five generations since Bertie Hadden swindled us out of it, and dozens of court petitions have upheld that swindling."

"Oh, please, Moreau," Bennett interjected. "Your family aren't the true owners of anything, let alone Summerlight. Talk about swindlers. Just how many times has your uncle Cecil tried to throw himself under a bus to bilk the city out of millions? How many emails has your aunt Rose sent out claiming to be a displaced Eastern European royal who needs our help? How many credit cards has your cousin Nanette opened in other people's names?"

Haven ignored him. Probably because she knew he was telling the truth. Sure, there may have been a time when the Moreaus were the cream of New York society. But, starting with Winston Moreau, the family had begun a slow downward spiral into scandal, chicanery and lawlessness. At this point, they were virtually all some kind of petty criminal. Haven was supposed to have been the one to lift them all out of that, after winning a place at Barnaby Prep. Instead, she'd run right back home to join them the minute she could. Maybe she wasn't a petty criminal, but she certainly hadn't risen to the levels she might have had she done something halfway decent with her life.

"Anyway," she continued, "like I said, not to sound ungrateful, but...why me? Why a Moreau at all?"

Mr. Crittenden gave her a reassuring smile. "Aurelia experienced quite a lot of disappointment and loss in her life. She was orphaned as a child and raised by family members who were none too pleased to have her join them. She and her husband had hoped to have children of their own, but that never happened. She then lost him far too young after nursing him through a terrible disease. She knew a lot of heartbreak in her life. A lot of wrongs she wasn't able to put to rights. I think, Ms. Moreau, she thought that bequeathing Summerlight to you and Mr. Hadden together would be a wrong that she *could* right. Because she felt that, in a sense, the house does belong to both families. By throwing you together this way, she thought it would force a resolution that would put your families on better footing."

Haven thought about that for a moment, then said, "Mr. Crittenden? I have another question."

"Yes, Ms. Moreau?"

"If the conditions of Mrs. Hadden's will are effective today, does that mean Hadden and I have to be moved into the house by tonight?"

"I'm afraid it does, yes."

"But that doesn't give us much time."

"No, it doesn't."

"I mean…we'll need to pack our stuff and make arrangements for travel. That could take a while."

Bennett didn't see the problem. "The Finger Lakes are only a five-or-six-hour drive, even with Sudbury being halfway toward the north end of Cayuga Lake. How long does it take you to throw a few things into a bag, Moreau? You can buy whatever else you need in Ithaca, on the way."

"Speak for yourself, Hadden," she countered. "I don't have a car. I don't even know if there are any buses that run to Sudbury from New York."

"There aren't," Mr. Crittenden told her. "But there are several that run from here to Ithaca, and from Ithaca, you should be able to arrange for a cab or rideshare to the house. It's only about thirty miles. Less than an hour's drive on the local road."

"Oh sure, and how much is all that going to cost me?" she asked. "Provided I can even get a bus at the last minute? Not to mention I have to go all the way back to Staten Island to pack and then come back here to the city to catch said bus. Provided they haven't all left by then and there's still a seat left on any that might run later. Hadden here will be unpacked and enjoying a cocktail on the front porch before I even get my toiletries zipped into a baggie."

"Summerlight doesn't really have a front porch," Bennett told her. "It's more like a veranda that wraps all the way around, and—"

He stopped talking when he realized Haven wasn't listening. She'd whipped out her phone midway through her rant and was typing frantically, presumably to address all her concerns, many of which she was still voicing. Bennett supposed he could have helped her out by offering her a lift, but he stopped himself. For one thing, they hated each other's guts. For another, he was reasonably sure she wouldn't accept anyway, since that would mean being beholden to her sworn enemy. There was also the small chance that helping her out that way could hold them both up enough that neither of them would make it on time, and then the town of Sudbury would end up with the house. But mostly he didn't offer because of their mutually hated guts.

Sure, it was petty to hold a grudge from high school. But holding grudges was practically engraved on both families' coats of arms. Whatever the Latin words were for *Enmity over Honor*, that should have been both their mottos.

"I mean, especially if the reading of the will is going to take a lot of time today," Haven continued, still scrolling on her phone, "God knows when I'll even be able to make it back to Staten Island in the first place, and then I have to—" She snapped to attention in her chair. "There's a bus to Ithaca that leaves at four thirty this afternoon that still has a couple of available seats. It'll take five and a half hours to get there. That'll put arrival time at around ten. There shouldn't be much traffic between there and Sudbury that time of night, right? That should work." Then her eyes went wide. "Are you kidding me? Two hundred dollars? That's robbery!"

Even so, Bennett could tell she was booking the ticket as she spoke. Seriously, she couldn't even afford a two-hundred-dollar bus ticket? He thought plumbers made good money. So much for Barnaby Prep's claim that 100 percent of its alumni were placed in lucrative positions within two years of college graduation.

"If it will help, Ms. Moreau," Mr. Crittenden said, "we can dispense with the reading of Aurelia's will today, since that part is simply a formality and not legally binding. You and Mr. Hadden can read it at your leisure and contact me with any questions."

"That would help enormously," she told him, already standing and gathering her things. "Is the address for Summerlight in the folder?"

"It is," the attorney told her. "As are keys for the front and back doors, as well as a floor plan and a map of the grounds."

"Great," she replied as she began to make her way to the door of the meeting room. "Then, I should be good to go."

And she was. Gone, Bennett meant. She didn't even shut the door behind herself. Bennett looked at Mr. Crittenden. Mr. Crittenden looked at Bennett.

"Was there anything else?" the attorney asked.

"No," Bennett told him. "Guess I should be going, too."

Not that he was worried about making it to Summerlight before the end of the day. He totally would. He just hoped like hell—though God knew why, since sworn enemies and guts-hating and all that—that Haven made it by then, too.

Chapter Two

Haven made it to Summerlight in time. Barely. But by the time she climbed the front steps, at 11:37 p.m., all she had left in her wallet was her ID, her library card, a plastic tooth flosser and a Pikachu Band-Aid. The rideshare driver she'd had to hire in Ithaca, once she saw where she was dropping Haven off, suddenly told her that, oops, she forgot, the fare was actually twice what she originally quoted. Then she locked all the car doors until Haven ponied up. And when Haven had argued that the rideshare company the other woman worked for didn't allow for stuff like that, the driver had just muttered, "Oh man, my bad," then proceeded to not unlock the doors and continued to look at her expectantly.

Haven hadn't had time to argue. But she'd also only had sixteen dollars in her wallet. So she'd tried to pay the rest with a Starbucks gift card, an Old Navy store credit and a Metro Card with an $8.75 balance. When that still hadn't been enough to settle her so-called debt, she'd withdrawn from her duffel two unopened boxes of Tastykake Butterscotch Krimpets she'd grabbed from her pantry before leaving. And when the driver said they were her favorites, but she hadn't seen them in Ithaca for years, Haven used the revelation to inflate their recommended retail price until they were valuable enough to not just make up for the rest of her fare, but to also constitute a 20 percent tip, so, hey, unlock the damn door. The only thing that had gotten Haven through the day was the promise of digging in to those Krimpets tonight, and now her frump-battle-axe-witch-harridan of a driver would be enjoying them instead. *Hmpf.*

As she watched the rideshare driver complete the rotation around the circular driveway to leave, Haven noticed a shiny, cream-colored Bentley parked on the other side of the fountain, so she knew Bennett was already here. He'd doubtless been here for hours. He could have chartered a helicopter from Manhattan if he'd wanted to. But then he would have missed out on all the fun of sitting on a bus for six hours next to a creepster with bad hygiene who pretended to be asleep while trying to cop as many feels as he could, the way Haven had been forced to do, so, ha ha, joke was on Bennett.

She fished her key chain out of her pocket and easily located the ones for Summerlight—since, prior to today, she'd had only two keys on her chain to begin with: one to her apartment and one to her bike chain. After unlocking the door, she pushed it open with an ominous *creeeak*. She halfway expected to see Bennett poised at the top of a majestic double staircase, dressed all in black and holding a candelabra, with a raven perched on one shoulder. Instead, she found herself alone.

There was indeed a staircase, but it was neither double nor majestic. In fact, even from a distance and in the sparse illumination of the foyer light, she could see that the carpet covering the steps was faded and torn, and one of its bannisters was listing. She made a quick survey of what she could see of the house. The giant crystal chandelier overhead was grimy, the marble floor was cracked in places, and wallpaper that had probably once been ivory flocked with gold was now blemished and fraying. There were stains on the ceiling medallions and gaps in the crown molding. Clearly, it had been a while since Aurelia Hadden had been able to tend to the place. Apparently, she really had been brokenhearted by the tragedies of her life.

Haven had no idea where she was supposed to go or what she was supposed to do. She'd left Mr. Crittenden's office so quickly, she'd forgotten to ask Bennett for his phone number, so she had no way to contact him now. And thanks to the size of the house, he could be anywhere, most of it not even within shouting distance. Not that she necessarily wanted to contact him. It had been bad enough seeing him this morning. And she'd been so surprised by his appearance after so many years of giving him no thought—okay, fine, of doing her best not to give him any thought, even though thoughts of him crept in from time to time—that she'd barely been able to process her feelings. Then she'd been too focused on the chaos of trying to get to Summerlight that she hadn't given much thought to what it would mean to have Bennett back in her life.

She made herself think about it now. And the moment she did, her stomach clenched into a knot, her anxiety skyrocketed, and she felt like she wanted to cry. Because there had been a time in her life when she honestly thought she…had feelings for… Bennett. And she'd been foolish enough to think he might…have feelings for…her, too.

As she always did when she started beating herself up over her stupidity, she reminded herself she was barely sixteen when she fell for his cruel joke. And that she'd been completely naive about the ways of the real world back then, having been sheltered by her parents all her life. She had been completely unprepared that summer day before her junior year, when she went to meet him in the city for what promised to be the most romantic event of her young life—a carriage ride around Central Park, then tea and pastries at *this little place I know on Park Avenue. Trust me, Haven, you'll love it.* He'd make sure she'd be back on Staten Island by her curfew, he promised. He'd ride the ferry with her himself and cab it with her the rest of the way to her house. *Don't you worry, Haven,* his last text to her that long-ago day had said. *I'd never let anything bad happen to you. I promise.*

Except he'd broken that promise and did let something bad happen to her. Hell, he'd been responsible for it. She'd arrived at their designated meeting place— Bow Bridge, because where else would anyone meet in Central Park for a romantic tryst?—only to be joined by, instead of Bennett, a dozen of his cronies and cousins he sent in his place. All of them knew why she had come—he'd obviously arranged for them to witness her humiliation—and they'd all needled her relentlessly about her presumed rendezvous. Some of them even quoted parts of the texts Bennett had sent her over the previous weeks. Clearly, he'd let them read those, too, along with the many she'd written to him in return, in which she had bared her teenage heart and soul.

It had been all she could do to keep herself together long enough to escape them, and she didn't stop running until she rounded the lake to Strawberry Fields. But their laughter and jeers stayed with her. Attending Barnaby every day after that had been a hellish experience, even though Bennett had graduated, because his friends and cousins who were left continued to humiliate her daily. There were still times when she could hear their sneering and taunting loud and clear.

She reminded herself that more than ten years had passed since that day. They were both kids then. Yes, his prank had been heartless and mean-spirited, but that was the way of Haddens. She should have known better than to trust that he was a decent guy in the first place. And she'd gotten her revenge, even if it hadn't been of her own making.

Did she have to forgive him? No way. Did she have to forget? Nope. Did she have to let it define any part of her or continue to eat her up inside to this day? Absolutely not. And she wouldn't. She was a grown woman. She'd come a long way from the bullied teenager she used to be. She could handle herself in all kinds of scenarios now, including the stressful ones. No, it wasn't going to be pleasant spending the next year here in the boon-docks with Bennett. But she could do it. She could be civil to him. She would make it work. Once she stopped being shell-shocked by the day's developments and was coherent enough to think clearly again.

Man, she was exhausted. She looked longingly at the stairs leading to the second floor. She didn't care how decrepit they were. She needed some sleep. She remem-bered from the floor plans she'd inspected during her bus ride that that the bedrooms were all on the second and third floors—save those of the servants' quarters, which were mostly gathered in a fourth-floor attic. So she made her way to the upper level and looked first one way, then the other. Here, too, there was just enough light to see that the house was a shade of its former self, with more threadbare carpets, more dingy wallpaper and more spotty ceilings. The west wing was dark, but at the very end of the east wing's hall, light spilled out of a room. She walked cautiously toward it.

She passed a half-dozen other rooms along the way, none of which Bennett seemed to have claimed yet, because they, too, were all dark. So she paused by one and flipped a light switch. When she saw it was a bedroom—albeit dusty and musty and not particularly well illuminated—she dropped her duffel and back-pack just inside the door, then slipped off her wool peacoat to leave with them. At this point, she honestly didn't care what condition the room was in, as long as there was a bed. She'd changed into reasonably clean blue jeans and a black turtleneck before leaving home, along with her beloved thrifted Doc Martens, but her hair was still bound in its stubby ponytail. Well, mostly bound, she realized, when she felt a few strands brushing her jaw. It had been a long day.

She found Bennett in the last room on the left, one that looked like a study or salon, depending, she supposed, on whatever gender had used it back in its heyday. Though, like the rest of the house, its heyday was long gone. The furniture was still in good shape, however, if clearly neglected. There was a rolltop desk and a bookcase situated on one side of the room and an arrangement of chairs and small tables on the other, near a fairly substantial fireplace. All of it had probably been in the house since it was built. Bennett was seated in one of those chairs, reading what appeared to be an old book he'd plucked from those very shelves and looking fresh and comfortable in a pair of faded jeans and a forest green crewneck she'd bet good money was cashmere.

He looked up at her arrival in the doorway. "You made it," he said, sounding only vaguely surprised. He looked at his watch. "And on time, too. Way to go, Moreau."

She nodded. "Yeah, sorry to disappoint, Hadden."

"I'm not disappointed."

Wow, he almost sounded convincing. She wished she could be as fake-pleased about his presence. But they'd both know that would be pushing it.

"Really," he added when he must have detected her skepticism. "If nothing else, both of us being in this situation might finally settle the dispute between my family and yours once and for all."

She strode carefully into the room, stopping at the other chair but not sitting down. "How do you figure that?" she asked. "The house being occupied by a member of your family for generations hasn't settled it. A century of litigating it in a million different ways hasn't settled it. Both of our families being at each other's throats for a hundred years hasn't settled it. Why would this?"

He lifted his shoulders and let them drop, looking supremely unconcerned. "Maybe it's time for a new tack. Maybe this will be it."

She couldn't imagine what kind of tack throwing a Moreau and a Hadden together under one roof would be, other than a ridiculous and kind of malicious one.

"Look, be honest," he said. "Do you really care who owns this house? Deep down inside, has it ever been a thing for you, personally, at any point in your life, which one of our families calls this house theirs?"

She hesitated a moment before replying, giving the question some serious thought for the first time. And she was surprised to realize there was a part of her, however small, that did indeed feel as if Summerlight was a part of her. Even though this was the first time she'd actually seen the place in person, she did feel a strange kinship to it. When a long-ago memory floated to the front of her brain, she understood why.

Finally, she told Bennett, "When I was little, my dad used to tell me bedtime stories about how he and my mom and I lived in a fairy-tale castle in a faraway land, on a magical sea, surrounded by a beautiful garden, with an enchanted village nearby."

At this, Bennett smiled, the same sort of smile she imagined he would give to a child telling him such a fairy tale. He didn't seem to be feeling smug or superior, though. He seemed to be charmed by her recollection. Weird. She never would have thought a Hadden could find something whimsical or charming.

"I always loved those stories," she continued, "even though I knew they were just that—fairy tales. When I got older and started to understand the feud between our families, I realized my dad had been talking about Summerlight when he told me those stories."

"How old were you when your parents told you about the feud?" Bennett asked.

"I actually first learned about it from my aunts and uncles and cousins," she told him. "It really wasn't a big deal to my parents. Whenever I asked them about it, they always brushed it off as ancient history. They told me the house didn't belong to us and that we would never live here."

When she said nothing more, Bennett eyed her thoughtfully and said, "You haven't really answered my first question."

She looked back at him, surprised. "I didn't?"

He shook his head and repeated, "Have you, personally, ever really cared which one of our families owns this house?"

She sighed. "I guess, when I was a kid, I formed an idea from my father's stories that, yeah, the house could kinda belong to my parents and me, and maybe we did belong here. And, technically, if Summerlight had stayed in the Moreau family, it would belong to me now, since my father died when I was twelve. But then, technically, had it stayed in the Moreau family, my father never would have been born and neither would I. The Moreaus would have married in their own social station. So realistically, at least, no. It never mattered to me who it belonged to."

And, realistically, it hadn't. She'd never thought about living here with her parents beyond a childhood fantasy that only could have happened in an alternate reality. As nice as that fantasy had been. Even so, being here now, there was something about the situation— about the house—that made her feel as if maybe she belonged here after all.

Before she could put voice to that, though—not that she really knew how to put voice to that anyway, Bennett said, "It hasn't been a concern of mine, either. Even though I was always told Summerlight will belong to me someday, I've never felt much of a connection to the place."

His admission surprised her. She would have thought he'd be chomping at the bit to live here. Why wouldn't he? A gorgeous Gilded Age mansion sitting lakeside in one of the most beautiful areas in New York? Even if it was just for a retirement plan, who wouldn't at least make some kind of long-term plans for that? Hell, her own extended family, who hadn't owned the house for generations, regularly made plans for what they would do when Summerlight was returned to its rightful owners—i.e., them. Haven had always thought they were being silly. Now that she really would become an owner of Summerlight after the year was up, now that she knew the house *was* a concern for her, now that she saw how her childhood fairy tale could, in a way, come true, she felt…

Well, honestly, she still wasn't sure how she felt.

"We both own the place now, Moreau," Bennett said, scattering her thoughts. "Or we will, once the year is up. This stupid feud could be settled once and for all, because neither of our families will be able to accuse the other of gaining or losing possession by nefarious means."

Oh, wouldn't they? There was a part of her that suspected both families had put so much energy into hating each other for so long that they wouldn't make it through the day without that keeping the feud alive.

Thankfully, she didn't have to think about any of that right now. She'd spared enough time before leaving Staten Island to call her mother and tell her what had happened, but she'd asked for it not to be revealed to the rest of the family until Haven was on better footing. The moment her uncles and aunt found out she was a half owner, they were going to start making plans to figure out a way to make her full owner, short of asking her to murder Bennett in his sleep. Then again, considering some of the things she'd overheard over the years, she wouldn't put it past Uncle Cecil, at least.

And even if she and Bennett did remain co-owners of Summerlight after the passage of the upcoming year, she still wasn't sure how it was all going to work. She couldn't stay here forever. Her family, her friends, her work—her entire life—was on Staten Island. Even if her business, Right at Home, wasn't yet fully off the ground—and this sojourn in the Finger Lakes certainly wasn't going to help in that regard—she knew she could make a reasonably good living out of it. And now that she was beginning to see how Summerlight wasn't exactly the shining gem it used to be, her concern about its fate was as troubling as her concern about her own.

But fine. Let Bennett think whatever he wanted about their two families potentially coming together over this thing. They had a whole year to figure it out. Not that that was especially comforting, either. She knew the enormity of what was happening hadn't quite yet hit her. She was still too stunned by the day's events. A year was a long time to spend in a place you'd never visited and hadn't planned to occupy but were suddenly dropped into, unprepared. Not to mention, winter was on the horizon, and those could be pretty daunting this far north. Even autumn was further along up here, just hours from the city.

Seriously, she should just go to bed and think about all this after she'd had a good night's sleep. For some reason, though, she didn't want to go to bed. Not in this strange place after this strange day, with all the strange thoughts and strange feelings that were coursing through her.

"And what happens to the house after a year?" she asked Bennett, since that was the biggest question mark of all. "I'm gonna go out on a limb and assume neither of us wants to live up here forever. Especially under one roof, together."

He shrugged again. "I guess we have a year to figure that out."

She just hoped a year was enough time to undo a century and a half of ill will. Then she noticed a cut crystal glass with a couple fingers of something amber splashed into it on the table next to him. "You found the bar, I see."

He looked at the glass, too. "There's one in the cabinet by the desk over there. Pretty well stocked, but I don't think Aunt Aurelia was much of a drinker. A lot of what's in there is long past its prime. If it's even made anymore. I was lucky enough to find an unopened bottle of Lagavulin, so Uncle Nathaniel must have liked his Scotch. It's still good, by the way," he added as he lifted the glass and silently toasted her before sipping.

Haven wasn't much of a drinker, save a cold beer after a long day or a glass of wine on special occasions, and she rarely touched spirits. She knew from the house plans that there was a wine cellar in the basement. No way was she going to go down there to check it out in the middle of the night, though. That was just asking for ghosts to follow her back upstairs and then hang around forever.

Despite that, she made her way to the cabinet and located the bottle of Scotch easily, then grabbed a glass to pour herself a small amount. Why was Bennett being so nice to her? she wondered as she made her way back to the other side of the room. He should have been furious with this turn of events. The whole Hadden clan had to be. The very idea of a Moreau even stepping foot in these hallowed halls would have been enough to make them spontaneously combust.

Haven didn't know all the particulars of the lawsuits her uncles and aunt and their forebears had filed against the various generations of Haddens over the years. But her cousins had always been sure to keep her informed of everything Hadden-related in the way kids who didn't understand anything about life did. As a child, Haven had known only that it was her birthright and destiny to be their enemy, so that was what she had gone with. Then, when she was at Barnaby Prep and witnessed how the majority of Haddens behaved, she'd realized the family had earned every epithet her cousins ever used. They were villains, pure and simple.

Even if Bennett hadn't been particularly villainous since their reacquaintance this morning, she knew his proclivities well. Malice didn't just go away for no reason. It only festered over the years. If he was being nice to her now, it was only to lull her into a false sense of security for what he had planned for the long game. Haddens were excellent at the long game. She'd seen that for herself, too.

She didn't sit down when she rejoined him, but she couldn't quite make herself leave the room, either. As tired as she was, she was in no way sleepy. And, frankly, the idea of going to bed, all alone, in some creaky old room in this creaky old house wasn't exactly helping. She sipped her drink warily, then was surprised at the smoothness and earthiness of its taste. She liked how it warmed her going down. With any luck, it would eventually make her drowsy.

After another, less wary sip, she leaned over the chair she'd moved behind—since, somehow, having a barrier between her and Bennett, even just a chair, made her feel a little better—then asked, "How did your family handle the news of your inheritance?"

He lifted his glass and swirled the liquor inside it, focusing on that instead of Haven. "I haven't told them yet."

This surprised her. She assumed the first thing he did when she left the meeting that morning was call his parents to first reassure them that Summerlight was still in their miserly grasp, then ask what might be the neatest and least conspicuous way to dispose of the pesky Moreau that had come with it.

"Naturally, my parents and grandparents have been wondering when Mr. Crittenden would be in touch with them about the particulars of Aunt Aurelia's will, but he's evidently been very good at stalling. How did your family react?"

"I only told my mother," she said. "And I asked her not to let the others know yet."

Her revelation seemed to surprise him as much as his had her. "Seriously?" he asked. "How can you be so sure she hasn't already told all of them?"

What kind of question was that? Of course her mother would keep her secret. That was what people who loved you did. Besides, her mother had always been mystified by the whole Hadden and Moreau feud, coming into it as an outsider. Not that that had stopped anyone else who married into the Moreau family—they'd embraced the same vitriol as their spouses. Her mother had found the idea of suing for possession of a house that had been out of the family for five generations to be a waste of time, money and emotion.

In response to Bennett's question, however, she only said, "Because that's what moms do. They stand with their kids."

She could tell by his expression that he didn't believe her. Though whether that was because he didn't think a Moreau was capable of something like loyalty and affection or if his own mother wasn't like hers, she didn't know.

"They're all going to find out eventually, though," he continued.

Now Haven was the one to stare into her glass. "Yeah, I know."

"Your family is going to be delighted."

"Maybe."

"It's what they've been fighting for for generations," he pointed out.

She supposed. Though she still wondered what was going to happen now. What would the rest of the Moreaus have done if, by some miracle, the courts had restored ownership of the house to her family before now? Would they have all moved into it together? Just leave behind their lives and livelihoods to relocate to the wilds of upstate New York? And even if they did that successfully, then what would they do with their lives? It would have been her grandfather who owned the place at this point, and he wasn't even of sound enough mind to enjoy it. Uncle Cecil would have considered the place his. And he probably would have been forced to sell it right away to pay off all the uncollected debts he'd accrued over the years. In which case, the Moreau family would have lost Summerlight all over again, with no way to recover it after that.

She sighed and took another sip of her drink. She needed to go to bed. She couldn't think about this anymore tonight.

"I need to turn in," she said. "It's been a hell of a day."

"I feel that," he replied.

He stood. For some reason, that made Haven straighten and take a step back. He noticed and opened his mouth to say something, then seemed to reconsider and closed it again. Instead, he moved back to the cabinet and retrieved the bottle of Scotch.

"Need a top off?" he asked as he uncorked it.

She shook her head. "I'm good. With any luck, this will be enough to help me sleep."

He splashed a little more liquor into his glass, then replaced it. "The other wing is better tended than this one," he told her. "Looks like that was where Aunt Aurelia spent most of her time. The bedrooms down that way aren't as decrepit and are a lot cleaner. I put myself in one at the end of the hall."

If that was the case, then Haven would stay down here, regardless of the condition of the rooms. The farther away from Bennett she was, the better. As long as there was a lock on the door, she'd be good. She was *pretty* sure he wouldn't try to strangle her in her sleep, but, as her cousin Daphne had always said, *You just never can tell with a Hadden.*

"I left my things a couple rooms up," she said. "I'll be fine there."

"Even with the spiders?"

And there it was. His first step toward making her feel unsafe. That was the sort of Hadden she knew and didn't love. Even if he'd said it jokingly and with a smile, Haven wasn't buying it. It was textbook Gaslighting 101.

"Bugs can figure pretty prominently in my line of work," she told him. "I once knocked down a wall that was teeming with roaches, and I've had to remove more than my fair share of hornets' and wasps' nests over the years. Bugs don't bother me. Not nearly as much as, oh, say, snakes in the grass and weasels do."

His smile fell. "Well, then. I hope you sleep like a log."

Oh, sure. So she wouldn't hear him when he sneaked into her room to shove a pillow over her face.

"Thanks," she said.

As one, they lifted their drinks in a silent toast, a sort of "may the best person win." Then Haven spun on her heel and left. And for once, she did something very significant where Bennett Hadden was concerned. She didn't look back.

When Bennett awoke on his first full day in Summerlight, it was to the pelt of rain on the window and the rumble of not-so-distant thunder. It had threatened rain during his entire drive north the day before, so he wasn't much surprised. And, really, the weather was kind of fitting. There had been a gray, chilly pall over the mansion ever since he entered it. The place bore little resemblance to the house he'd visited when he was a kid.

He rolled over in bed and stared at the ceiling in the ashy morning light. The clock told him it was just past seven thirty, but it felt much later. He closed his eyes and made himself remember the last time he'd been there. It had been nearly twenty years ago, for Aunt Aurelia's seventy-fifth birthday. He remembered her looking frail and tired, even though seventy-five wasn't all that old. Frail and tired and sad, as if she were still grieving her husband's death, decades after the fact.

The house had looked incredible that day, though. His great-aunt had employed a few full-time servants back then to keep it that way, right down to the last delicate rosebud in the garden. Bennett remembered his mother saying in passing, some years later, that Aunt Aurelia dismissed all her staff not long after that birthday party, as if it had been her last hurrah. Then she'd shut herself up in the house and spent the rest of her life alone. Bennett couldn't imagine loving someone so much that you lost a part of yourself with them when they died, but that seemed to be what had happened to his aunt. It was reflected in every neglected corner of the house. Summerlight, too, seemed to have been in mourning for decades.

He had no idea what to do with the place. Not that the decision was entirely his, since Haven had as much right to the house as he did. But he couldn't see her wanting to live here any more than he did. They both had lives back in the city that had nothing to do with Summerlight. He planned to return to his as soon as was legally possible. Haven must want to return to hers just as much.

It would make the most sense for them to sell the house at the end of their year here and split the proceeds fifty-fifty. The place was too far gone to be habitable, and the cost of renovations for a house this size would be astronomical. Certainly more than he was willing to invest or than Haven could afford. As sensible as the idea of selling was, however, something about it felt wrong. The house had been a part of both Hadden and Moreau history ever since it was built, for coming up on six generations. Even if that history was full of contention and hostility, it was still a huge part of both families. To think of it belonging to someone else felt off somehow. But to think about keeping it when neither of them had use for it was silly. Of course, they had a whole year to think about that.

A year. The enormity of that was just hitting him. He had to stay here for a year. With Haven Moreau. Yesterday had been so surreal, he hadn't had time to think about the repercussions of Aunt Aurelia's bequest. Now that he did…

He jackknifed up in bed and turned to plant his feet firmly on the floor. Now that he did, he still had no idea what to think about it.

He rose and threw a sweatshirt on over the T-shirt and pajama pants he'd slept in, then shoved his feet into his slippers. Coffee. That was what he needed before anything else. Of course he had no idea what to do about his current or future predicaments without caffeine coursing through his system.

He was surprised, as he made his way down to the first floor, to be greeted by the aroma of the very coffee he sought. He'd explored the mansion yesterday, so found the main kitchen easily. Like the rest of the house, it was a ghost of what he remembered. Its once crisp black-and-white tile seemed to have bled into a dull gray, and what he recalled as sunny yellow walls were now as gloomy as the day outside. Many of the kitchen's fixtures—such as the Hoosier cabinet, the double-basin sink, and the massive L-shaped gas stove—were original to the house, or nearly so, and had seemed so charming before. Now their once-lustrous white was as dreary and abandoned as everything else.

Thankfully, there was a modern drip coffee maker on one countertop, its glass carafe half-empty, so he knew Haven must be around here somewhere. After filling a delicate teacup—the only vessel for a hot beverage he was able to locate in the only cabinet holding dishes—all of them antique-looking fine china—Bennett moved to a door leading to the screened-in portion of the veranda. There sat Haven in one of the house's many Adirondack chairs, wrapped in layers of fleece, with an ancient wool blanket thrown over her lower half. It couldn't be more than fifty degrees out there. Why the hell was that where she'd decided to have her coffee?

He pushed the door open and was met by a jolt of air that called his assessment of the temperature into question. There was a bone-chilling mist blowing under the eaves that gave him an involuntary shiver. She looked up at the sound of his arrival, gave him a quick once-over, then returned her gaze to the vista—a tangle of brambles that were once the garden, then a sprawl of lawn dotted by tattered trees, then Cayuga Lake rippling beyond, as gray and gloomy as everything else today.

"Morning, Hadden," she said, clearly as an afterthought and with no more warmth than the weather.

There was no *good* attached to the greeting, either, he noted. Not that he disagreed. Although it was indeed morning, there wasn't much good about it. And not just because of the weather.

"Morning, Moreau," he replied just as frostily.

Damn. Day one, and they were already feeling belligerent about each other's existence. Evidently, last night's truce had just been a result of their fatigue and confusion. Call him an alarmist, but this didn't bode well for the 364 days they had left.

Be civil, he told himself. He wasn't sure he could ever make himself be nice to Haven, but he could be civil. If he tried hard.

He stepped through the door, battled another wave of frigid air and seated himself in a chair two down from hers—keeping a civil distance between them.

"Nice morning for coffee on the veranda," he said wryly.

"It is, actually," she told him. "I love mornings like this."

Of course she did. Moreaus must thrive in cold and murk.

Civil, he reminded himself. "Thanks for making coffee," he told her, not quite able to keep the grudginess out of his voice.

She obviously noticed. "I didn't make it for you," she replied blandly.

Bennett persevered. Civilly. "We're going to need to go into Ithaca for groceries today," he said. "I only stopped long enough yesterday to grab a few things for breakfast and lunch today. There's a Wegmans and Trader Joe's, both. Do you have a preference?"

She looked at him as if he'd just asked her whether she preferred the rack or the iron maiden when it came to torture. "Um, no, I don't have a preference. I don't do much grocery shopping. I usually just grab something for breakfast and dinner on my way to and from work, then wing it for lunch."

"That can get expensive."

Now she looked at him as if to say, "Are you effing kidding me?" Except that she probably wasn't thinking the word *effing*.

And, okay, maybe he could afford expensive things a lot more than she could. That was exactly his point. Haven couldn't afford to waste money. None of the Moreaus could. Not that he was going to apologize for his family's wealth. For one thing, he hadn't been the one to accrue it. And even if he had, it would have been through hard work and perseverance, the same way his family had earned it. Just because Winston Moreau had given Bertie Hadden Summerlight as a bribe so his chauffeur would keep his mouth shut about Winston's many, *many* transgressions, it hadn't turned Bennett's ancestors into millionaires overnight. Yes, it had been a very nice start. But Bertie and his family had been smart enough, and industrious enough, to parlay that initial windfall into several generations' worth of profit. Unlike the earlier Moreaus, who had succumbed to the same profligacy as their ancestor and lost every nickel their robber-baron patriarch had owned.

Instead of hammering that point home—*be civil*—he moved on. "All I grabbed yesterday—besides the coffee, I mean—was bread, skim milk and some fruit and veg."

She winced noticeably at the announcement. "Wow, you're right. We definitely need to pick up some groceries."

"You talk like you never eat fruit or veg or drink skim milk."

"That's because I never eat fruit or veg or drink skim milk."

"That's a good way to get scurvy."

"I'll be sure to alert my commodore in the Royal Navy."

Bennett sighed. "Look, Moreau, we're going to have to coexist under this one roof for a year. Do you think we could at least get through the first day without fighting?"

She turned to look at him again. "Hey, I'm not the one who started the day by denigrating the other's spending and diet habits."

She was right. That was on him. "I apologize," he managed to make himself say. "But we're still going to need to make a trip into Ithaca for supplies. We can fill a cart with provisions for both of us and just split the cost fifty-fifty. Does that sound fair?"

She suddenly looked worried about something. "You go ahead and get what you want for yourself today. I'll go in and get a few things for myself later."

"And how are you going to do that? You don't have

a car." And, although he didn't point it out, because he was being civil, a rideshare back and forth to town was going to be pricey. Especially for someone who'd barely been able to afford the bus ticket here.

"I'll manage," she told him.

He wanted to argue but stopped himself. Seriously, though, how was she going to fend for herself if she wouldn't even accept the smallest offer of help? A round-trip rideshare to Ithaca would cost more than the groceries and would eventually bleed her dry. But what did he expect of someone who ate carryout all the time?

"Fine, Moreau," he said, standing. It was getting way too cold out here for him. And not because of the weather. "While we're living in Summerlight, we'll each do our own thing and go our own way. You on your terms, me on mine. It's a big enough house that the two of us can survive for a year without having to see too much of each other."

Still looking out at the bleak scenery, Haven replied, "I'm sure we can, Hadden. Piece a cake."

Somehow, Bennett managed to make it back into the house without asking her any of the million things that were suddenly ricocheting around in his head. Like, why was she was so damned stubborn? And how did she expect to get through the next year if she couldn't even have a halfway cordial conversation with him? And, dammit, why did it still bother him to this day that she had been more vindictive and diabolical when they were in high school than he'd thought even a Moreau could be? But more than anything else, how could he suddenly find her more than a little attractive?

That last, especially, was going to be problematic in light of the fact that he was going to have to live under the same roof with her for a year. Summerlight was a big house, sure. But it wasn't that big. Not big enough to hold five generations' worth of animosity and resentment. It was going to be a long fall. And winter. And spring. And summer. He just hoped they were both still standing at the end of the year.

Chapter Three

Ultimately, Haven had no choice but to accept Bennett's offer to drive them both into Ithaca for groceries. She might be stubborn, but she wasn't stupid. She only had two choices. Either be beholden to a Hadden for a lift into town or eat the kind of things Bennett ate and be beholden to a Hadden anyway for letting her eat his stuff. If she was going to have to be beholden to him regardless, she was going to at least do it on her own terms and with her own culinary team—Marie Callender, Little Debbie, Cap'n Crunch, and Sara Lee.

"I'm not paying for that," Bennett said as she dropped the fifth member of her tribe into their shared cart—Chef Boyardee. "I'm not paying for anything on your side."

"I never asked you to," she assured him. "You're the one who suggested splitting our purchase fifty-fifty."

"That was before I realized how…different…your diet is."

It didn't escape her notice that he had actually been kind of polite in insulting her food choices during this trip. He could have called them a lot worse things than *different*. Even so, he had still insulted her food choices. In one breath, he had been both rude and civil. Just what kind of Hadden was she dealing with?

"Hey, way more people in this country eat what I eat instead of what you eat," she told him. "Meaning you're the one whose diet is different." She picked up a bottle of…something…on his side of the cart and read the label. "I mean, what even *is* kefir?"

He snatched it out of her hand and placed it back in the cart on his side, as if he feared she would lob it into the next aisle. "It's like drinkable yogurt. This particular brand is made from fermented sheep milk. It's full of probiotics."

She bit back a gag and eyed him suspiciously. Was he trolling her about the fermented sheep milk? Who would actually consume something like that? Then she remembered she was dealing with a Hadden. Of course he was trolling her. No one in their right mind would consume fermented sheep milk. Even a Hadden.

"Aren't probiotics just germs with a fancy name?" she asked.

"Yes, but they're good germs," he assured her.

"Are you sure? Maybe they're just regular germs with good PR."

Why was she baiting him? she wondered. Who was

being the troll now? For some reason, though, she just couldn't help herself.

He frowned at her. "At least they're organic whole foods, not processed crap."

"At least my food has had the germs processed right out of it."

"To be replaced by even more crap. How do you even know to buy all this stuff? You said you never go to the grocery store."

"I don't. But this is what my mom got me when I was a kid."

"Your mother fed you artificial dyes and flavors?" he asked, aghast.

"Your mother fed you fermented sheep milk?" she asked, even more aghast.

He opened his mouth to say something, seemed to think better of it, then closed it again. Hah. She was right. He *had* been trolling about the sheep-milk thing.

"So you can keep your kefir to yourself," Haven told him. "I'm not paying for that."

He expelled a frustrated sound, gripped the handle of their cart as if it were a bazooka and made his way down the aisle, not bothering to check to see if she was following. Reluctantly, Haven did follow. But she really wasn't going to pay for his kefir. Hell, she was barely going to be able to pay for her own stuff. She had to watch what few pennies she had in her bank account like a hawk while she was at Summerlight. Her income was going to be nonexistent while she was here if she didn't find some way to make money.

It had occurred to her last night, as she lay wide-awake in bed, that there might be some odd jobs in the town of Sudbury, which was within walking distance of Summerlight. She could potentially pick up a few bucks that way. But she'd be going into it cold, with no reviews or references from anyone who could vouch for her work. Still, even mending a fence or tightening a gutter could bring her enough to at least buy food. Not that fall and winter were exactly prime time for home improvement, but there should still be *some*thing she could do. She'd go into the village tomorrow to have a look around. Today was too rainy to do much more than stock the kitchen anyway.

She caught up to Bennett in the next aisle over and saw him adding canned tomatoes to the cart. All kinds of tomatoes, from diced to crushed to whole to some that were mixed with green chilies. Haven had had no idea just how many ways a tomato could be canned. Although her own mother was a decent cook, she'd never really diverted much from good ol' American standards, such as spaghetti and tacos, with the occasional meatloaf or tuna croquette thrown in for good measure. Thanksgiving and Christmas had been the usual assortment of traditional dishes, but food had never really been more to Haven's family than something to stave off hunger. The only seasonings in the Moreau household had been salt and pepper, and the only condiments had been mayo, mustard and ranch dressing. Certainly, her mother had never brought home things like…

Haven glanced at one of the cans Bennett had added to the cart before moving on. Sun-dried, julienne-cut tomatoes with basil. Wow.

He slowed at the beans section, which she naturally assumed he would go right past, but then he stopped and started stocking up again. *Ew.* He didn't seem to agree with her opinion, however, because he loaded up on four different kinds—black, cannellini, kidney and garbanzos.

"Are you actually planning to cook with all that stuff?" she asked as she watched in horror.

"Of course I'm planning to cook with it," he told her. "Black beans and garbanzos are great in soup. The cannellini beans are for this chicken-and-caper dish I like, the kidneys are for red beans and rice and—" He halted. "Why are you looking at me like that?"

"I just… I don't know." She hesitated. "I guess I didn't figure you for the cooking type. Your mom must have cooked a lot more creatively than mine did."

He dropped a few more cans into the cart, giving them an inordinate amount of attention. He must really like that chicken-and-caper dish.

"My mother never cooked," he said.

"You taught yourself?" she asked, not quite able to mask the incredulity in her voice that even she thought sounded uncharitable.

He glared at her. "No. Our cook, Mrs. Tobin, taught me. Because, like she said, everyone should know how to cook."

"Okay, yeah, I probably should have learned." She nodded. "I mean, learned a little better," she continued, backpedaling. "I do know how to cook. I've just never really had an interest in it. Picking something up somewhere that someone else makes is a lot more convenient for me. Which makes it worth being more expensive," she added pointedly.

Instead of arguing, Bennett began pushing the cart forward again. Together—and mostly in silence—they roamed up and down every aisle of the grocery store, each pausing long enough to add something they liked to their collection, always placing whatever the item was safely on one side of the cart or the other. Only once did they both reach for the same item at the same time—a gigantic bag of mini chocolate–peanut butter cups. Both halted abruptly the moment their hands came into contact, but neither pulled away. Which was weird, Haven couldn't help thinking, since there were a dozen other bags just like it in the bin. It was as if they both had to have this specific one.

"I thought you didn't eat processed food," she said, not letting go of the bag.

"Well, there are some processed foods that are worth dying for," he replied, not letting go of the bag, either.

"I mean, you're even buying a big jar of that crappy organic peanut butter that you have to stir up before using," she reminded him. "Which is ridiculous when you can just grab a spoon and go right to town on the jar of regular extracrunchy I bought."

"Your peanut butter has added sugar," he pointed out.

"What, and peanut butter cups don't?"

Clearly, he couldn't argue with her logic. So he only tightened his grip on the bag. In turn, Haven clenched harder, too. Much more of this, and they were going to turn the whole bag into chocolate–peanut butter soup.

But at least neither of them would have given the other the slightest quarter. Victory in destruction. Yay.

For a long moment, neither of them released the package, but only stood toe-to-toe, glaring at each other. It was long enough for Haven to realize just how much taller Bennett was than she, even in her Doc Martens, long enough for her to see that the eyes she'd always thought were bittersweet brown actually had a ring of dark gold around their pupils, long enough for her to note a faint scar, no more than a half inch, near his right eye that marred an otherwise perfect cheekbone. It was all she could do to battle the urge to lift her free hand to skim her fingers lightly over it and ask him what had caused it.

Oh, this was not good. She'd buried her adolescent attraction to Bennett in the deepest hole she could dig inside herself, and she'd filled it with more rancor than any Moreau had ever felt for a Hadden. Then she'd jumped up and down on it with the force of a thousand hateful Moreaus to really tamp it down. Then she'd torched it with enough fiery indignation to satisfy the hundreds of generations of Moreaus that would be born after her. *Any* good feelings she had *ever* had for Bennett had been completely eradicated the summer he broke her heart. And she would *never* be foolish enough to fall under his spell again.

At least, that was what she'd thought. How could her attraction to him have escaped from such an entombment so easily? How could she be looking at him now with a pounding heart and heat swirling in her belly? How could her blood be racing and pooling in places it had no business pooling? How could she want to lean forward and close the scant inches separating them and cover his mouth with—

She somehow managed to stop that thought before the image that came with it erupted in her brain. Bennett Hadden had hurt her worse than anyone she'd ever known. He'd humiliated her in front of his family and opened her up to endure years of more ridicule and bullying. She hated him. For good reason. What twisted, depraved part of her could have forgotten that and be betraying her so badly now?

She released the bag of candy as if it had burned her. Without grabbing another, she pushed the cart to the end of the aisle, needing all the distance from him she could manage. It happened so fast that, by the time she came to a stop and turned around to look at him, Bennett was still gazing down at the bag of candy in his hand. When he finally glanced up at her, he looked confused. Good. Let him feel as off-kilter right now as she did. Put them on equal footing for once.

He started to ask, "Don't you want—"

"No," she assured him. Whatever he had, she wanted no part of it. Even if it was her most favorite candy in the world.

"But—"

"Is there anything else you want?" she said, interrupting him again.

Belatedly, she realized just how badly that question could become a double entendre. Fortunately, he hated her, too, so there was no danger of him taking it that way. Except that somehow, the look he gave her in response made her think he was taking it even more double-entendre-y than even she was thinking it.

For another moment, he only stood staring at her as if she had lost her mind. Which, of course, she had. But there was no reason he had to know that. Then, cautiously, he made his way to where she stood and dropped the bag of candy into the cart. But he didn't put it on any specific side. He put it right in the middle. Then he easily wrested the cart from her grasp and began pushing it forward again.

"I just need to make a quick run through personal care," he said. "I didn't realize how low I was at home on shampoo and razor blades."

Without awaiting a reply—again—he trundled off with their cart. Haven followed, still keeping a distance between them, then pretended to have a huge interest in some bath bombs while he finished up his shopping. When they finally hit the checkout counter, with her still trailing behind, he swept a hand forward to indicate that she should go first. So she piled her items onto the belt and dropped the little plastic divider behind them. She knew to a penny how much she had in her spend account, and she held her breath as she watched the screen while the cashier rang up her purchases, hoping like hell she'd added them all up correctly in her head as she shopped. When the total came to fourteen dollars less than she had in her account, she breathed a literal sigh of relief and inserted her debit card into the scanner. Then she helped the bagger finish bagging her purchases and stowed them all back on her side of the cart.

When she looked up again, she saw Bennett gazing

at her instead of at the screen, where his own items were scrolling by. Two things hit her at once. One, that he was looking at her as if he were deeply concerned about her welfare, something she knew she had to be misreading, because why could he possibly care about her well-being? And two, that she couldn't imagine what it must be like to not have to keep track of every item you were purchasing or worry about every nickel you spent.

Not that Haven was struggling to get by—well, not that much. She did have a savings account, as meager as it was, and she did her best to add to it regularly and to never dip into it unless she had an emergency. Which, she supposed, actually made it more of an emergency account than a savings account. But that was just it. If she didn't watch her money closely while she was living in the wilds of upstate New York, not working regularly, she wouldn't have an account at all. Her business had just begun to turn a profit when Summerlight fell into her lap. Now she was going to have to abandon it for a whole year in order to keep her inheritance. What few regular customers she'd managed to collect were going to have to look elsewhere for their fix-it needs while she was gone. The home renovation business was supercompetitive and its customers, supercapricious. She was by no means the only person on Staten Island who could install flooring or drywall a basement. And in the days of YouTube DIY tutorials, jobs were even scarcer. What was a small-business owner to do?

As Bennett paid for his groceries, Haven made a mental note to move some money from her emergency fund to her spend account. She'd completed her last job

for Right at Home a week ago and had been paid in full
for it, but that was the last she'd see of any money coming in for the foreseeable future. Although she'd had a
few jobs on the horizon, scheduled prior to learning of
her inheritance, there was obviously no way she could
complete them now—she'd have to give the jobs to a
colleague who was as much in need of work as she was.

Still, she couldn't rely on Bennett to be the sole pro-
vider of food. Especially when he didn't even know
to buy normal peanut butter. That, if nothing else, ce-
mented her resolve to go into Sudbury soon to look for
work there—any work. This time of year, there should
be plenty of gutters to clean and HVAC filters to replace. No job was too dirty or too small when you had
a year of unemployment breathing down your neck. She
just hoped she would make it through the year without
losing everything.

Somehow, they made it through the first week of
October without killing each other. Though that was
probably only because they both did their best to avoid
each other. Bennett learned fairly quickly that Haven
was an early riser, so he made sure to sleep in a bit later
than usual to allow her to have her coffee and breakfast alone before he infiltrated the kitchen. He had the
time, since he no longer had to make the commute into
the office. And it was kind of nice to suddenly have
some leisurely mornings. Normally, he hit the alarm at
5:00, hit the kitchen at 5:10, hit the gym in his building at 5:30, hit the shower at 6:30 and hit work at 7:15.
He liked being the first one in at Greenback Directive,

because it gave him a chance to catch up on email and other tasks that would fall by the wayside once his staff started trickling in at eight. Even though green consulting was still in its infancy in a lot of ways, there was always plenty to do on any given day.

Actually, the fact that it was such a new field made it even busier. He spent a good bit of his time just explaining what he could do for a company and why integrating environmentally friendly policies into their organizations was good business. He just wished more corporations were interested in reducing their carbon footprint and making themselves more ecologically responsible. It wasn't as if there was a Plan B for the planet once it was bereft of its resources.

It also helped that, although Bennett would be working remotely now, it didn't mean he had to work "from home." Since Ithaca was less than an hour away, he could work from the Cornell University Library if he and Haven started getting on each other's nerves—their internet was probably better anyway.

Though it didn't get to that point during their first week at the house, since he barely saw Haven on those days. While he worked from a makeshift office he set up in the library, she spent most of her time cleaning up in other parts of the house. He often heard her thumping around and vacuuming—though who knew where she'd even found a vacuum. And he regularly saw her dart past the library door with a broom, mop or bucket. Or all three at the same time. Once, when he passed the billiards room on his way to the kitchen to make lunch, he saw her in there on an impossibly tall ladder—seriously, where was she finding this stuff?—wiping down the gigantic chandelier. It was all he could do not to run into the room and grab the bottom of the ladder to make sure she didn't tumble to her death.

She didn't go near his wing of the house, however, he couldn't help noticing. Not that he expected her to clean up the parts of Summerlight she wasn't even using—well, not really, even though she had scoured the smoking room, too, and he was reasonably certain she would never be in there puffing on a stogie—but it did pressure him into spending his evenings cleaning that wing himself. After that first week, he had to admit the house looked a lot better than it had when he and Haven had first entered it. It was still dingy, run-down and kind of sad, but at least the first two floors were—mostly—clean.

Midway through their second week in residence—yay, only fifty-one weeks to go!—Bennett was in the middle of a Zoom call in his library office when a pounding that had erupted upstairs midmorning became more than he could bear. It had been occasionally interspersed with an even louder clanking—and once by the whirring of a power tool—and since all the noises had been coming from directly overhead, they'd all been loud enough that his associates with whom he'd been in session had asked about them. The moment he was able to conclude their business and close his MacBook, he rose to search for the origin.

It didn't take long for him to follow the sound down the hall toward the room Haven had chosen as her own bedroom. But the noise wasn't coming from her bedroom. He knew that because he peeked in there first—hey, the door was open, so it wasn't as if he was snooping. In fact, it was the first time he'd traveled to this part of the house at all since that first night, because he had started to think of this as Haven's wing.

He was surprised by how comfortable she had made the space, considering how little she had arrived with. His first day in Summerlight, he'd inspected the living areas thoroughly before choosing which room would be his. All the bedrooms had obviously been guest rooms, save for the big master bedroom joining both wings that had clearly been Aunt Aurelia's. Bennett hadn't wanted to claim that room, though, both out of respect for its previous occupant and because he hadn't wanted to create an imbalance of power between himself and Haven. All the other rooms had been plain by the Victorian standards of Summerlight's time, with only functional furnishings, impersonal touches and no memorabilia to speak of.

But whereas his bedroom still looked like a guest room, Haven had collected bits and pieces from elsewhere in the house, probably during her travels while cleaning it, to make this room more hospitable. Cozy, even. There were tapestry pillows on the bed, and potted plants lined the window seat. A fringed, paisley shawl draped an overstuffed chair. She'd hung a number of old framed photos, including a wedding portrait from what looked like the 1920s—all people from Bennett's family even he couldn't have identified. A mirrored dresser held colorful bric-a-brac and more old photos of unidentified people.

Why she would want to invite the odds and ends of people to whom she had no connection—people who were her sworn enemies, even—into her personal space was beyond him. But he had to admit the room was a lot more inviting than his own.

The noise erupted again, in a bathroom two doors down from where he stood. He found Haven in there, sprawled on the floor, her lower half wrapped in cargo pants covered with dozens of stains that might have been paint or filth—or both—her upper half gobbled up by a decrepit vanity housing an even more decrepit sink. The bathroom was large enough that she had room to scatter tools around herself—which she had—and she reached for one when there was a momentary break in the action, tossing aside another. It hit the dingy honeycomb tile with a clatter, only to be followed by more clanging when her hand with the new tool disappeared into the vanity.

"Moreau," he said, hoping to interrupt whatever she was doing. But she must not have heard him over the clatter. "Moreau," he tried again, a little louder this time. Still, she kept working.

He started to call out her name a third time, then realized it was probably pointless, thanks to the din and the sink enclosure. So he took a step into the room and nudged her booted foot with his toe. She jerked hard at the contact, enough that he heard another thump, this one he recognized as a head making contact with wood. Then she scooted herself out from under the sink, rubbing her forehead.

A forehead, he couldn't help noticing, that displayed a

streak of grease running from her hairline to her cheek-bone. There was another smudge of black on her chin. Bennett didn't think he'd ever had a conversation with a woman who had pipe grease on her face. Or who was wearing suede work gloves that were at least a size too large for her. Somehow, on Haven, though, both features were weirdly...attractive?

She really had grown into a beauty since they were in high school, he thought, not for the first time. The dark blond hair that had been so scraggly and unkempt then was silky smooth now—if still a tad unkempt, falling as it was out of a tattered ponytail that had also been a feature in high school. Now, though, the messiness of her hair looked kind of chic. Like those models in magazines that they probably spent hours making look all rumpled and sexy. Though why he suddenly found the rumpled look kind of sexy when he'd always been attracted to women who were perfectly put together and in no way rumpled was a mystery.

It was her eyes, though, that he found most compelling. He couldn't remember ever being very physically close to her when they were in school, in spite of sharing a couple of classes, but even from a distance, her eyes had always been remarkable—large and thick-lashed, and a startling shade of blue unlike any he'd ever seen. Since he'd been up close to her lately, he'd come to realize that the reason for their unusual color was a tinge of violet that was mixed in with the blue, making them seem deeper somehow, more expressive.

Now those eyes were glaring at him—but they were no less beautiful. She tugged an earbud out of one ear—

so that was why she hadn't heard him—and a stream of what sounded like some fabulous forties' film torch singer flowed out to greet him. The music surprised him. It just seemed too romantic and old-fashioned a genre for her.

"What the hell was that?" she asked.

And why was he suddenly attracted to women who swore a lot? He'd always preferred women who were articulate and well-spoken and only relied on profanity when there was no other way to express their disdain or frustration.

"I called your name twice," he said, "but you didn't hear me."

She looked as if she didn't believe him. "What do you want?"

Immediately, he was carried back to that morning last week in the grocery store, when she'd asked him something similar. *Is there anything else you want?* He'd known she meant anything else he wanted in the store. But somehow, for some reason, it had come out sounding as though she was asking him if he wanted her. And, weirdly, in that moment, he kind of had wanted her. Only for a moment. Only long enough for him to realize that he had completely misunderstood the question, and that she hadn't been asking him that at all, and that his libido, which he'd been neglecting for far too long, had been the body part listening, not his ears. His libido must be listening now, too. Because there was still something about the way she'd asked the question that made him think she was asking him if he wanted her. And there was still something about her that made him want her.

Ridiculous, he immediately told himself. Haven wasn't asking him if he wanted her, and he wasn't wanting her the way he thought. She couldn't be. He couldn't be. He'd just gone too long wanting what he hadn't had in a long time—namely a halfway decent partner, one who was well put-together and didn't swear all the time, with whom he could spend hours and hours, all night long in fact, doing the kinds of things that made two people—

"What are you doing?" he asked, reining in his thoughts and shoving them to the furthest corners of his brain.

She jutted her thumb toward the underpinnings of the sink. "The water pressure in this bathroom is terrible, and it seems to be getting worse every time I use the shower. It's better in the one by your bedroom but still not as good as it should be. That made me hope the problem is just in here, since a single room is a lot easier to deal with than a whole floor. Or, worse, a whole house."

She'd checked his bathroom at some point? he wondered, barely hearing the rest of what she said. When had she done that? Presumably while he was working and not while he was sleeping, but it was still kind of creepy. And maybe kind of weirdly arousing. But mostly creepy, he assured himself when he started feeling weirdly aroused.

"So far, I haven't found anything out of the ordinary up here," she continued, "except that everything is really old and almost certainly original to the house. I've never seen pipework like this, and I've worked on buildings that are a hundred years old. I just hope whatever's wrong isn't a problem for the whole house. Because that would end up being a *major* problem for you and me."

Putting aside, for now, how her use of the phrase "you and me" made something inside him tilt a little off-kilter, and in spite of his realization that the house wasn't in the best of shape, it hadn't occurred to Bennett that its condition could pose a problem for him and Haven while they were living there. He truly had been focused on just biding their time over the next twelve months, by which point, they would have figured out what to do with the place. If there were going to be problems between now and then, they would be the ones responsible for dealing with them, and that could get expensive. He hadn't yet taken the time to read the particulars of Aunt Aurelia's will. There was a chance she had set up a fund or trust that would cover any kind of additional expenses he and Haven might accrue while living there. But there was also a chance she *hadn't* set up a fund or trust for that.

"That doesn't sound good," he said with much understatement.

"Maybe, maybe not," she replied. "Depends on a number of factors."

"Such as?"

She sat up and pulled her legs up in front of herself, then rested her arms on her knees, looking thoughtful. And still clutching the tool that looked way too big for her to manage. It wasn't that he was a sexist, thinking women weren't capable of wielding tools as well as a man. He knew they could. Hell, he wasn't all that great at fixing things himself. But Haven barely topped five feet, and the tool in question looked nearly half that length. The too-big gloves didn't help. There had to be someone out there making work gloves that fit small hands. Yet, for some reason, she had shunned those to wear some that could easily fit both of her hands into one.

"It could be a lot of things," she finally said. "For one thing, I assumed the house was on the same water system as the village, but this far up from Sudbury, it could be using a well." She gritted her teeth, as if that would be a Very Bad Thing. "I mean if there's a well, then there's a well pump, and if it's centrifugal-style, and the well is deep..."

Here she launched into an explanation of why that could be a problem, followed by a variety of other things that could also be the cause of the bad water pressure, not a single one of which Bennett understood. All he knew was that he hoped it didn't affect his showers, because a winter without hot showers would be like, well, a winter with cold showers. And that would indeed be a Very Bad Thing.

Finally, she ended with, "How many bathrooms are in this house? I don't think I counted when I was looking at the plans."

"Seven," he told her. "Two on the first floor, three up here on the second, two on the third. No, wait, there's one up on the servants' floor, too. So eight all together."

She looked thoughtful again for another moment. "I wonder if Mr. Crittenden has any kind of blueprint for the house that would include the plumbing and electrical plans. It would be superhelpful to know where the main water valve is. Among other things. Now that I think about it, since we're going to be here for a year, and with winter breathing down our necks, I probably should check this place over thoroughly. If your aunt Aurelia let the underparts of the house fall into the kind of bad shape the obvious parts are in, it's a good bet the stuff behind the walls and under the floors is giving away, too."

Bennett suddenly felt defensive on his aunt's behalf. Even if he hadn't been particularly close to her—he'd barely known her—she'd still been family. Elderly family, at that, grief-stricken and probably mentally compromised by the end, too.

"Aunt Aurelia was old," he reminded Haven. "And she lived here all alone. And she was still in mourning for her husband. If she neglected the place, it wasn't through…neglect."

To her credit, Haven looked contrite. "I'm sorry. I didn't mean to speak badly of your aunt. I just…" She sighed heavily. "When I look at a house, I don't see its owners. I see the state it's in. When it's in this kind of shape, all I see is how it hasn't been taken care of the way it should have been. How it's been mistreated. How it's lost its spirit. Its life. Houses like this were the American equivalent to palaces when they were built. We'll never see architecture or details or finishes like these again. Summerlight was a treasure once upon a time, Hadden. It was magnificent. It should have been spoiled and pampered instead of deserted and ignored. It deserved better."

She spoke of the house the way she might have spoken of a person. And not just any person but someone who made the world a better place just by existing, and who then was left to perish alone and heartbroken. Bennett would have thought she would think places like this were excessive and obscene in light of the way a lot of people had been forced to live when they were built—crowded into sagging tenements, lined up at soup kitchens, slaving in factories and sweatshops alongside their children. Truth be told, that was kind of how Bennett felt about places like this himself. Instead, she seemed to admire the house and be saddened it was no longer viable.

Then again, her father had told her stories about it when she was a child, which had turned it into a fairy-tale castle. Maybe there was a part of her that still thought it was.

"This house was radiant in its prime," she said softly, seeming to read his mind. "A time when there was little beauty in the world to be had. Hell, there's little beauty to be had in the world now. And anything that's beautiful should stay. Instead, the majority of houses like this got torn down and discarded in the name of progress. Progress that did nothing to make the world a better or more beautiful place. I'd hate it if the same thing happened to Summerlight."

Hearing her talk about the house the way she did, Bennett was filled with a sense of…something. Something not particularly good. When he'd first entered

Summerlight, he'd decided almost immediately that it was a lost cause. It would cost a fortune just to repair and update the things he could see. As she said, if the things he couldn't see were in comparable shape, they might as well multiply that fortune tenfold. The house's time—and its splendor—seemed long past to him. Haven, though, seemed to think differently. That maybe there was a reason—and even a way—to save the place. A way to really turn it into some kind of magic, fairy-tale sanctuary.

Surely, he was misreading that. Surely, she wasn't thinking there was any real potential for rehabilitation of the place. Surely, she was as confident as he was that the place was a lost cause and should be sold for whatever they could get for it at the end of the year. Surely, she was.

Surely.

She opened her mouth to say something, and he braced himself for her telling him she wanted to start renovating the house ASAP. Instead, she said, "I have to go into Sudbury tomorrow. I need to find a job."

He almost laughed…until he realized she was serious. "What? Why?"

"Because I'm going to run out of money if I don't," she said. "I talked to my mother this morning, and she told me one of her friends has a daughter who's interested in subletting my apartment until I get back. But even with my rent and utilities covered for the year, I'm gonna go out on a limb and say that you and I are going to have more than a few expenses where Summerlight is concerned between now and the end of our time here. I don't want to end up broke."

He started to tell her she wouldn't be broke after they sold the place. Even in its current state, it would bring in a decent amount, if for no other reason than the land it was sitting on could be worth a lot—provided there was someone out there who wanted to develop it, and provided the town of Sudbury would allow development this close to their sleepy village. Then he remembered that neither of them had mentioned selling the place. Until they talked about it, he couldn't assume anything. Especially after just hearing Haven talk about Summerlight with such affection.

But he was reasonably certain she would want to sell the place as much as he did. Surely, she would.

Surely.

Chapter Four

The town of Sudbury, Haven realized not long after she made the twenty-minute walk down to it the next morning, wasn't in much better shape than Summerlight was. Though it was clear it had been a picturesque little village at one time, which had probably drawn a fair share of holiday-goers. She noted a number of small, seasonal shops, a small microbrewery, a small inn, a small grocery store, a small café… Well, suffice it to say that pretty much everything in Sudbury was small. Charming, too, in a once-upon-a-time kind of way that made her feel as if she'd wandered into the fairy tale her father had told her when she was a little girl. Sudbury had to be the enchanted village he'd described.

The enchantment, though, was failing now. There was a fatigue about the place that was also unmistakable. More than one of the shops she passed looked closed up tight, though whether for the season or for good she couldn't have said. A sign at the entrance to the—small—marina was still advertising a regatta that had taken place over a year ago, and another announced that there were still plenty of huts available to reserve for the upcoming ice-fishing season. Obviously, the demand for those wasn't what it used to be.

Even the people Haven passed on the street looked tired and strained. The few she encountered smiled, and some even offered a half-cheery hello. But mostly, they reminded her of Summerlight. Somber and weary and in dire need of life. Sudbury's glory days had clearly waned, too, and the little town was holding on for dear life.

At the end of what looked like the historic section of town—though, honestly, the whole town looked like it was stuck in the early twentieth century—she found the business she'd specifically been looking for: Huxley's Habitat. Haven had done some googling last night and discovered that Sudbury had its own version of Right at Home, run by one Finn Huxley, who, like she, seemed to be the only employee. With any luck, he, like she, could use a hand with some of his jobs. With even better luck, he, *unlike* she, could afford to pay someone a decent wage to be such a hand. Hey, at least he had an actual storefront, so he must be doing something right. Haven still worked out of her apartment, using a PO box for her professional address to mask that.

A sign on the door was flipped to the open side, so she turned the knob and entered. Her arrival was accompanied by the tinkle of a small bell overhead and followed by a booming "Be right out!" from somewhere in back, before she even closed the door behind herself. True to his word, the speaker appeared within seconds, a big bear of a man with blond hair and the greenest eyes she'd ever seen. He was so tall, he had to duck to clear the door to the store's front room, and his big frame was wrapped in enough flannel and denim to clothe every contestant in the Lumberjack World Series. If, you know, there actually were a Lumberjack World Series.

"What can I do for you?" the man she presumed was Finn Huxley asked without preamble.

"Hi," she said. In light of his right-to-the-pointness, she stated, flat out, "My name is Haven, and I need a job. I was wondering if you were hiring."

His pale eyebrows shot up to his hairline. Like everyone else she encountered for the first time in her work, he was probably thinking she was too girly and too small for any kind of hard labor. She wished she'd worn her tool belt. The one that had a special loop for her impact driver.

"Do you have any experience?" he asked skeptically.

"I have my own shop," she told him—seeing absolutely no reason to elaborate that her "shop" was actually a desk in the corner of her four-hundred-square-foot apartment that was decked out with all the accoutrements a person could buy at OfficeMax—right down to the plastic three-shelf, side-load desk organizer and letter tray that had set her back a full twelve bucks.

Finn Huxley, though, remained dubious. Okay, fine, she had stopped using the plastic three-shelf, side-load desk organizer and letter tray when she realized how much of her billing and receiving she could do online and had instead turned it into a catchall for her Nintendo Switch games and individually wrapped bags of matcha. So she explained her situation as quickly as she could. She told him how she was one of the new owners of Summerlight and would be wintering there—and springing and summering, too—and was hoping to support herself in the meantime with a few odd jobs here and there. He asked her some questions about handiwork in general and her own work in particular, and she replied easily and confidently to each one.

Her replies must have satisfied him, because he gave her a long, thoughtful look, then told her, "I don't really need a full-time employee, and it's not exactly high season for work right now, but yeah. I could probably find a few things for you to do. It would free me up to work on a couple of bigger projects of my own." He cited her an hourly rate that was only slightly less than the absolute-rock-bottom-dollar amount Haven had promised herself she wouldn't take less than, and she told him it would be perfect.

"Even ten or fifteen hours a week would be great," she told him. "There's a lot to do up at Summerlight, too, and I'd like to have time to see to those jobs, as well."

He nodded. "Shame about Mrs. Hadden. She was a nice lady. I used to go up to Summerlight with my dad when I was a kid to help him out with the occasional odd task up there. She always made fresh lemonade for us and sent us home with a bag of her homemade spice cookies."

"I never had the privilege of meeting her," Haven told him. "But I gather she led quite an eventful life."

Finn looked surprised. "You never met her, but she left you her house?"

"Well, me and her nephew, yeah. It's kind of complicated," she rushed to add before he started asking too many questions—many of which Haven probably still wouldn't be able to answer. She tried to clarify as quickly she could by saying "But my family had something of a claim to the house, too. She didn't just pull my name out of a hat."

Now Finn nodded knowingly and said, "*Ooohhh.* You must be one of those Moreaus." He smiled. "Funny, but you don't have horns or a pointed tail *or* reek of brimstone like I've always heard."

Haven was surprised that the Hadden-Moreau feud was that well-known in Sudbury, even if one of the family members only lived a stone's throw from the village. Thanks to her bequest to both Bennett and Haven, Aurelia Hadden hadn't seemed to be especially wedded to the conflict. Then again, four generations of Haddens had lived there before her, so at least that many generations had called Sudbury home before now. Who knew how many earlier Haddens had badmouthed earlier Moreaus? It made sense that the townspeople would side with their neighbor, regardless of the time period, and it made sense that they would share the lore with their respective families, regardless of the generation.

"It's cool," Finn said, seeming to read her mind. "Mrs. Hadden never had a bad word to say about anyone. I think her husband might have had a thorn in his side about your family, but he died before I was born. According to my dad, though, you Moreaus were never the most popular people here in Sudbury."

Great, Haven thought. She'd traveled behind enemy lines without even realizing it, and now she had no backup. *Note to self: Never give your last name to anyone while here.*

"Nobody really talks about it much anymore," Finn assured her. "Except maybe some of the old-timers. You should be fine."

Should be fine, she noted. Not *would* be. She wasn't sure how much import to put on the distinction. But she really would avoid revealing her last name to anyone she came into contact with.

Finn Huxley pulled his phone from his back pocket and began scrolling through what she assumed was his calendar. "I don't really have anything much coming up for the next week or two," he said, still scrolling. "But there might be something—"

He stopped scrolling then backed up a bit. Then he looked at Haven again.

"Actually, let me make a call. I had a potential client about a month ago that needed some small jobs done around her house, but when she found out I'd be the one doing the work, she said she'd find someone else to do it instead. Unfortunately for her, I'm the only one in town who knows how to do the work. No one from Ithaca will come this far for small jobs like hers. Far as I know, she still needs the work done, and maybe she wouldn't object to you doing it."

Haven wanted to ask for clarification, since Finn

Huxley seemed like a nice enough guy, and she wasn't sure why he wouldn't be welcome somewhere. But she said nothing, since the two of them were still pretty much strangers, and it was none of her business. Her confusion must have shown on her face, though, because he smiled and proceeded to give her an explanation anyway.

"Her daughter and I had a thing back in high school, but she never approved of me. She still doesn't. So the farther away she keeps me from Alice, the better. She'd probably be fine with you. And you and Alice will probably get along great. She's kind of a town outcast, too."

He seemed to say that as if being a town outcast weren't such a bad thing, but Haven wasn't crazy about having such a distinction. Whatever. If he had a job for her, and that job paid an almost-living wage, she'd take it.

"Sounds good," she told Finn. She pulled her wallet from her back pocket and gave him one of her business cards. "Just shoot me a text if you have anything for me." She smiled. "My schedule's pretty free for the next, oh... year."

Bennett was just prepping for dinner, getting his *mise en place* in place, when he saw Haven outside through the kitchen window, returning to Summerlight from Sudbury. Today was still chilly, but there was a bright sun sinking toward the horizon, and the blue sky was clear, stained now with the pinks and oranges of early evening. The trees that had looked so frayed the morning after their arrival had bounced back, gleaming with hints of the auburns and ochers of autumn. The lake that had roiled gray and gloomy that day was now blue and flat, throwing back the late afternoon light as if it were limned with gold. He'd give Winston Moreau credit for one thing—he couldn't have chosen a more beautiful spot on which to build his family getaway all those years ago.

As if cued by the thought, the robber baron's great-great-great—how-many-greats-was-it-again?—granddaughter appeared in the door of the mudroom, which led from the kitchen to the back door. Her cheeks were pink from the brisk air and exertion, and the hair beneath her cap was again falling in thick strands from the ponytail at her nape. He wondered why she even bothered. Not only did her hair seem to be adamant about not being restrained but it was far too nice to not be allowed to roam free.

Having avoided each other as much as they could during their two weeks in residence so far, they still stood on shaky ground, neither ever seeming to know what to say or how to act around the other when they did find themselves in the same place. Although they'd managed to maintain a decent degree of courtesy, their lack of interaction hadn't exactly allowed them an opportunity to be much more than tolerant of each other's presence. Right now was no exception. Bennett had no idea what to say or do. And the fact that Haven was looking at him as if she were just as uncertain as he was didn't help matters. Nor did the fact that, as always, he couldn't help noticing how beautiful she'd grown since the last time they had to be around each other, when they were in school. He really needed to stop noticing that.

"Hi," she finally said. Cordially. Uncertainly.

"Hi," he replied in exactly the same way. "How did it go in Sudbury?"

"Good," she told him.

But she didn't elaborate. She unzipped her jacket—an army green canvas bomber jacket that, like her work gloves, was a couple of sizes too big—and hung it on a peg just inside the door of the mudroom. It was followed by a too-long knitted scarf and the too-big beanie, its removal causing her hair to really fall out of its confines. Hastily, she unfastened the band that held her ponytail in place and, without even seeming to pay attention to what she was doing, she gathered her hair again at her nape and twisted the band back around it…only to have those same stubborn strands as before immediately fall free. Not that she seemed to notice that, either. Or maybe she just didn't care. Her clothes today mirrored the ones she'd arrived in, her sweater dark blue and falling past her hips over faded jeans, and worn work boots.

Bennett didn't think he'd ever encountered another human being who seemed so unconcerned about their appearance. He'd grown up in a family where first impressions were everything. And second, third, fourth and every other impression was just as important. As a child, he and his sisters had had to dress up for everything, and woe betide them if any of them had ever had a hair out of place. It had been the same for every kid he knew. Maybe there were some rich kids out there whose parents didn't care about things like image, but Bennett had sure never met one. Every family member he had, every kid he'd known at school, everyone he'd ever worked with, all of them made sure to present a perfectly well-put-together self to the outside world.

Even at Greenback Directive, where he tried to nurture a fairly casual work environment—every day was casual day at his office—his employees showed up looking cultivated and polished. He supposed they were just following the example he set by being their boss, but he wished they'd all loosen up a little. Just because he didn't know how to do that himself didn't mean no one could.

Haven moved to the fridge, which was as old and energy inefficient as everything else in the kitchen was, and withdrew a bottle of beer. She did, at least, have good taste in that, he'd noted when she dropped the six-pack of IPAs into the cart at the grocery store that first day. Then she twisted off the cap with an inelegant hiss.

"What's for dinner?" she asked, somewhat awkwardly but striving for civility. Hey, at least she was trying. "I mean, I'll probably just stick a potpie in the oven when you're finished in here," she added, "but what are you fixing for yourself? Smells good."

All he'd done so far was chop up some onions and garlic. But the fresh basil he'd been delighted to find still growing along with some other herbs out in the garden smelled pretty good, too.

"I was just going to throw together a little pasta *pomodoro*," he told her. Then, reluctantly, since he wasn't sure how she'd take the offer, but trying to be more accommodating, too, he added, "I'm happy to make enough for both of us."

He could tell she was about to decline—it was probably an instinct for her by now—then was surprised when she told him, "That'd be nice. Thanks. I can do the cleaning up afterward."

Okay, so the kind words came out sounding a little resentful. She had offered to help out, cleaning up when they were done. She really did seem to be trying to at least move past their animosity. He didn't kid himself that the two of them could ever be friends. There was too much ill will between both them and their families. But it was likely they'd each stopped plotting the other's murder. That was a huge step forward. Maybe if they both kept making conscious efforts at civility, they could end the year on a note of decorum. And wouldn't that be something?

"Can I do anything to help?" she asked, going one step further than civility.

"Um, sure," he told her. "You can open the wine. I brought up a bottle of Pinot Noir from the cellar."

She looked at her beer, then back at him.

"I need it for the pomodoro," he told her. "But yeah, you could pour me a glass, too." When she looked at him expectantly, he rolled his eyes and added, "Please."

Haven was as good as her word. She not only helped by opening the wine but she opened the cans of tomatoes, too—shame they didn't have fresh, but what could you do in October?—then grated the Parmesan. She even went so far as to set the table in the corner of the room with more of the fine china with tiny rosebuds and gold trim that seemed to be the only dishes in the house.

"And, as always, I have no idea where to find napkins," Haven said after disappearing into the butler's pantry for a moment and returning empty-handed. "I've been using paper towels when I eat, but that just doesn't seem right for an actual table setting."

"Pretty sure Aunt Aurelia only used cloth. Check the china cabinet out in the formal dining room," he added. He'd found the napkins his first day here.

Haven disappeared again, returning with two silky-looking bits of fabric. "I've heard these existed," she said, "but I've never known anyone who used them."

"Oh, come on," he replied. "Everyone's grandmother had cloth napkins when we were growing up."

She looked up from where she'd been placing the napkins on the table. "I never knew either one of my grandmothers," she told him. "They both died before I was born."

Bennett sobered. She had been matter-of-fact in her delivery. But there was something sad in her demeanor. "I'm sorry, Moreau," he told her. "That was a thought-less thing to say."

She lifted one shoulder and let it drop, then made a bigger-than-necessary deal about straightening the silverware and dishes. "No need to apologize. You couldn't have known."

Except that he could have. He knew plenty of things about Haven's family. He knew her aunt Rose had made her way in the world as a young woman by being "kept," as his mother said, by lonely Park Avenue widowers. He knew her cousin Nanette shoplifted handbags from Bergdorf. He knew her cousin Dexter was constantly tossed out of SoHo bars for creating some kind of scene. He knew her uncle Desmond sold counterfeit Cartier online. He knew her father had never graduated from high school. Bennett just didn't know any things about the Moreau family that didn't paint them in a bad light. Evidently, no one in his family had ever considered anything else than that possibility, so they'd never bothered to learn more. Or, if they did learn something good about the Moreaus, they decided to overlook it.

"I'm still sorry," he told Haven. "Everyone should have a chance to know their grandparents."

She looked up at that, her expression blank, as if she were trying to figure out if there was some kind of double meaning behind what he said. He guessed he couldn't blame her for thinking the worst of him. She'd probably heard similar stories about his own family over the years. About how his aunt Renee was currently on her seventh husband. About how his cousin Phillip ran a multilevel marketing company that preyed on college students. About how his uncle Harmon's ex-wife had a restraining order in place. About how his cousin Alvy was only successful in the stock market because of insider trading.

Finally, she said, "My mother's father died when she was a teenager, so I didn't know him, either. But I still have my grandpa Moreau."

Who, Bennett also knew, had been in a memory care facility for at least a decade, so it had probably been a while since she'd been able to have much of a relationship with him. But he didn't say anything about that. He'd already brought up enough unpleasant memories for her. Unfortunately, he wasn't sure how to move on to something more cheerful. She didn't seem to know, either, because she went back to arranging the place settings that had already been well set into place.

After a few moments of awkward silence, she looked up and said, "I got a job today."

Bennett looked back at her, surprised. "Just like that?" He'd thought she was being overly optimistic, thinking she could just walk into Sudbury, introduce herself to a couple of people and come home employed. But it looked like that was exactly what she'd done.

She nodded. "There's a guy in town who has a business similar to mine, and he said he could use someone part-time for small jobs. It's exactly what I need, since there are some projects I wouldn't mind tackling here at Summerlight, too."

That announcement surprised him even more than the one about her finding a job. They'd been at Summerlight two weeks. How many projects besides the one in her bathroom could she have found?

"Like what?" he asked. "I mean, I know you want to look into the plumbing situation, but the rest of the place seems solid enough for now." In spite of the misgivings he'd been having about the house, he added, "The only problems I've noticed are cosmetic. We can fix those ourselves if we have to. Or hire someone from town to take care of them."

She smiled. "Great. I'll let my new employer know you're willing to pay his part-timer to tackle a few things up here. Much obliged, Hadden. Here I thought all the work I'd be doing around Summerlight would be labors of love."

Okay, he'd walked right into that one. It didn't mean

he was going to pay her for work she was willing to do anyway. Probably. Once he figured out how to walk back what he'd just said.

She continued, "Anyway, for now, sure, a lot of the obvious challenges are cosmetic. But just taking a look around while I was cleaning the last couple weeks, I found a lot of places that could potentially go beyond challenging. And not just cosmetically," she clarified.

"Are they challenges that can't wait a year?" he asked.

She looked confused. "Why would we wait a year to address them?"

"Because after that, they'd be someone else's challenges."

Now she looked even more confused. "I don't understand. If Summerlight has problems, then it's up to its owners to fix them."

"Exactly. In a year, we could sell this place to someone else. Then everything would be a concern for the new owners."

Bennett hadn't meant to just blurt out his intentions that way. Even though he'd been reasonably sure Haven would share his conviction that it was unrealistic for either of them to keep the place, never mind both of them, he hadn't planned on throwing that possibility out there until the two of them had settled in better and had a more realistic idea of what kind of shape the house was in and then had a chance to sit down and discuss it. And, okay, after they'd had a chance to stabilize their relationship—whatever it was. But she'd brought up the perfect opportunity for them to talk about it now. So what the hell. They might as well at least get the conversation started.

To soften the blow a bit, and because the idea had occurred to him more than a few times—and because she was suddenly looking at him as if he'd just stolen her favorite Beanie Baby—he told her, "I mean, if nothing else, someone in my family might want to buy it from us, just to keep it in Hadden hands. And most of them have the means to make any repairs or do any updating that needs to be done. Who knows? My parents might even want to buy it from us to move here. They're getting to that age where they're talking about what they want to do when my dad retires."

In spite of her stolen–Beanie Baby expression, Haven didn't seem all that surprised or averse to his suggestion. Then she told him, "I'm not certain yet we should sell Summerlight."

Well, damn. Bennett wasn't as good at hiding his own surprise and aversion. He turned away from the stove to look at her. "You can't honestly be thinking we keep the place."

She shrugged. "Why can't I be thinking that?"

"Why *would* you think that?"

She shrugged again. "I don't know. But we've only been here a couple weeks. It's too soon to make any decisions one way or another."

"Yeah, and you've already said you've found problems with the house that could go beyond cosmetic. What do you think you're going to find after being here a whole year?"

"I don't know," she said again. "That's just the point.

If it's in better shape than I think it is, it wouldn't be that hard or that expensive to rehab it."

He couldn't believe she was actually suggesting what she seemed to be suggesting. "What? You mean renovate it ourselves?"

"Sure. Like I said, depending on its condition."

"Moreau, that could cost a fortune."

"Hadden, I can do a lot of the work myself. And I know people who can give us a good deal on materials. For the jobs that require more than one person, we can hire outside labor. You'd be surprised how many rehabbing businesses there are in Ithaca."

"What? You've already checked?"

She looked a little panicked. *Busted.* "Maybe?"

He crossed his arms over his midsection. He knew she'd probably read it as a defensive gesture. But, hell, he was beginning to feel a little defensive. "Okay, fine," he said indulgently. "Say we somehow magically find the funds and workforce to make over Summerlight, right back to its original glory. Then what? We live here together happily ever after? A Hadden and a Moreau? A million miles away from our real lives?"

"Of course not," she was quick to assure him.

"So then we what? Turn it into a tourist attraction? Assume people are going to drive all the way to Sudbury to see a house that has absolutely no significance other than that it's old?"

"Why not?" she asked. "The Finger Lakes has tons of tourism. There's all kinds of stuff to do up here, especially this time of year, when the autumn colors are coming out."

"And there are already a lot of places to draw those tourists," he pointed out. "We'd be competing in a market full of other way-older, way-better-established businesses, run by people who, unlike us, know what the hell they're doing when it comes to the tourist industry."

At that, she seemed to retreat a bit. All she said was, "Maybe we could turn Summerlight into a hotel."

He struggled to keep his expression neutral. "Do you know how much work goes into running a hotel? It's insane. And a hotel for what? There's nothing nearby, except Sudbury, and it's on its last legs as much as Summerlight is."

She looked as if she wanted to argue, but instead, she relented. "I just think it's too early for us to make any long-term plans for the house," she finally said. "We have a whole year. And I'd like to do a more thorough inventory of the place and see what's what before we make any decisions one way or another."

Bennett told himself to cut her some slack. They'd been here less than a month, and he'd seen for himself how she'd started to romanticize the house. He remembered her story from that first night about how her father had turned Summerlight into a fairy-tale castle for her when she was little. She'd pretty much said herself that she saw places like this as more human than their owners. He should just drop the subject and let her do her investigating. Let her do her dreaming. Let her make her plans. Once she saw how unrealistic they were and how impractical it would be for the two of them to do anything with the house besides sell it—though he really hated to think about how a development like that would go down with either of their families should neither step up to buy it themselves—she would come around to his way of thinking. Their families, on the other hand…

Well. It wasn't up to their families, he reminded himself. They weren't the owners of the house. He and Haven were. Or would be, once they made it through the year. Looking at her now, however, and the way her blue eyes were flashing, and the way her chin was jutted up with just the slightest hint of challenge…

Well *again*. He was starting to wonder if maybe it wasn't up to him, either.

Chapter Five

By the end of her third week at Summerlight, Haven was starting to form an impression of what exactly she and Bennett had gotten themselves into. Or, rather, what his aunt had gotten them into. Although she was certain Aurelia never meant for either of them to have any problems with her bequest, the fact was that there were definitely problems with her bequest. Because although Summerlight had been constructed at a time when houses were built to last, this particular house was starting to fail and wouldn't last much longer, thanks to its not having been maintained the way it should have been for the last few decades.

Although she wasn't convinced the place would need to be gutted, it definitely needed a lot of work. More work than Haven could perform by herself, even having a year to complete it. More work than she could afford financially to put into it. More work than Bennett could probably afford financially to put into it. His family and extended family might be able to cover the costs, as he had said, but why would they, when a Moreau would ultimately benefit from the outcome? God forbid they should contribute to anything that would help out the enemy. Even so, it wouldn't hurt to at least ask Bennett to put out some feelers to his family, to see if any might be inclined to help pay for the restoration of the house they'd fought so hard, for so long to hold on to.

And she would ask him that. As soon as he got back from his errands in Ithaca, and after she got down from the roof—once she found a way to access it.

Since the weather had continued to be clear, if chilly, she'd spent a lot of time outside this week, surveying the exterior of the house. She'd found a number of places where the bare minimum of work had been done to prevent the worst damage, but there were nearly as many places where water—the most evil enemy a building could have—had done its share of damage.

Houses were built according to their environments, of course, so Summerlight had been protected against the severe upstate New York winters as well as it could have been. But that had been nearly a century and a half ago. These days, there was a lot more that could have been done to weatherize the place, but Aurelia had clearly decided not to take advantage of those options. Certainly not because of the expense, since she'd had money to burn. More likely just because she'd felt too overwhelmed or had still been too lost in her grief for her late husband to really care.

What work had been done had been done well. Probably by Finn Huxley and/or his father, so her new employer was obviously as good at his craft as she was. But there was only so much a craftsperson could do if their client couldn't—or wouldn't—go the extra mile.

Which was what had brought Haven to attempt to access the roof of Summerlight. A house's roof was its first line of defense. If moisture got in up top, it eventually found a path all through the house, right down to the foundation. And once the foundation succumbed, well, that was the end of everything. If the roof was in good shape, then there might be hope for the rest of the house. If the roof wasn't tight, well…

First things first. Haven wasn't going to worry about that until she had a look topside.

She found her way up to the fourth floor for the first time since her second day in residence, when she'd made a brief inspection of the whole house. It was really little more than a garret that had been sliced up into eight small rooms, four on each side of a narrow hallway. The first one, she discovered upon opening the door, was a closet filled with boxes and linens that smelled of dust and cedar oil. The next room was a small bathroom with a toilet and sink but no shower. The rest of the rooms were bedrooms with no windows or frills. This apparently really had been the servants' quarters when the house was built. And it looked as if none of the rooms had been used—or cleaned—in a long, *long* time.

It did relieve—and surprise—her that there had been no sign of pest infestation anywhere in the house, including these obviously ignored rooms. Either there were no small rodents or bats living this far north in the state—unlikely—or Aurelia had at least had pest control come in regularly to treat the place. It was another hopeful indication that the house wasn't so far gone that it was beyond rehabilitation.

At the end of the hall was a tall window that opened onto a slender widow's walk. Its latch was painted shut, Haven realized when she reached it, something that didn't surprise her. She'd come prepared, tugging a wrench from the back pocket of her cargo pants—there were various and sundry other small tools in her additional pockets—which was how she usually traveled through her days here at Summerlight. She first scraped away some paint on the latch, then wrestled the fixture free. The moment she opened the window, a blast of fresh, cold air rushed inside, a welcome cleanse for the staleness that had surrounded her. She climbed through the window, sitting first on the windowsill and then gripping the sides firmly as she extended a leg to test the integrity of the metal walkway. It held firm, so, still clinging to the window, she extended her other leg down and exerted more weight onto the foot-wide extension. Finally, never letting go of the window, she put her whole weight onto the walk. It didn't so much as tremble. Okay, then. More reason to expect that the rest of this part of the house was as sound as she hoped.

The view up there was incredible, she realized once she'd climbed through the window. She could see for miles. On the other side of Cayuga Lake was another Victorian village much like Sudbury, its mostly clay and metal roofs and stubby chimneys looking like something out of a Charles Dickens novel. The slate-gray sky behind it only added to the image. The lake, too, was gray again today, and the leaves on the autumn-stained trees between them looked like old copper-and-gold ornaments. For one whimsical moment, she imagined herself a servant for the original owners of Summerlight—her own ancestors, so really, she should have imagined herself as a socialite, but that for sure didn't feel right—sneaking out onto the roof to enjoy the last bit of the vista before packing up the family to return to the dark, dingy city.

What must it have been like for all of them back then? How must it have felt to be a young woman of any social station calling a house like this home, even if only for part of the year? Haven had grown up in the upstairs half of the Port Richmond duplex where her mom still lived, with half a backyard, lined by a leaning privacy fence, and half a front porch that was more stoop than anything else. Her window views as a kid had been of the houses across the street and behind them; she'd mostly seen Mr. Klosterman tending to his roses in the summer and his compost pile in the winter and Mrs. Mancini sitting on her own front stoop, bending the ear of anyone who made the mistake of walking by her house too slowly to escape her interest. Haven's home had been minimalist before minimalist was trendy, and the scenery of her everyday life had been urban and working-class. To live in a grand home such as Summerlight, looking out at views like this every day...

Well. It really would have been like living in a fairy-tale castle.

She shook off the uncharacteristic whimsy in her head and took a few more careful steps along the walk. The surface was definitely secure. So, without further concern, she scrambled up onto the roof proper. It had a steep pitch, but it was no worse than a million other roofs she'd been on in her line of work. Moving as quickly and efficiently as she could, she assessed what she needed to, then returned to the widow's walk, moving to the next section of the house. She had circled from the back to the front, nearly completing her inspection, when she saw Bennett's cream-colored Bentley rolling up the long drive. So she planted herself on the roof and watched until he came to a stop in front of the house. He exited the car without seeing her, grabbing a couple of bags from the back seat, then started to make his way toward the house.

Unable to help herself, she cried out, "Hi, Hadden!" and waved vigorously to him.

He glanced up but didn't wave back. Instead, he glared at her and yelled, "What the hell do you think you're doing, Moreau?"

Had the question been written in text, it would have been all in italics—probably capital italics—and it would have been followed by at least three question marks and even more exclamation points. He was obviously that angry.

"Looking at the roof!" she yelled back with no italics and only one exclamation point, since sound carried really well in a semirural environment like this one, and she probably wasn't telling him anything he hadn't already figured out for himself.

His next words, she was certain, were going to be something along the lines of "Come down from there this instant!" Instead, he just glared at her some more. But she knew that was what he was thinking. Complete with excessive italics, caps and punctuation again.

"I just need to finish giving it a good once-over!" she called down. "Gimme ten! I'm almost done!"

Then she started crab-walking along the roof again, since the widow's walk had ended on the east side of the house and didn't pick up again until the west side. She told herself she only imagined the gasp of fear from Bennett, since he was way too far away and sound didn't carry *that* well in a semirural environment.

When she finally made her way back around to the garret window, he was waiting for her. And he was even angrier than he'd been on the ground. Okay, okay, so maybe it had taken more like twenty minutes to get back instead of the ten she'd promised. There had been a place that had looked like a few shingles were loose, but it had turned out to just be some scrub that had blown off a tree. Anyway, there was no reason for him to be so mad. And there was certainly no reason why he had to grab her with both hands the way he did, the minute she was within reach, and yank her through the window with enough force to land her in the hallway, pitching forward until she was toe to toe with him, close enough to feel the heat of his anger.

Or maybe it was the heat of his body, since it wasn't just their toes that connected. He had his hands wrapped tight around her upper arms and had pulled her close enough that she was enveloped by the fabric of his open coat. Close enough that the cables of her dark wine turtleneck fairly knit with the fine, sea green cashmere of his. Close enough that she could smell the scent of him, something savory and herbaceous that made her want to…taste him. He'd gone a few days without shaving, and there was something about his newly adopted scruffiness that made something inside her respond with a zing of desire. He looked less like the buffed and polished urban professional she knew him to be and more like the guys she was usually attracted to— guys who were a little rough around the edges. Who were a little graceless. A little uncultivated. Guys who were nothing like the Bennett Hadden she'd known— and fallen for—in high school. She liked this version of him. More than she wanted to admit. She hoped he started shaving again. Soon.

For one interminable moment, they stayed entwined, his hands encircling her arms, her fingers curled into his sweater, their gazes locked. His brown eyes were even darker than usual somehow, his mouth set in a firm line that still couldn't quite harden the beauty of his full lower lip, his cheeks burnished from what could have been the cold, or his fury, or…or something else she probably shouldn't even consider. Mostly because thinking about that feeling would make her feel it, too. And feeling that way for Bennett was unthinkable.

And then the moment was gone, because he was setting her away from himself, as far as he could. Unfortunately, in the confines of the cramped hallway, she only ended up pressed into the wall behind her, mere inches away from him, their gazes still locked. Belatedly, she realized she was still gripping his sweater, so she hastily released the garment, pressing her hands flat over the place where she'd bunched it to smooth it out, even though it had snapped back just fine. Bennett must have realized that, because he hastily grabbed both her wrists and jerked her hands from his chest, holding them firmly in the air between them, as if he had no idea what to do with them.

Okay, she'd lied. The moment wasn't gone at all. In fact, just then, the moment turned into something else. Something no less intense, but infinitely more intimate.

Her breath caught in her throat at the depth of her reaction to him then. God help her, she wanted to grip his sweater even more tightly than before, then pull him toward her to cover his mouth with hers. Passionately. Then she wanted to shove his coat off his shoulders, unfasten his belt and pants, then unfasten her belt and pants, then demand that he take her, right then and there, against the wall, in front of the open window, her legs wrapped around his waist as he thrust himself in and out of her.

The image came upon her so fast, and so fiercely, she honestly had to battle the demands building inside her to act. For one insanely wild moment, she nearly did act. For another, even more insanely wild moment, she thought Bennett was reading her mind and that he was every bit as eager as she was to act, too. He even started to lower her hands toward his waist and dip his head toward hers. It was only with the most supreme effort—and conjuring the image of his friends and cousins assailing her on Bow Bridge in Central Park—that she freed her hands from his and took a giant step to the right to escape both him and herself. Then another step. Then another. Until she was halfway down the hall.

Which, admittedly, only put a few feet of space between them. It was enough for her to recapture both her composure and her sanity. Mostly. Okay, some. Enough that she didn't do anything stupid.

For a long time, neither of them said a word. Bennett continued to stare at the wall, as if it hosted the most amazing work of art that had ever graced the planet, and Haven did her best to stare out the window, at the overcast sky. Her gaze kept straying to him, though, and she couldn't help wondering what he was thinking. Probably, it was best not to know.

Suddenly, she had no idea what to do with her hands, so she jammed them into the pockets of her cargo pants. Bennett, in turn, shoved his into the pockets of his coat. Then, very slowly, he turned to look at her. And, in that moment, something shifted, and things almost—almost—returned to normal.

Well, except that both of them were still breathing kind of hard and looking at each other in complete and utter confusion.

"I'm, um, I'm sorry," he said, the words coming out dry and raspy and not especially sincere. "For overreacting, I mean. When I saw you up on the roof like that, I just…" He looked at her more intently, enough that Haven couldn't meet his gaze and dropped hers to the floor. "Moreau, you shouldn't have done something that dangerous when you were here alone," he told her. "You could've fallen, and there wouldn't have been anyone to help you. You could've ended up—"

Here he halted and said nothing more. Probably because he was wondering what the repercussions of her death would have been, and if that might mean he'd inherit Summerlight outright, all for himself, or if it screwed everything up.

Stop it, she immediately told herself. He wasn't thinking that. They'd been getting along fairly well during their occasional encounters. Although they probably wouldn't be enjoying a meal together again after the dinner he'd cooked for them had ended up passing in mostly superficial conversation and awkward silences. They had at least managed to not be petulant when they did see each other. Of course, what had happened between them just now went way beyond *not petulant*. But what *had* just happened between them, Haven couldn't say.

"I wasn't in danger," she assured him. "I've been on lots of roofs, Hadden, some in a lot worse shape than this one, and I've lived to bill the client for my time. I know what I'm doing."

Now she lifted her head to look at him, too, to pin him with as steely a gaze as she could manage, to let him know she meant business. Instead of feeling like a woman of steel, however, she felt like a woman of noodles. Being this close to Bennett in a narrow hallway with only one way out, having experienced with him what she just had… That scared her way more than being fifty feet off the ground without a net.

So she did the only thing she knew to do. She mumbled something about having to go make some notes on the roof while her thoughts were still fresh and escaped as quickly as she could.

Bennett wasn't sure how long he stood by the window after Haven left. Or, rather, fled. That had definitely been fleeing, not leaving. Not that he blamed her. If she hadn't beat a hasty retreat when she did, he would have done it himself. Because if the two of them had spent even one more minute looking at each other the way they had been, standing as close as they had been, with tiny bedrooms and tiny beds mere steps away...

Oh, he really shouldn't let his mind wander in that direction. That way lay madness.

He had no idea what he was supposed to do next. It was the weirdest thing. Never in his adult life had he not known what he was supposed to do next. He'd been criticized for planning too well. But right now, in this place, after what had just happened with Haven...

What the hell had just happened with Haven?

He had no clue. One minute he'd seen her up on the roof, just sitting there, waving at him, not even holding on to anything for support, and the next minute, he'd been racing up the back stairs in sheer panic, not even sure where he was going, and the next minute, he'd been pulling her through the window as if she were about to fall to her death, and the next minute, she'd been in his arms. It had felt like the most natural, most right thing in the world to hold her that way, and the next minute...

Holy hell. The next minute. The next minute, she'd been backed against the wall with her eyes wide and her mouth open, looking at him as if she wanted him to take her right there, no questions asked. And he'd come so close—so close—to doing exactly that. With her wrists already in his hands, all he would have had to do was press them above her head, then push aside her sweater and unfasten her pants to dip his fingers inside to find out if she was as ready for him as he'd been for her. God help him, he had been so ready for her in that moment, as stiff and full and ready to—

He looked out the window in an effort to clear his head. But as beautiful as the view was, the only thing his brain—or something—wanted to focus on was the sight of Haven only inches away from him, looking at him as if she wanted to devour him as hungrily as he wanted to consume her.

He told himself he had to have been mistaken. The last person on earth she would want to get close to was him or any other Hadden. He'd just transferred his own feelings—his own wants—onto her for a moment. But just what were his feelings? What were his wants? The last person on earth *he* should want to get close to was a Moreau. Especially Haven Moreau. How could he have any wants or feelings where she was concerned? Other than bad ones, like those he'd had all his life.

He could not think about this right now. Best if he never thought about it again. He was having a weird enough day as it was. A weird enough month as it was. A weird enough life as it was.

Tomorrow, he was flying into the city for a few hours to meet with a client who had some misgivings about some of the ideas Bennett's most senior associate had put together for her business. Maybe getting away from the Finger Lakes and back into his normal life in Manhattan, even briefly, would help him focus and get his head back on straight. Yeah, that was it. Put some distance between himself and Summerlight—and Haven—even if it was just for a day. Hit the reset button on his brain and win himself a do-over. With Haven. With the house. With everything.

He'd spent the last few weeks telling himself everything could still be business as usual for him, for the most part, when in fact, nothing was going to be usual for at least a year. A year that would necessitate spending a lot of time with a woman whose family had hated his for generations and who had been petty enough at one point in her life—even if she had just been a teenager at the time—to sabotage his entire future.

That was what he should be thinking about, he told himself. How he had been denied entry into Stanford University—his dream school, near his dream city of San Francisco—because of Haven. Not how much he wanted to—

He growled a frustrated expletive and closed the window, jamming the latch back into place. Then he strode to the end of the hall and closed that door behind him, too. Not that he expected anyone else in Sudbury to be able to Spiderman their way along the roof the way Haven had and break into the place. The nights were just starting to get a lot colder, and heating a house like this for even a month cost more than most people's biweekly paycheck. He made his way slowly down the back staircase until he was in the kitchen again, where he'd dropped everything he'd been carrying onto the table when he rushed up to rescue Haven.

Rescue Haven, he repeated to himself. Right. As if she were the one who needed rescuing, when he was the one losing his mind.

A trip back to Manhattan, even if only for a little while, was exactly what he needed to put himself back to rights. He needed to be back amid the hustle and bustle—and noise and chaos—of the city, to remind him what real life was all about. All this peace and quiet and pastoral splendor could drive a person mad.

Chapter Six

Haven was outside inventorying the contents of Sum-merlight's storage shed at the edge of the garden—none of which looked like it had been touched in decades, in-cluding the shed itself—when she realized the sky had taken on an ominous color she'd never quite seen be-fore. When she checked the weather app on her phone, she realized it was still set for Staten Island, where it was a clear day, with a pleasant high of fifty. When she pulled up the info for Sudbury, however, that forecast changed dramatically. There was a cold front moving in fast from the west that would be hitting them right around dark. Not just a cold front, but a supercold cold front. As in borderline-freezing cold. As in rain-mixed-with-snow cold. With icy patches. And fog. And isobars that were doing stuff she'd never seen isobars do before.

And she'd come down to make coffee this morning

to find a note from Bennett saying he would be making the roughly ninety-minute drive to Syracuse today—to the east of Sudbury—to meet with a potential client and wouldn't be back until sometime after dinner. She looked at the sky again and wondered who would make it to Summerlight first—Bennett or the ice and rain and crazy isobars.

He'd spent a lot of time away in the past week. Ever since that day in the attic when the two of them had nearly… Well, anyway, he'd spent a lot of time away. First in Manhattan. Then in Rochester, a couple hours away. He'd even found reasons to go into sleepy little Sudbury. She couldn't remember the last time they'd spoken more than a dozen words to each other. And even those dozen words had been stilted and superficial.

But she'd be lying if she said she wasn't kind of grateful for the distance. She was still rattled by what had happened that day in the garret, and she was uncertain how to act around him. She knew she shouldn't beat herself up over what she'd wanted to do that day. What she'd almost done. There had been a time in her life—even if it was a decade ago—when she'd had a fierce crush on Bennett and had thought he returned her feelings. A time when she had genuinely believed that the two of them could be together, regardless of their family history. A time when she'd honestly thought she was in love with him. Well, as in love as a sixteen-year-old who'd never even been kissed before could be with an imaginary version of a guy who was just flat-out beautiful to behold.

Clearly, there were still remnants of that naive infatuation lurking somewhere inside her, and they'd somehow made their way to the front of her brain that afternoon. Not to mention, it had been a while since she had dated anyone, and she wasn't exactly the most sexually experienced person in the first place. A person had needs. And if those needs went neglected too long, they got a little desperate. So did the person having them. Bennett might be a Hadden, but he was a damned hot one, especially for someone like Haven. She shouldn't be surprised that her libido had jumped up to respond to him the way it had that day. She just had to make sure it didn't happen again.

By the time she finished up in the shed, the sun was beginning to set, the sky was spitting rain, and Bennett still wasn't back. Haven fixed herself a grilled cheese sandwich and popped open a can of tomato soup for dinner, listened to the wind whistle menacingly around the kitchen window as she ate, and forced herself not to text him to ask for an ETA because the weather was turning rough and she was worried about him.

She wasn't worried about him. She wasn't. He was a big boy, entirely capable of keeping track of weather updates and finding his way safely back to Sudbury all by himself. She just didn't want to see anyone—even a Hadden—get stranded in the middle of nowhere in freezing temperatures or wind up driving into a ditch someplace they wouldn't be found for days. Or, worse yet, ending up at the bottom of Cayuga Lake, still seat-belted into their car, their rotting corpse discovered decades later, after climate change turned the whole world into a barren desert, so the lake has gone completely dry, finally revealing all of its ugly secrets for the last few centuries. They'd likely be found next to an early Puritan, probably someone named Epiphany Lamentations Freemason or something, who accidentally jerked their oxen right instead of left and drove off the path of righteousness and straight into Cayuga Lake.

Anyway, she didn't want to see anything bad happen to anyone. Even a Hadden.

After washing up her few dishes, she checked to make sure the house was locked tight, made her way upstairs—still not worrying about Bennett, by the way—took a shower, brushed her teeth and settled herself into bed with a book. And still she didn't worry about him. She didn't. Just because she kept having to read page 81 over and over again, and then page 82 over and over again, and then page 83 the same way, it was just because there was a plot point in there that was hard to follow. It was only through sheer exhaustion—and okay, maybe a couple glasses of wine, toothbrushing be damned—that she was able to finally nod off to sleep. Still not worrying about Bennett.

When she awoke, the clock by her bed, an old windup alarm clock with radium hands, told her it was a little after one. The precipitation smacking against her window told her the rain had turned to ice. And the way her breath left her mouth in a frosty streak told her the temperature in her room was a lot colder than it should be. Yeah, the windows of the house weren't exactly snug—caulking was one of the many projects she was hoping to get to before Thanksgiving—but she and Bennett had agreed to keep the thermostat at sixty-five at night, which meant the house temperature actually stayed around sixty. Her breath should not be foggy at sixty degrees. When she tried to switch on the lamp, nothing happened. Great. Now the power was out. And there was only one blanket on her bed, under the already-thin quilt.

Did Bennett make it back okay?

That, even more than the cold, was what drove Haven out of bed. She grabbed her College of Staten Island sweatshirt from the foot of her bed and tugged it on over the cotton undershirt and flannel pajama pants spattered with cartoon power tools she'd gone to bed in—normally, she slept hot but not when there was no heating. Then she wriggled on her thick rag-wool socks and made her way down the hall to Bennett's bedroom. When she saw that his door was open and his bed was still made, something in the pit of her stomach clenched tight. She was heading back to her room for her phone to text him—no way would she get any sleep until she knew he was okay, even if he was a Hadden—but hesitated at the top of the stairs when she thought she heard a sound coming from the first floor.

It had to be Bennett. No home invader in their right mind would be out on a night like this. Not that anyone who would invade another person's home was in their right mind to begin with, but they would have to be certifiable to attempt a break-in when Haven hadn't even had a chance to salt the front walk, since everybody, even home invaders, knew how unpredictable and dangerous black ice could be.

Anyway, it had to be Bennett.

She padded down the stairs and started for the kitchen, then slowed when she saw a soft glow coming from beyond the library entry and turned that way instead. There was a fire going in the fireplace, and in its amber glow, she saw a man's socked foot hanging over the arm of the sofa in front of it, a chunky knit throw tossed over the lower part of its leg. Bennett had made it back in one piece.

She was surprised by the depth of the relief that wound through her when she saw he was safe. When she'd been thinking about how she didn't want anyone, even a Hadden, to be thrust into dangerous circumstances, she'd been kidding herself. She hadn't wanted a specific Hadden—a specific person—to be thrust into a dangerous situation. She *had* been worried earlier. And she'd been worried about Bennett. Which could only mean she must still have feel—

Which could only mean something she would think about tomorrow. Right now, she needed to find an extra blanket or two and make her way back up to bed. Even if it was a lot warmer in the library, she couldn't help noticing, even this far away from the fire. She didn't want to wake Bennett. Not while all the weird feelings and thoughts that she would think about tomorrow were swirling around inside her.

She took a step back into the hallway, only to have a loose floorboard creak loudly beneath her foot. Dammit. She knew she should have worked on the floors before now. Bennett stirred at the sound and sat up, looking at her over the back of the sofa, shoving his dark hair back with one hand.

He grinned a little sheepishly. "Hi, Mom, I'm home."

Even with her heart still pounding with what had been her earlier panic, and her breath still a little wonky, she managed to grin back and say, "Hi. I didn't hear you come in."

He straightened taller and turned on the sofa to look at her more fully. "It was nearly midnight by the time I got in. I figured you'd be in bed asleep, and I didn't see any reason to wake you."

Oh, except for the one about how it took two glasses of wine—in a mouth that had already been coated with toothpaste, which, in a word, *ick*—and more than a dozen readings of pages 84 through 90 of a book that wasn't even making any sense before she could fall asleep. But other than that, nah. No reason at all.

"Especially after I came into the house," he continued, "and discovered it was as cold in here as it was outside. It didn't take much to figure out we lost power, so there was even less reason to wake you up, just to make you cold, too. I figured I'd just start a fire and sleep down here instead."

She nodded. "Yeah, well, I woke up anyway and wanted to, um…" She didn't want to admit she was worried about him, so she hurried to say, "I mean, it's freezing upstairs, so I wanted to grab a couple more blankets."

His eyebrows scrunched up in confusion. "Which, if memory serves, are in a hall closet upstairs where the bedrooms are."

"Right," she agreed. "But I wanted a glass of water, too."

"Which you can also find upstairs. Modern convenience called 'the drinking glass in the bathroom.'"

She sighed and bit back a growl of frustration. "I wanted to see if you made it back safely, okay?" she finally told him. And, because she couldn't quite stop herself, she added, "I was worried about you."

He tried to turn again to look at her even more fully, but his position was awkward and clearly uncomfortable. So Haven reluctantly made her way into the library proper, rounding the sofa at one end so he didn't have to tie himself up into a knot to look at her. Then—what the hell, in for a penny, in for a pound, whatever that meant—she seated herself on that end, as far from Bennett as she could. Since he was still pretty much in the middle of the couch, though, that wasn't very far. Nor did he move himself farther away when he resituated himself to look at her after she took her seat. Meaning that, at the moment, she was physically closer to him than she'd been for a while. Like, since that day in the garret, by the window, when—

And she was closer to the fireplace, too. Which must be the reason for the heat that suddenly began coursing through her. Not Bennett. Though there was a window not far behind from where she was sitting, and she could feel the cold air from outside rattling through it, despite its being a good five or six feet away. Bennett must have felt it, too, because he tugged the bulky throw up higher over himself, then kicked the extra at the other end toward her. He didn't have to offer twice. She turned and pulled her legs up toward herself, covering her lower half with as much of the throw as she could.

"Thank you for worrying about me," he said in response to the comment she had to remember making. "Gotta say, it wasn't a fun drive from Syracuse. The weather was a lot worse than I thought it would be. When I left Sudbury this morning, the forecast was just for a cloudy day followed by a little overnight rain."

"They changed it midafternoon," she told him. "A storm that was supposed to head up into Canada suddenly decided it wanted to visit New Hampshire instead, by way of—ta-da!—the Finger Lakes."

He smiled again. Haven did her best not to swoon. "I hate when that happens."

She chuckled. "Me, too."

"I ended up having to stay later in Syracuse than I planned, but the weather there was fine when I left. I was about halfway home when I hit rain. Then sleet. Then snow. Then ice. I was probably only going about ten miles an hour when I finally turned into Summerlight. I was so happy when I finally made it home."

Home, Haven repeated to herself. It was the first time either of them had referred to the house that way. And Bennett had just done it twice. Not only that but he'd also expressed happiness at arriving here. At home.

Only because he'd been feeling uneasy in the nasty weather, she hurried to remind herself. His happiness at being home—at being back at the house—was a result of his relief at his safe arrival. Not because he had become fond of Summerlight. Or of its other resident.

He seemed to realize the significance of what he'd said, too, because he quickly backpedaled. "Summerlight, I mean. I'm glad I made back to Summerlight."

Haven was glad, too. But she didn't see any reason why she had to voice it. Especially with her feelings being all wonky at the moment.

Another gust of icy air sliced through the window behind her, eliciting an involuntary shiver that had her wrapping her arms around herself. Bennett noted her action and nodded toward a chair in the corner of the room.

"I brought down an extra blanket. It's in the chair over there. Help yourself."

"It's okay. I can grab another one on my way back to my room."

"Why go back upstairs?" he asked. "It's freezing up there. Stay down here where it's warmer." He smiled. "There's brandy, too. Grab a glass from the bar and help yourself to that, as well. It's right by the chair with the blanket."

She noted then the empty snifter on the end table at the other side of the sofa. Oh. So that was why he was being so chatty and so nice to her after a week of being so distant. He'd obviously already had a glass himself, and it had mellowed him out. Unfortunately, the effects of her bedtime wine had waned, as had her desire for sleep. Seeing Bennett's empty bedroom had sent a shot of adrenaline through her along with the panic. She was wide-awake now.

The wind rattled the window again.

And cold. She was still supercold.

She rose and made her way to the blanket—and the brandy—Bennett had indicated, pouring herself a glass of the latter before snatching up the former. As an afterthought, she held the bottle aloft in a silent query if

Bennett wanted a refill, and he nodded. So she brought the bottle with her when she returned to the couch. As he poured himself a second snifter, she tucked her lower half under the throw again, then wrapped the blanket around her shoulders and snugged it closed as well as she could with one hand. Then she sipped her brandy carefully, stared into the fire and let the liquor do its thing. After a few sips, she finally began to thaw, both inside and out.

Then Bennett said, "Do you ever wonder what would happen if our families just sat down in a room together to talk?"

The chill came back. The question had come out of nowhere. Although both of their families knew by now what had happened with Aurelia Hadden's will—Bennett had informed his parents a few days after his and Haven's arrival in Sudbury, and she had told her mother it was okay to let the rest of her own family know right around the same time—neither the Haddens nor the Moreaus had done much to stir up any trouble. Well, okay, Bennett's father had hired another attorney from a different firm than Sterling Crittenden's to go over the will to make sure there were no loopholes they could use to cut Haven out entirely, and Haven's uncle Cecil had demanded to see a notarized copy of the will, even though notaries weren't necessary for that in New York. But they hadn't come after Haven or Bennett in particular. At least, not yet.

Anyway, Haven had no idea how to answer Bennett's question. But he obviously expected a reply, because he looked at her intently, his gaze locked with hers.

Finally, she told him, "Not really. For one thing, I can't

imagine our families talking about so much as what kind of toppings to put on a pizza. For another thing, my parents rarely mentioned the family feud. Even if my father was still alive today, neither of them would show up for a talk about something they thought was ridiculous."

Bennett looked at her for a long moment, his handsome features gilded by the firelight. He looked mellow and sleepy and wistful, and Haven wanted very much to reach over and trace her fingertips over the elegant line of his cheekbone. Instead, she gripped her glass tighter.

"You said you were twelve when your father died?" he asked.

She nodded.

"That's a tough age to lose a parent."

"Any age is a tough age to lose a parent."

"I know, but…twelve. That's about the age when we really start getting to know our parents." He enjoyed another long taste of his brandy. "Not that we always end up liking them once we get to know them."

Haven waited to see if he wanted to elaborate on that, but he said nothing more. So she told him, "I actually knew my dad pretty well. He taught me everything I know about being handy. I followed him on his jobs whenever I could, even when I was really little." She smiled. "I used to sit beside him and hand him his tools until I was old enough to learn how to use them. He was a great dad."

"Those are his tools you use now," Bennett guessed.

She nodded. "And his work gloves. And his jacket. And a million other things that used to belong to him." She hesitated only a moment before pushing up her sleeve to show him something she rarely showed anyone on purpose. "I got this tattoo because of him," she said.

He bent forward to look, squinting in the dim light of the fire. "It's words," he said softly. "They say…'A work in progress'?"

"Yeah," she replied, pushing her sleeve back into place. "That was what he said about everything. Buildings, people, you name it. To him, everything was a work in progress. To him, everything could be fixed or made better."

It was the first time she'd thought about her father's catchphrase since everything that had happened with Summerlight, and somehow, it suddenly seemed to hold so much more weight than it had before. When she was a girl and her father said that, she hadn't really thought much about it. It was the sort of thing a dad would say when things went wrong or when he thought his child could do better. But sitting here now, with Bennett, and Summerlight surrounding them and their history unwinding with every passing day…

They really were a work in progress, she thought. All of them.

"So…anyway…that's interesting about your parents not talking about the feud much," Bennett said. "Because my family talked about it a lot. They thought you Moreaus were a huge pain in the…" He smiled again. And even more of the cold inside Haven melted. "…neck," he finally finished. "They thought you were all a huge pain in the neck."

"Well, my aunts and uncles and cousins certainly felt the same way about you Haddens," she admitted. "They all hated your family *so much*, always talking about how much better their lives could be—how much better all our lives would be—if your grandfather Bertie hadn't been such a crook. Even though I never thought my life was all that bad, I guess some of their animosity rubbed off on me, and I adopted this sort of vague all-Haddens-are-bad attitude."

She dropped her gaze down to her brandy and told herself to leave it at that. But because she couldn't quite help herself, because the hurt of what had happened in high school still lingered not-so-far below her surface, because she still couldn't quite forgive Bennett for what he had done, she couldn't quite keep herself from adding, "But then, after what you did to me in high school, and the way your cousins treated me for the rest of my time at Barnaby after that, I guess I felt like I had a really good personal reason for hating all of you."

She stopped herself from going into any detail about that day on Bow Bridge. They both knew the details, even if it felt like it happened a lifetime ago. Maybe Bennett was sorry for what he'd done now that he was older and more conscious of how damaging youthful cruelty could be. Maybe he thought Haven had forgiven him because she was older and more conscious of how cruel youthful people could be without realizing the damage they did. And, as hurtful as the experience had been, it had happened a long time ago. She was a different person now. So was Bennett. The two of them were getting along reasonably well these days. There was no sense in bringing up the details of old wounds and retaliations and bad blood. Even if he hadn't ever apologized. And even if she hadn't forgiven him. Not really.

When she finally looked up again, Bennett was gazing at her and seemed genuinely confused. "What are
you talking about?" he asked. "What do you mean what
I did to *you* in high school? I didn't do anything. If you
want to talk about high school, let's talk about what
you did to *me*."

Now Haven was the one to be confused. "I didn't do
anything to you. You were the one who played the cruel
joke on me. Not that I thought it was much of a joke. It
was totally cruel."

He pushed himself to the far end of the couch, taking
the throw with him. Haven pulled her knees up in front
of herself more tightly and wrapped what she could of
the blanket around them, too. It was a defensive posture.
So was Bennett's. But what could he possibly have to
defend himself from? He was the one who'd behaved
badly. Not her.

"I never played any kind of joke on you, Moreau," he
stated adamantly. "And I was certainly never cruel to you.
If anyone in this room did something cruel, it was you."

"Me?" she asked incredulously. "When was I ever
cruel to you?"

He shook his head in clear disbelief. "Oh gee, there
was that small matter of lying to our teachers about me
and making sure my acceptance to Stanford was revoked. Not to mention every other school I applied to,
including all the Ivies. I had to go to Colgate because of
you. And I had to start a semester late and play catch-up
the whole time I was there."

Putting aside for now the fact that Colgate University
was an excellent school Haven herself had considered

before deciding she would be happiest at home in Staten Island, she told him, "I didn't lie about anything. What happened is totally on you, Hadden, not me. Actions have consequences. Your action. Your consequences."

"My action?" he echoed. "What the hell are you talking about?"

Now Haven sat up straighter, too. She inhaled a fortifying gulp of her brandy, then said, "I'm talking about that day in Central Park when you sent your legion of friends and cousins to attack and humiliate me on Bow Bridge. I'm talking about how you stringed me along for a month with your texts, making me think you liked me and wanted to go out with me. I'm talking about how I told you things about myself, personal things I never told anyone else, only for you to laugh about them with your cronies and then send them after me. If that isn't cruel, I don't know what is."

His expression was gradually growing horrified. Good. He should be horrified, even a decade later, by the reminder of what he did to her.

When he said nothing in response—seriously, he looked like the wheels inside his head were spinning out of control in every direction—she expelled a single, humorless chuckle. "Though now that I think about it, maybe I should blame myself as much as I blame you. How could I have ever thought someone like you would give someone like me the time of day, let alone want to meet me for a romantic tryst? I humiliated myself more than you or your cousins did."

Now he was looking at her as if she'd been speaking to him in Sanskrit all this time. "Moreau, what the hell are you talking about?"

His bewilderment was almost palpable. Almost convincing. *Almost.* But there was no way he could have forgotten about that day any more than she had. Behavior that malevolent left a stain on a person that never came out.

To humor him, however, she said, "I'm talking about the summer after you graduated from Barnaby. When you started texting me, telling me how you wanted the family feud to end with us."

At this, he only looked even more dazed. Or, rather, pretended to look more dazed. So she decided to turn the screws a little tighter.

"That summer when you told me in your texts how you not only wanted to mend the family rift but how much you'd liked me since you were a junior and I was a freshman. How you were too afraid to act on it at school, because you knew if your family found out, they would never accept it. And you told me the reason you liked me was because I was so different from the other girls at Barnaby." Here, Haven couldn't help but expel another humorless chuckle. "Yeah, I was different, all right," she added miserably. "I was naive and stupid enough to think the most popular guy at school would have anything to do with a geeky nobody like me. Especially when he was a Hadden and I was a Moreau. I still can't believe I actually had a massive crush on you for two years."

By now, Bennett was gazing at her in what she could only liken to dread. For a long time, he only gazed at her in silence. Slowly, he lifted his brandy to his mouth and drained it.

Then he told her, "Moreau, none of that ever happened."

She couldn't believe he would deny it. She opened her mouth to harangue him again, but he held up a hand to stop her.

"I never texted you," he assured her. "Not that summer. Not ever. I never told you I wanted the feud to end with us—though, interesting that it seems like that could happen now. I never told you I liked you—even though, yeah, okay, I always thought you were kinda cute, in a weird, gawky, oh-come-on-this-person-is-my-mortal-enemy kind of way. And I certainly never asked you to meet me in Central Park at Bow Bridge."

Something inside Haven clenched tighter with every word he spoke. He was just that staunch in his denial. Was he telling the truth? Had she really hated him for a decade for something he didn't even do?

She looked at him hard. He *seemed* to be telling the truth. But could she really trust a Hadden? And if he hadn't texted her, who had?

"Tell me exactly what happened to you," he said.

She still wasn't sure she believed him. But she did as he asked. She told him how, a few weeks after school ended his senior year, she got a text out of nowhere, from a number she didn't have in her contacts, from someone who identified themself as Bennett. The texts were tentative at first—Hey, hi, how's your summer going? Got any plans?—and after her cautious replies, they gradually grew more casual. Then more friendly.

Then more intimate. The texter told Haven things she already knew about the Haddens and about Bennett himself. They mentioned things that had happened at Barnaby and people at school they both knew. She had no reason to think it wasn't him. The texts were funny and charming. They made her feel as if he really did like her and really did want to get together with her before he took off for Stanford in the fall. By the time he asked her to meet him in Central Park, she trusted completely that it would be for a fun date together. Presumably, the first of many.

Instead, she was greeted by a host of his friends and other Haddens—none of them Bennett, all of them abusive. His cousins, especially, had surrounded her and began hurling one hurtful, humiliating comment at her after another. They made fun of her for having a crush on Bennett and thinking he could ever return it. They even read back to her some of the texts she'd sent to him, things she'd told him in private, which she was mortified he'd shared with others. And they'd laughed. Oh, how they had laughed. They'd physically prevented her from escaping for as long as they could, pushing her back and forth among them as their taunts grew more and more brutal, until she finally managed to break through two of them and run. She told him how she hadn't stopped running until she encountered Ms. Pérez, the English teacher for one of the two classes she and Bennett had had together, who was strolling in the park that day with her wife and their twins. And how Ms. Pérez had demanded to know what had Haven so shaken, so Haven, through her tears, had spilled everything.

And she told Bennett how, after that, every day for her remaining two years at Barnaby, his cousins had continued to ridicule her. To bully her. To make her life a living hell. When she finished talking, she realized she hadn't been looking at him during her entire account. She'd been gazing into the fire or down at her glass, sipping her brandy as she went, to give her courage to continue. Now her glass was empty, too. She didn't want to look at Bennett to gauge his reaction to everything she'd just told him. He'd been silent the whole time. She had no idea what he was thinking.

Finally, very softly, he said, "That was why Ms. Pérez went to so much trouble to make sure my recommendations to all the colleges I applied to were revoked. Because she thought I had done something terrible to you."

And those losses of recommendations, especially the one to Stanford, had to have cost him a lot. Had to have changed the course of his life. And he'd done nothing to deserve it.

"I'm sorry," Haven said. "It never occurred to me she would do something like that."

It didn't escape her notice that she was the one apologizing first. Of course, Bennett hadn't been responsible for the actions of his family, so he didn't owe her an apology for anything he had done. Then again, Haven hadn't been responsible for his losses of recommendation—his cousins had been the ones at the heart of that, too. So it wasn't so much that she was apologizing for anything she'd done as it was expressing her regret for the situation as a whole. Still, an apology from Bennett would have been nice, too, even if he wasn't responsible for any of it, either. An expression of regret for the situation as a whole from him would have meant a lot, as well.

"Moreau, I promise you," he continued, speaking even more adamantly than before. "I never did, I never would have—I never could have—done something that mean. To you or anyone." He expelled a sound of derision. "My cousins, on the other hand. Yeah. They could absolutely do something like that. One of them must have texted you, pretending to be me. Probably Everett, that dick. Or Cricket. They're both awful, and they always got bored when they had to summer at their family compound on Martha's Vineyard."

Haven wasn't sure what was worse. Finding out it wasn't true that Bennett had been the one to text her back then or finding out it wasn't true that he'd liked her back then. He seemed to be denying both, even if he had admitted he thought she was cute when they were both teens, albeit in a backhanded kind of way. But, really, what difference did it make? He hadn't done the thing she'd hated him for for more than a decade. Her humiliation had come at the hands of his cousins, not him. His cousins had, in fact, screwed up both their lives.

Had she told him earlier she didn't hate his whole family? Because now she kind of did. Except for one of them. Maybe. She still wasn't sure how she felt about Bennett.

Because she still wasn't convinced he was telling her the truth.

Chapter Seven

All through her account, Bennett had watched Haven carefully, bathed in the golden light of the fire, her eyes dark and her expression haunted. And he wondered when, exactly, everything in his life—everything in the world—had changed. When she'd first started describing what happened to her the summer after he graduated from Barnaby, he'd wondered just how much she'd had to drink before he got home. When he realized she was sober, he'd wondered if she was lying. Or just flatout delusional.

Then he'd remembered how much his cousin Everett loved pranks and how his cousin Cricket had taken the term "mean girl" to new heights. Although Bennett truly hadn't ever been wedded to the feud between the Haddens and Moreaus the way the rest of the family had, he'd never exactly divorced himself from it, either.

Certainly, he'd never said anything against any other family members who perpetuated it. Even at school, where he knew his cousins sometimes gave Haven a rough time, he'd never stepped in. He hadn't wanted to make waves in the family. And, hey, Haven was a Moreau. Why should he show any concern for her or her family when she and her family had never shown any concern for him and his? But had he realized just how badly his cousins were mistreating her, he would have—

—*what?* he asked himself. Told them to knock it off? As if that would have actually worked? Like most of his family, his cousins were total narcissists who didn't give a damn about anyone but themselves. Like most of his family, they despised the Moreaus. He didn't spend that much time with his extended family anyway, since he'd never really liked any of them that much. But he had known they weren't very nice to Haven. And he'd never said or done anything about it. Which, maybe, had given them the impression that he would think a prank like the one they'd pulled was as funny as they'd clearly found it themselves.

"Moreau, I'm sorry," he said. "They had no right to do that to you. It was inexcusable."

Instead of looking at him, she looked into the fire. He couldn't imagine what she was thinking. He'd never been bullied himself. On the contrary, he'd traveled in all the best social circles at Barnaby. He'd hung out mostly with the populars because, duh, he was a Hadden. But he'd been at home with the jocks, too, thanks to his excelling on the lacrosse and polo teams. The arty kids had welcomed him because he liked books and

movies. He'd run around with the brains sometimes—
not because his grades were that great, but because the
teachers loved him, so the scholarly students did, too.
He'd even gotten along fine with the counterculture
types—the goths, the burnouts and the loners.

The one group he hadn't had anything to do with was
the geeks and nerds. Haven's group. Not that she'd really been welcomed there, either, he knew, thanks to her
blue-collar background. Even the outcasts at Barnaby
had cast her out. But Bennett had moved fluidly among
the other groups, enough that he had been connected to
pretty much everyone at school and knew whose status
was what. Haven's status, from day one, had been per-
sona non grata. The Haddens, other than he himself,
had taken it one step further, though. To them, she'd
been Public Enemy Number One.

"Truly, Haven, I am sorry," Bennett said again. "If I'd
known what was going on that summer, I would have—"
His voice halted the same way his brain had a moment
ago. He honestly didn't know what he would have done.
Nowadays, he would have made clear to his cousins that
they were behaving barbarously and put an immediate
stop to it. Back then, though, as a self-absorbed teenager? He hated to admit it, but back then, it was entirely
possible he might have just looked the other way.

She did finally turn to look at him when he spoke
again, her expression one of clear surprise.

"What?" he said.

"You called me Haven," she told him.

He did? "I did?"

She nodded. "You've never called me by my first name.

No one in your family has. I've always been 'Moreau.'
As if my last name was the only thing that defined me."

"You've never called me by my first name, either," he
pointed out.

Now she was the one to say nothing. She only dropped
her gaze back to her empty glass.

He sighed heavily and set his empty glass on the floor.
When he looked at her again, it was to find her gazing
back at him with an intensity he couldn't begin to understand.

He sighed heavily. "I guess neither one of us has ever
really been anything to the other but our last name."

"Until now. Bennett," she said, surprising him this
time.

She was wrapped in the blanket, but not so tightly
that he couldn't see her sleepwear—a City University
of New York College of Staten Island sweatshirt and
pajama pants spattered with cartoon power tools. Those
things defined her as much as her name did, but he
didn't go around calling her CUNY or Band Saw. Then
again, he evidently wasn't calling her Moreau anymore,
either. He still wasn't sure why his brain had decided
to make that change. But she also wasn't calling him
Hadden anymore.

Just what the hell was going on between them tonight?

"So, Haven," he began again, deliberately using her
first name now, surprised at how natural it felt to do it,
"now that we both realize that the grudges we've been
carrying against each other personally for a decade should
really be directed at my insufferable cousins—most likely

Everett and/or Cricket, but, honestly, any of them could be responsible for what happened because they're all pretty awful—what are we going to do about it?"

Her response was a body-shaking shiver from a blast of cold air from the window behind her, one so strong, it made Bennett shudder, too. Instead of saying anything in reply to his question, she tugged her blanket closer around herself and moved off the sofa and onto the richly colored Persian rug on the floor, scooting herself as close to the fire as she dared. It was obvious she wanted to put some distance between them and was using the cold as an excuse to do that. But something about the conversation they'd just shared made him uncomfortable sitting above her the way he was, so he moved down to the floor, too. Then—what the hell—he pressed his luck further by moving closer to her anyway, sitting cross-legged near the spot where she sat with her knees tucked up in front of her, her blanket cinched even tighter.

Everything about her posture screamed that she was in defense mode, and he told himself not to push her, not to get too close. Something inside him, though, wanted to be close to her. Whether that was because that would put him nearer the warmth of the fire or because he suddenly felt weirdly protective of her in light of the way his family had treated her, he couldn't have said. He only knew she didn't move away from him when he joined her. That went a long way toward making him feel as if the metaphorical chasm between them could eventually be closed, too.

He said nothing, though, reminding himself that he'd

been the last one to speak, so it was up to her whether or not to continue the conversation. For several long moments, she didn't. Finally, still looking at the fire instead of at him, she said, very quietly, "I always thought you were kind of cute, too."

Bennett smiled at that. And he was surprised at the curl of pleasure that unwound inside him at hearing her confession. "Um, yeah, you kind of already admitted that," he said. "I mean…you did use the words *massive crush*."

Now she did look at him, her cheeks pink with her embarrassment. Or maybe it was the heat of the fire doing that. Or the effects of the brandy. But he was pretty sure it was embarrassment, because she didn't say anything to deny it.

Instead, she said, "I, um, I wasn't really thinking straight when I said that. It wasn't actually a *massive* crush. Just, you know, your regular, garden-variety crush. I had crushes on lots of guys at Barnaby."

Oh, now he knew she was lying. Mostly because 99 percent of the students at Barnaby were self-entitled jerks. He hated to admit it, but he couldn't quite rule himself out from that percentile. How Haven had managed to have a crush on him, he had no clue.

Just to playfully needle her—they did seem to be moving past the unpleasantness of their earlier discovery, and he was eager to lighten the mood—not to mention she was kind of smiling now—he said, "Right. Lots of guys at Barnaby were totally worth crushing on. I mean, who could resist Rockford Leopold Beddington IV? Rocky was such a charming guy."

Rocky's claim to fame at Barnaby had been his ability to recite the alphabet in one long, loud belch. Which he had done every day while standing on a table in the center of the commissary. Truly an irresistible dude. But the suggestion made Haven's smile go a little wider, something that made Bennett's pulse race a little faster.

Heartened, he continued, "And then there was Dylan Yamada. Yeah, I can absolutely see how you would want to spend as much time with him as possible."

Dylan's fixation on entomology had been so fierce that he brought specimens from his cockroach collection—*live* specimens from his cockroach collection—to the biology class Bennett and Haven had shared three days a week, each specimen large enough and gross enough to make every member of the class want to heave.

At this, Haven wrinkled her nose in disgust, obviously remembering their classmate's proclivities as well as he did. But she did chuckle a bit, too. She had told him, after all, that bugs didn't bother her. Bugs the size of Greenland, though, as most of Dylan's had been, obviously made an impression.

"And, hey, let's not forget Keaton Blanton," Bennett continued, hoping to elicit a full-on laugh, since he didn't think he'd ever heard Haven actually laugh at something, and that suddenly bothered him a lot for some reason. "I mean *there* was a guy to crush on. Who could resist someone who made flowcharts for all his teachers about his homework, where every reply led to the conclusion, 'Why am I getting in trouble for something I didn't do?' Jeez, that guy had beauty and brains, both."

That, finally, did elicit the laughter Bennett had hoped for. Maybe it wasn't a lot, but it was there. And it made what little icy barrier that still hung between them melt the rest of the way. Or maybe it was the fire that did that. Or maybe the brandy. Or maybe the fact that it was the middle of the night, and neither of them had slept much. Or maybe it was just the fact that they both realized now that there was no reason for them to be enemies. That there had never really been a reason for them to be enemies. That maybe, possibly, perhaps, they didn't have to be enemies anymore.

She sighed, but the sound was more wistful than it was melancholy. "I forgot about Keaton and his flowcharts," she said, still looking into the fire. "He was actually one of the few people at Barnaby who was usually nice to me."

Now she turned to look at Bennett, and his breath caught at the image. The glow of the fire seemed to soften everything about her, and she had already been pretty soft tonight to begin with. Her hair, usually bound in its messy confinement, danced around her shoulders in loose waves, the firelight staining the tresses amber and gold. Her blue eyes, always so startling in their color and clarity, were darker and mellower. All of her just seemed so much softer, so much more approachable. In that moment, she did cease to be Bennett's enemy, and she became…something else. He wasn't sure what. But he was liking whatever it was. He was liking it a lot.

She wasn't clinging as snugly to the blanket now, and it slipped from her shoulders a bit, making her look even more relaxed. Which was something else he couldn't ever recall her being during their time at Summerlight.

"It's strange, isn't it," she said quietly, "how you always remember the bad times and bad people more than you do the good times and good people. It shouldn't be like that."

"No, it shouldn't," he agreed. And to him, at least, it wasn't like that—not really. After what he'd learned from Haven tonight, though, he wasn't surprised that was how she felt. "But you and I remember each other," he continued. "And it wasn't bad between us. Was it? Before that summer, I mean?"

He hated to realize he honestly didn't know the answer to that, at least not from her point of view. Whereas his own memories of Barnaby were pretty fond ones, it was because he'd been at the top of the food chain. He knew too many of his classmates hadn't been particularly good people, and if he made himself dig deeper, he would probably recall things about the school and its population that were awful. The way Haven did, living at the bottom of the food chain as she had. But surely there had been some good things about her time there that she could look back on now and remember fondly. She'd said she had a crush on him before his cousins' interference. Although he didn't blame her for having nothing but bad thoughts about him and their school after that, there must have been some before then that made her happy.

She met his gaze levelly. "No. It wasn't all bad while you were at Barnaby. In a lot of ways, you were what made my time there bearable. Until you graduated, I mean."

Her admission shouldn't have made him as happy as it did.

Before he had a chance to consider that, she turned to look back into the fire and continued, "I so didn't want to go to school there. I wanted to stay on Staten Island and go to Port Richmond with my friends. But my mom was so excited about the scholarship and all the opportunities it would afford me. And my aunts and uncles were practically frothing at the mouth about how this could be our ticket back into New York society. All of them were telling me how proud of me my dad would have been if he could be there to see me. There was no way I couldn't not go Barnaby and disappoint all of them."

She sighed again, but this time there was indeed a melancholy sound to it. "The whole time I was growing up, I almost never left Staten Island, and suddenly, going to Barnaby, I was going to be in Manhattan every day. This huge place I'd mostly only ever looked at from across the water. It might as well have been the Emerald City from *The Wizard of Oz*. I didn't know anyone who lived there. Or anyone who went to Barnaby. Oh, except for my mortal enemies, the Haddens. And even them, I wouldn't have recognized, since I'd never met any. Sure, I could look for the horns and cloven hooves, but…"

Here, Bennett chuckled. But, tellingly, Haven didn't. Even more tellingly, she continued to gaze into the fire instead of at him. He could almost see the uncertain teenager she had been back then. The one who had no social graces and had just been thrust into an arena where society was at its most vicious.

"I was walking into that school blind," she said, "without even knowing who my potential friends or enemies were. I was terrified that first day. Terrified. The minute I walked through the door, I felt like I was going to throw up. No one spoke to me. But everyone looked at me. As if I were something they'd stepped in and needed to scrape off their shoes. Then they talked to each other behind my back after I walked by, saying awful things about me. And then, suddenly, the crowd parted for a group of kids who, it was obvious, even to a newcomer like me, were the absolute cream of Barnaby society."

Here, she finally did look up, and she met Bennett's gaze completely. "You were in the middle of it. And when you walked past me, you said, 'Oh, hey, new girl. Welcome to Barnaby.' And you said it like you meant it. And even though you kept right on walking afterward, I think I kinda fell in love with you right on the spot. It was the only thing that kept me from bolting that day. And it was the only thing that brought me back to school the next."

Bennett didn't even remember the episode. It actually kind of surprised him that he'd done something like that. Not that he'd ever been hostile to anyone at school, but he hadn't exactly been the Welcome Wagon type, either.

"And then, when I found out later who you were, I couldn't believe it. I couldn't believe a Hadden could be so..." Here, she shrugged. "...so nice. So beautiful.

So completely opposite what I'd always been told you all were."

She scrunched up her shoulders a little, then relaxed them, a gesture that punctuated how complicated and weird their one-on-one relationship had been from the get-go. He knew how she felt. He'd been kind of baffled about her after finally realizing who she was, too.

Even though he couldn't recall greeting Haven that first day, Bennett did remember when he first found out she was a Moreau. Because she'd been so advanced in English and because Bennett hadn't—even if he'd loved books, he'd never been good at articulating his thoughts—they'd landed in the same literature class the second semester of her freshman year. When Ms. Peréz had taken roll that first day and called out Haven Moreau, Bennett had searched the classroom wildly for the name's owner. By then, he'd known one of his and his family's mortal enemies was a student there, but because she was two grades behind him, he'd figured he would never cross her path. And he hadn't wanted to. He'd heard from his cousins what an ungainly, unappealing creature she was and how badly she fit in among them.

So imagine his surprise when the creature that raised its hand and said, almost defiantly, *I'm here, Ms. Peréz*, as if she were daring the rest of the class to make her leave, was actually, well, not all that unappealing. Not to Bennett's way of thinking, anyway. Yeah, she was kind of gangly, but she was also kind of…appealing. In a cute, chaotic kind of way. As the semester had worn on, he'd also come to realize she was appealing in other ways, too. She was smart. And funny. And gutsy in light of the way people treated her. And her eyes…

Damn. Her eyes. Even from the other side of the room that first day, he'd never ceased to be startled by how blue they were. How expressive. How full of… At the time, he hadn't been able to think of a word for the quality he'd always seen in her eyes while they shared that class. Looking back, he realized he still couldn't. *Passion* was as close as he could come now. But even passion seemed too weak a word to describe the impression he'd had of her back then.

"Anyway," she said, more softly now, "you surprised me that day, being so decent when everyone else was being so horrible. After that, I looked for you at school every day. And even if I only saw you once, it made me feel like I could handle whatever else was thrown at me."

Bennett inhaled a deep breath and released it slowly. He'd had no idea—none—that Haven had felt that way about him. And he was kind of ashamed now that he'd not just been so unaware, but that he hadn't done anything to deserve the distinction.

He wanted to apologize again, but there were just too many things to apologize for. So he only said, "I wish things could have been different back then."

"Yeah, me, too," she told him.

Those three little words tore a pretty big hole in the way he'd been feeling about Haven Moreau. Maybe because he really did wish things could have been different back then. Maybe because the mood that had started to grow lighter was beginning to dim again. Maybe because her smile had vanished, and he wanted desperately to see it come back.

For one of those reasons—or maybe all of them—he heard himself ask, "What if it had been different back then at Barnaby? For us, I mean? You and me?"

She looked puzzled. "How could it have possibly been different? Our courses were preset before I ever came through the school's front doors, thanks to our last names."

"Yeah, but that first day, that first contact we had, neither one of us knew who the other was. What if that anonymity had gone on for a while? What if we'd had a chance to talk or hang out without knowing who the other was? Could we have become…friends?"

She started shaking her head before he even finished with his questions. "It just would have delayed our animosity. We would have found out who we were to each other at some point and then started hating each other after that."

"You didn't hate me after you knew who I was," he reminded her. "You just said so yourself."

Her cheeks went pink again. And this time, he knew the warmth of the fire had nothing to do with it.

"And I didn't hate you after I found out who you were in Ms. Peréz's class."

And he hadn't. Once his initial surprise had worn off that Haven wasn't the fire-breathing dirtbag bent on destroying his family the way she and the rest of the Moreaus had always been painted, and once he saw more of her in class—even if they hadn't interacted one-on-one—he'd kind of grudgingly liked her. At least until the end of the year. After school let out for the summer, Bennett hadn't given much thought to it or anything about it, including Haven. And even when the two of them landed in the same anatomy class his senior year, he'd been way more interested in his lab partner, Kimani, than he had anything else about that class.

She hesitated, then asked, "What *did* you think of me once you knew who I was?"

Although he'd set himself up for the question, Bennett wasn't sure how to answer it. Truly, on any given day at Barnaby when he encountered her, he'd mostly just shaken his head in bemusement—whether at the weird way she chose to accessorize her uniform or her lack of grace when she tripped down the hall.

So he only reiterated what he'd been thinking earlier about his immediate impression of her in Ms. Peréz's class. "I thought you were kind of cute," he admitted. "And I admired your defiance."

His reply obviously surprised her. "Defiance?" she echoed. "In what way was I ever defiant at Barnaby?"

This time, he was the one to chuckle. "You came back every day, for one thing. Even though you weren't exactly the most popular person there."

"Understatement of the millennium," she muttered dryly.

"And even though you didn't exactly fit in," he continued.

He was afraid she would take that the wrong way, when he'd actually meant it as a compliment. Looking back, he wished he hadn't fit in so well at Barnaby.

So he was relieved when she laughed again. "I take it back. *That* was the understatement of the millennium."

He smiled. "And even though no one, not even me, ever gave you a reason to tolerate any of us, never mind have a crush on one of us."

She sobered at that. So did Bennett.

But he made himself return to his original question, since neither of them had really answered it. "I'm serious, Haven. What if we had somehow become friends at Barnaby? Or what if we even...?" At this point, he honestly had no idea what part of his brain was driving his line of questioning. All he knew was that it made him finish what he started to say. "What if we'd even started dating or something?"

She gazed at him in silence for a long time. Finally, softly, she said, "I don't know. I can't even imagine something like that happening. Not after everything else that did."

"But what about before all that?" he asked.

Why he was belaboring this concept, he had no clue. It just seemed really important for some reason. Maybe by setting up an alternate scenario for what had been such a bad experience at the hands of his family...

Oh hell, he didn't know why it seemed important. Only that it did.

They somehow seemed to have moved closer to each other as they were talking. Bennett couldn't remember ever changing his position, and he hadn't noticed Haven changing hers. Yet both of them must have, because whereas they'd sat a good foot apart when they initially moved to the floor, now their bodies were nearly touching. And neither was in the spot where they first started.

So, what the hell. He scooted himself over the scant inch that still separated them, until his thigh was aligned with hers and their shoulders were touching. Her eyes widened at the contact, but she didn't move away. Instead, after a second or two, she tipped her head toward his, just the slightest bit. So he tipped his toward hers, the slightest bit more. She, in turn, touched her forehead lightly to his. He, in turn, after the merest hesitation, just enough time to allow her to stop him if she wanted—but she didn't—covered her mouth with his.

It was by no means a passionate kiss. In a lot of ways, Bennett kissed Haven the way one young kid kisses another when it's the first time for both of them. Because in a lot of ways, they were kids again tonight. And in a lot of ways, this was a first. For both of them.

He pulled away without doing more than brushing his lips against hers, once, twice, three times, four. Even so, his heart was pounding as if he'd just run a marathon. Haven seemed to be just as moved, because her breathing was as erratic as his, and when she opened her eyes, her pupils were large and dark.

She swallowed hard. "Why did you do that?" The words had come out barely a whisper.

"I don't know," Bennett replied, his own words just as quiet. And he didn't. "It just felt like the right thing to do." And it had. "I guess I was just wondering what it could have been like for us. If things had been different, I mean."

Her expression revealed nothing of what she might

be thinking, and he was surprised by just how badly he wished he knew. Very quietly, she asked, "Do you really think you would have ever asked me out on a date at Barnaby if you didn't know who I was?"

She spoke the question dubiously, as if she didn't believe he ever would have. And, truth be told, Bennett didn't know, either.

So he told her honestly, "I don't know. But maybe—"

"Maybe what?" she asked when he didn't finish.

"—maybe we could try it now."

Her eyebrows arched delicately. "What? Dating?"

He lifted a shoulder and let it drop. "Yeah. Why not?"

He really hoped she didn't have a response for that. Because, suddenly, he really wanted to take her out on a date. The fact that she said nothing weirdly heartened him.

"Seriously," he continued, "why shouldn't we? We're adults now. And I think it's kind of obvious after tonight that we're not exactly enemies anymore. And we don't have to deal with our families."

For the first time since he kissed her, she smiled, and something that had been wound tight inside Bennett slowly began to unravel.

"Oh, don't we?" she asked lightly.

"Okay, fine. We'll have to deal with them eventually," he conceded. "But they're like three hundred miles and an ice storm away. We've got a good head start on them."

She chuckled at that, and what little tension still existed inside him dissolved away completely.

"So where does one even go for a date in Sudbury?" she asked.

Though it didn't escape him that she hadn't exactly agreed to go out with him. Yet.

"I'm not even sure there's anything open there right now," she added. "Every time I've gone in to do some small job for Finn, the whole place seems to be battened down and buttoned up."

Bennett had noticed that about the village, too. He assumed most of the businesses were closed and the population was so sparse because it was so long past the summer vacation season. But parts of the town did look like they hadn't seen much action for a long time. Like Summerlight, Sudbury seemed to be coasting into its twilight years, without much chance of ever coming back to life. Which was a shame. It really could be a picturesque little place, the way it undoubtedly had been once upon a time. It was probably one reason Winston Moreau had chosen to build his summer home here.

"There's a restaurant on Hoptree Street," he told Haven. "It's called Jack's. It's open. I had lunch there the other day."

She eyed him pointedly. "The other day when you had that superimportant errand to run in the village that you never said exactly what it was?" she asked knowingly. "That day?"

"Saw through that, did you?" he asked.

"Like a glass full of air," she assured him.

He expelled a restless sigh. "I've needed some space lately, after…you know."

She nodded, still knowingly. "Yeah. I did, too."

He looked down at the closeness of their bodies, then back at her. "Guess we both got over that, huh?"

She grinned. "Guess we did."

A moment passed that probably should have been awkward, but somehow wasn't.

"So what do you say, Haven?" he asked. "Want to have dinner with me this weekend?"

She nodded. "I'd like that, Bennett. I'd like it a lot."

"It's a date, then."

"Yeah. It's a date."

Chapter Eight

Haven hadn't been kidding when she told Bennett how out of service most of Sudbury seemed to be. And as they drove into the village three nights later in his cream-colored Bentley—which she'd been surprised to hear him tell her was actually an environmentally friendly vehicle—she wasn't ready to change her opinion. The village looked even lonelier in the dark, though still kind of adorable with the yellow glow of its Victorian streetlights warming the occasional row house or storefront.

Then again, the handful of times she'd traveled to the village since being hired by Finn Huxley, she'd mostly worked in the same area on the outskirts of town, where it was principally residential—tidy saltbox houses and Cape Cods interspersed with larger Queen Annes and Victorians. Though those homes, like everything else around Sudbury and Summerlight, had looked tired and battered, too.

But Jack's, the restaurant Bennett had discovered, was on the other side of town, where she had yet to visit, tucked down a side street off another side street, and she never would have found it by herself. The single block it sat on was dotted with other small shops and businesses, and it looked like the one place in town where things were still hopping.

Well, okay, maybe not so much *hopping* as just happening. Okay, maybe not so much *happening* as just occurring. Yeah, that was it. This block was definitely the occurring part of Sudbury. Woot. The buildings here were better tended than elsewhere in the village, and there were honest-to-God people moving from one to the other, even though the nighttime temperatures were dipping into the forties now, and the wind off the lake could gust it even lower. In addition to Jack's, there was a café across the street named Dragonfly, which was still open, along with what looked like a pub called The Bitter End. On either side of Jack's was a bookstore, Turn the Page, and a coffee shop, The Magic Bean. Both of those were closed for the day, but it was clear by their cheerful storefronts that they were still in business.

Yep. For Sudbury, this was definitely the occurring spot to be.

Which was fitting, since *occurring* could also be used to describe how she and Bennett had been existing since that night in front of the fireplace. Instead of their confidential conversation and that chaste series of kisses bringing them closer together, both interactions had somehow seemed to put them on even more fragile footing. Whereas before, their roles had been neatly defined by their families' animosity for each other and their misunderstanding about their own past, their new role as tentative friends—or something—was vague and uncertain. It didn't help that, for the last few days, they'd seen even less of each other than usual, thanks to Bennett suddenly having to focus on a new account for his work and Finn having a couple of jobs for Haven to do in town. On those few occasions when they had encountered each other, they'd seemed to walk on eggshells.

It was those kisses, she'd finally decided, that had introduced the most awkwardness. Even though they had been little more than a repeated brushing of their lips together, it had been a very nice brushing of lips. A very intimate brushing of lips. And it had taken what started off as apology and amends to a level of…something else. Something that went beyond both. Something she had yet to identify.

She had no idea what to expect from their date tonight. She wondered what Bennett was anticipating.

They made chitchat during the short drive and the walk to Jack's, and he held the door of the restaurant open for her when they arrived. She passed through ahead of him and was instantly thrown back in time. The place looked like something out of a classic Hollywood movie that hosted live jazz in the front room and bootlegging in the back. Dark wood, dim lighting and small tables, crowded together and covered with white linen. Only about half of them held diners, but considering how few people Haven had seen out and about elsewhere in town, the place looked packed.

Bennett told the hostess they had a reservation for seven o'clock, and when she asked them for their coats, he exchanged them both for a tag. Beneath hers, Haven wore the only dress she owned, a simple vintage shirt-waist in wine red that had also come from her favorite thrift shop. She'd packed it as an afterthought when she'd been frantically jerking clothes out of her closet the morning she'd learned of the bequest. Since she didn't have many in-between outfits, she had grabbed the few she owned just in case. In case of what, she couldn't have said at the time. Panic did that to a person. But she was glad for her decision now.

Bennett had dressed up, too, but he had opted for the in-between of a chocolate-brown cashmere V-neck over a linen T-shirt—because they had to be cashmere and linen—and dark trousers. He'd shaved, too, something about which she had mixed feelings. On one hand, his face was so beautiful, she liked seeing all of it that she could. On the other, he did look awfully hot when he was all scruffy. And she could still recall the faint scrape of his beard when he kissed her the other night, a luscious counter to the softness of his mouth on hers.

Her heart flickered at the memory, so she did her best to focus on something else instead. Such as the dozens of black-and-white photos on the walls she passed as they followed the hostess to their table. Seriously, they just went on and on, and a lot of them had been auto-graphed by the celebrities they featured—movie stars, rock stars, foreign dignitaries…and, holy cow, was that

Jackie Onassis? But none of them seemed to be more current than a time before Haven was born. Damn, Sudbury had been a lot more than *occurring* once upon a time.

The hostess seated them at a table by the window, leaving Haven and Bennett alone again. And, as had been the case all evening, Haven had no idea what to say.

So she went with the obvious. "This is a really cool place. All the photos on the walls? Just how many famous people have eaten here?"

"I asked my server about them when I had lunch here the first time," he told her. "He said the restaurant's original owner, Jack Parris, ran liquor to and from Canada during Prohibition—first Canada's, then ours. And that he had ties to the mob in New York and Toronto, both."

"Wow. That's kinda cool," Haven said.

Bennett nodded. "Not only that but the place had some major French chef during the twenties and thirties who was known for his crêpes suzette, and a lot of jazz greats came here to perform. With all that going on, Jack's drew a lot of impressive people back in the day."

Never in a million years would Haven have guessed sleepy little Sudbury had been home to such a notorious past. "Sounds like it was some kind of flashy waystation between New York and Toronto back then," she said.

"Because it was so off the radar of the big-city authorities," Bennett agreed. "According to my server, a lot of famous—and sketchy—people came through here when they traveled from one city to the other. Or they stayed here for a few days if they needed to lay low when the heat got too bad in the city."

Haven couldn't help chuckling at that. "I'm sorry, but it's just so hard to imagine Sudbury teeming with naughty-doers."

Bennett laughed, too. "But wait, there's more. Another time when I was here, my server that day told me that, in the seventies, there was this major annual music festival that brought in bands from all over the place for an entire weekend like some small-scale Woodstock, which is probably what inspired it. Sudbury Sounds, it was called."

Haven was shaking her head in disbelief before he even finished. "How could a place change so much in less than fifty years?"

"It gets better," Bennett said. "Sudbury Sounds was held on the grounds of Summerlight, believe it or not. My uncle Nathaniel and aunt Aurelia loaned out the land with their blessing."

"No way," she said, laughing in earnest now.

Although she'd never met Nathaniel and Aurelia Hadden, Haven did her best to conjure them in bell-bottoms and headbands and concert tees. Nope. Wasn't going to happen. She couldn't even imagine them dressed like rich people looking out fondly over the vast swath of concert-goers in their backyard who were tossing Frisbees and hurtling down homemade, mud-soaked Slip 'n Slides. She laughed harder.

"I know," he agreed. "I can't imagine Uncle Nathaniel and Aunt Aurelia doing something like that, either, but apparently, they were both big music lovers. The festival had all kinds of acts. I never heard any mention of Sudbury Sounds when I was growing up. I mean, it stopped happening after Uncle Nathaniel's death, but it still sounds like it was a pretty big deal in these parts for a while. That must have been some scandal for the city Haddens, to have the country Haddens rubbing shoulders with hippies and punks and thrashers."

Haven couldn't wrap her head around any of it. How could this quiet little rural community have such a rich, out-there history? And why had it all died off and become forgotten? How had Sudbury gone from a hotbed of arts and counterculture to an exhausted little hamlet where nothing of interest ever happened?

"How can I have never heard about any of this?" she said.

Bennett shrugged. "I've never heard about it, either. And, hell, my family has always been a part of this place. But it just goes to show, you can't judge a place's past by what it looks like in the present."

There was a wealth of significance in what he said. Because it wasn't just the true essence of Sudbury that neither of them had known about. And it wasn't just Sudbury's outside appearance that had been misleading. They'd misjudged and made too many assumptions about each other, too. From the way Bennett was looking at her now, Haven thought maybe he was thinking the same thing.

Fortunately, their server showed up tableside before the moment grew awkward. When Haven looked up, she saw a tall, curvy redhead whose name tag identified her as Alice. She had interacted with Finn Huxley often enough now that she'd heard the name Alice from him on a regular basis and couldn't help wondering if this was the woman he always talked about—and always with a glimmer of something wistful and sad in his voice when he did. Certainly, Alice wasn't an unusual name, but it wasn't hugely popular for women in Haven's age group, either, which this Alice definitely was. And in a town the size of Sudbury, it was a good bet there weren't too many Alices.

"Hi," she said, looking first at Haven and then at Bennett. "Can I get you anything to drink while you look at the menu?"

They each ordered a glass of wine, then Alice went over the night's specials before departing.

"Doesn't look like crêpes suzette is on the menu anymore," Haven said after giving it a perfunctory look, all the way down to the desserts.

"Yeah, well, when was the last time you saw crêpes suzette on any menu? I don't think it's been much of a thing since my folks were our age. The salmon looks good, though."

They discussed their options, then Alice returned with their wine, and they ordered their dinner. And then, suddenly, things grew awkward. Again. Outside the window, a slice of yellow lamplight lit the evening, but even though the weather had cleared since the storm the other night, no one was on the street. Stars dappled what Haven could see of the sky, and the full moon hung like a bright silver dollar. She looked at Bennett, only to see that he was looking outside, too.

"It's a beautiful night," he said unnecessarily. Then he turned to look at Haven. "You look beautiful, too."

Something warm and wild splashed through her belly

at the matter-of-fact way he'd spoken the compliment. As if it were something he told her every day.

"So do you," she said. Less matter-of-factly, since she wasn't used to giving anyone compliments, but especially not someone like Bennett, who had loomed so larger-than-life in her brain for so long.

He smiled. But all he said was, "Thanks."

And then silence fell again. *Why is this so awkward?* she wondered. They had spoken so easily and frankly that night in front of the fire, about a subject that was infinitely more difficult to discuss than a simple dinner date out. That night, they'd cleared the air for anything that might come after. Why was what was coming after so weird?

"So…" she began.

"You know…" he said at the same time.

They both stopped talking at once. Then they smiled at each other again.

"Go ahead," she told him.

"No, you first," he said.

She honestly didn't know what she had planned to say. Probably something she'd already said about the restaurant or some obvious observation about the world beyond its windows.

So she said the first thing that popped into her head. "Did you realize today is our five-week anniversary?" The question surprised her as much as it seemed to surprise Bennett. Even so, she hurried to say, "At Summerlight, I mean. Today marks five weeks since we moved in."

She truly hadn't meant to make the announcement

sound romantic. Somehow, though, it came out sounding a bit romantic.

"I didn't realize," he said. "That went fast. Only ten months to go."

It had gone fast, she was surprised to realize. What surprised her more was that, even after five weeks, they'd achieved so little. She'd only managed to make a few of the repairs it needed. There were still parts of the house she hadn't fully assessed. Neither of them was committed to a long-term plan for the place. Yes, there were still ten months to go. But if they were anything like the first one, then they would pass quickly, too. In less than a year, she and Bennett could be sitting here in Jack's again, still not agreeing on what they should do with Summerlight.

Though, after the exchange they'd just shared, Haven could feel the wheels starting to turn in her head.

"We need to start making some plans for the house," she said.

He nodded but said nothing in reply.

She tried again. "Especially since I know you want to sell Summerlight, but I'm not sure I do."

He inhaled deeply and released the breath slowly. "You know my reasons for wanting to sell," he said. "The place is a dinosaur. Neither of us wants to live there. It's not commercially viable. What are your reasons for *not* wanting to sell it?"

She smiled. "The place could be amazing if it's rehabbed. My mind could be changed about possibly living there after it's been rehabbed. It could potentially be extremely commercially viable once it's rehabbed."

His expression grew more dubious with every word

she uttered. "Could be, could be, could be," he echoed. "Rehabbed, rehabbed, rehabbed. That's a lot of *coulds* and no *woulds*. A lot of rehabbing with no funds to do it. And unless you have access to a crystal ball…"

"I don't. But after talking about what Sudbury used to be tonight, I'm starting to get a vision anyway."

Bennett eyed her warily. "What are you thinking about?"

She grinned. "Bennett, I'm starting to have the best idea."

Bennett gazed back at Haven, at once curious and fearful. Curious, because she still seemed to be weighing whatever she was thinking about. Fearful, for the same reason.

"What kind of idea?" he asked. Curiously and fearfully.

Her smile in response was dazzling. All of her was dazzling tonight. Not that he'd ever considered her anything less than beautiful, no matter how she presented herself. Even the day she came back from town after tiling someone's bathroom, with her clothes caked in grout and her hands covered with caulk, and her hair and face streaked with dust and god-knew-what else, he'd thought she looked adorable. But he'd never seen her dressed up this way, looking a lot more like the women he normally dated.

No, that wasn't actually true. She might be dressed tonight in a way that was comparable to other women he'd gone out with, but there was an air about her that was totally different from them. She had a different kind of confidence. A comfort with who she was, maybe. As if she no longer felt the need to apologize for herself because she knew there was nothing wrong with the way she lived. His family and friends at Barnaby may have done their best to bring her down a few pegs when she was there, but in the long run, all they'd done was make her stronger. They'd caused her to have a better sense of who she was and what she wanted, and she'd embraced that with her whole heart.

"What if," she said, pulling him back to the matter at hand, "in addition to rehabbing Summerlight, we revitalized Sudbury, too?"

Of all the ideas he might have expected her to have, that that one never would have made the cut. Certain he was misunderstanding because he'd been so lost in thought, he asked, "What? You mean fix up the parts that are kinda run-down? 'Cause that's, like, the whole town."

She shook her head. "No, more than that."

How could there be more? That was already more than enough.

Her smile widened. "What if we brought it back to the kind of place it used to be for people to visit the way they used to?"

Okay, that brought him up short. Barring the building of a time portal that people could pay admission to and go back a hundred years, he didn't see how Sudbury could ever be the place it used to be. And last time he checked, he was pretty sure no one had invented time travel yet.

"I mean it," she insisted when he remained silent. "If this town was that big a deal once, it could be again."

"Haven, that is a way, *way* bigger project than either of us can handle," he told her. "And it involves a lot more people than just you and me. What if the people of Sudbury don't want their town to go back to the way it used to be? Maybe everyone here likes the peace and quiet."

As he was speaking, Alice returned with their salads and placed them on the table. They both thanked her, but before she could walk away, Haven took it a step further.

"Alice, can I ask you a question?" she said.

"Sure," Alice replied.

"Do you like living here in Sudbury?"

A host of emotions crossed the server's face, something Bennett found both interesting and discomforting.

"I guess so," she said. "I mean, I grew up here and don't really know what it's like to live anywhere else. And I live with my mother, who can be a bit…challenging. But Sudbury is okay. I wish there was more to do, but it's not terrible or anything."

Haven gave Bennett a triumphant look, then turned her attention back to Alice. "So you wouldn't have a problem with it if someone came to Sudbury and started making changes?"

Alice looked confused. "Why would anyone come here to make changes? There's nothing here."

"But that's the point," Haven said. "What if someone came in and made changes so that there *was* stuff to do? A lot of stuff. What if Sudbury became kind of a vacation destination? Would that be a good thing or a bad thing?"

Alice thought about it for a moment. "For me, it would be a good thing. Not just because there would be more to do, but I'd make more money if we had more people coming in to Jack's."

Now the look Haven threw Bennett was one of challenge. So what could he do but rise to the bait?

"What about the rest of the town, though?" he asked Alice. "How would other people in Sudbury feel if some stranger—some outsider—came in and suddenly started changing everything? How would they feel if suddenly the town were overrun by other strangers—other outsiders—who created more traffic and more headaches?"

"And created more jobs and entrepreneurship and improved the entire town's infrastructure?" Haven added before Alice had a chance to respond. "And preserved the town's history and historic buildings? And protected the local wildlife and woodlands? And brought in more tax dollars to benefit the entire community?"

At this, Alice laughed lightly. "Whoa, whoa, whoa. You sound like you're going to turn us into a utopia overnight. And trust me. Sudbury is no utopia."

"But it could be," Haven said.

"There's no such thing as utopia," Bennett assured her. "With progress comes headaches. The more you build and reform, the more you have to be responsible for."

"And the more opportunities there are for..." Haven smiled again. "For everything."

Bennett started to protest again, but Alice saved him the trouble. "Any business you want to bring to Sudbury," she said, "you're going to have to take up with the town council and chamber of commerce. And a lot of those folks aren't exactly what I'd call progressive."

Another table summoned her, so Alice excused herself.

"She's right, you know," Bennett said. "It doesn't matter how many plans you or I make for Sudbury. The decision comes down to what the locals want. And they might like Sudbury the way it is just fine."

"Or they might miss all the fun stuff that used to happen around here." Before he could reply to that, she quickly added, "Bringing all that back would be a very good reason for people to want to vacation here. It would be a very good reason for us to turn Summerlight into a hotel."

"Haven, I'm not sure you're really considering all the—"

"Just listen," she told him.

The words were less a command than they were a petition. Fine. Bennett would listen to what she had to say. Then he would let her down as gently as he could. Because what she was suggesting just wasn't doable for the two of them. No way could they rehabilitate Sudbury the way they could rehabilitate a house. Hell, he wasn't even convinced they could do the house part yet. To renovate an entire town? Yeah, no.

"Look, I know what I'm about to propose is a massive undertaking," she said. "But if we tell the villagers about our plan to renovate Summerlight and turn it into a hotel, they might get on board with revitalizing Sudbury, too. The businesses that have closed for good could reopen. And the seasonal ones that are only open for the summer could stay open year-round."

Bennett said nothing. It wasn't that her idea wasn't good. He'd wondered himself during his few visits to Sudbury how some of its residents—if not all of them—were able to make a living. Tourism seemed beyond the town's reach, because there were so many other villages around the lake that had started capitalizing on tourism a lot sooner, and many of those towns were closer to highly populated areas. But if Sudbury had been a hot spot once, it made sense that it could be again. And yes, there was a chance the townspeople might get on board with that. But they might not. It was possible the reason for the lack of tourism was because the villagers just wanted to be left alone these days.

Even if they did want to draw tourism again, it would take a lot of time and work and money to manage it. And from what he'd seen of the town and its people, there may not be resources for any of those things.

So yeah, Haven's idea was good. It just wasn't practical.

"And Christmas!" she added impulsively. "Think how much fun we could have turning Summerlight into a Christmas getaway. A house like that is a Hallmark holiday movie just waiting to happen."

"Haven, I don't think it's going to be—"

"There could be all kinds of outdoor activities," she hurried to say before he could object. "Cross-country skiing, ice fishing, snow sculpturing. Snow sculptures would be supercool."

Yes, they would. But she had gotten so far ahead of herself that she was about to lap herself.

"But, Haven—" he tried again.

To no avail. "And a holiday craft fair for the locals," she said. "Or even for the students at Cornell. Everybody likes craft fairs. Especially during the holidays. And I bet a lot of those college kids don't get to go home for the holidays. Or their families could join them up here."

Her brain was clearly in full swing on the planning front, Bennett thought, and there would be no stopping her now. The wheels that had started turning were now zooming down the highway at Formula One speeds. Not that he was going to tell her that, since it would just give here ideas about building a racetrack around Cayuga Lake while they were at it.

"Haven," he said again.

But she was on a roll. She pointed to the name of the restaurant on the window beside them. "We could do a food-and-spirits festival in the fall, to tie in with Jack's history of that."

"Haven—"

"And nature hikes and baby farm animal visits in the spring."

"Haven—"

"And a music festival in the summer, like Sudbury Sounds used to be. We could have something for every season that would bring people in. We could make Summerlight events a year-round thing and call it Sudbury Seasons. Or Seasons in Sudbury. Or—"

"Haven!" he interjected again, raising his voice enough to turn the heads of the other diners.

And to shut up Haven, too. "What?" she asked.

"You are light-years ahead of anything we or this town might be able to manage."

"But we need to make plans," she said softly.

He chuckled at that. "We don't need to make a million plans in one night," he told her. "Baby steps. Please. One thing at a time. I don't even know yet if renovating Summerlight is a good idea, never mind an entire town. It's going to cost a fortune just to deal with the house. More than you or I can afford. Who's going to pay to rebuild an entire town? Who says the people of Sudbury even want to rebuild their town?"

They were all fair points, and he could tell she realized that. It was also clear from her expression—her defeated, demoralized, desolate expression—that she knew she was going out on a limb with her many, *many* ideas.

"They're good ideas," she said quietly, defensively, obviously reading his expression, too. "And they're not impossible." She expelled a soft sigh and sat back in her chair. "But I guess I could reel it in some. I'm just saying we have an excellent opportunity here, that's all. One with a lot of potential."

"And I'm just saying tap the brakes a bit," he countered. "First things first."

"Okay," she conceded with clear reluctance. "Then tell me, what comes first?"

It was a fair question. Especially in light of the fact that, as she'd pointed out earlier, they'd been in Sudbury for five weeks and were no further along in figuring out what to do with it than they'd been that morning in Mr. Crittenden's office. It really would take a lot of

time and money to turn Summerlight into a hotel. But…
if Haven was willing to donate her time to such an effort, then maybe Bennett could convince his family to
invest a little money into the place. The house had been
in the care of the Haddens for five generations. The last
generation, Aunt Aurelia, hadn't been in a position to
really care for the place, so it was up to the current generation, Bennett and his family, to step in and do that.

He would front what money he could himself. But the
rest would be up to his family. The Haddens might have
their drawbacks, but they weren't completely heartless.
Not all of them. And they certainly knew how to keep
up appearances. If it got around Manhattan that they'd
let the Gilded Age mansion they'd been hell-bent for
more than a hundred years on keeping in their possession deteriorate, they'd never live it down. He'd call his
parents tomorrow.

And wow, how weird. Just making that decision suddenly made him feel as if a huge weight had been lifted
from his shoulders.

He smiled at Haven. "What comes first?" he asked,
echoing her question. "I guess renovating Summerlight
does."

She looked as if she was afraid to hope he meant
what he was saying. "Are you just talking about fixing
it up enough to sell it?" she asked. "Or are you okay
with the idea of turning it into a hotel?"

"First things first," he repeated. "For now, I'm on
board with completely rehabbing the house."

She looked more disappointed than he'd thought she
would. And he hated seeing how she went from being

so excited and enthusiastic a few minutes ago to being so somber and discouraged now. He hated even more that he was the one responsible for it.

He hesitated just a moment before adding, "And I'm on board with turning Summerlight into a hotel."

And he was, he was surprised to realize. Hell, maybe the two of them could make a go of it. Not that he wanted to be the one running the place. And he was pretty sure that, deep down, Haven didn't want to, either, since her life was in the city as much as his was. But it might actually turn out to be a halfway decent investment at some point. If other people could get as excited about the place as Haven was.

Her spirit flickered to life once more, and the smile she gave him then was dazzling. "Do you promise?"

He expelled a restless sound. But he told her, "Yes. I promise. *If*," he added emphatically, "and I do mean *if*, Haven, turning it into a hotel looks like it will actually be a viable project once the renovation is done."

"It will be," she told him. "I know it will."

That remained to be seen. In the meantime, he looked down at their untouched salads and their barely touched wine.

"You know," he said, "this was supposed to be our first date. An attempt to get to know each other as something other than mortal enemies and co-heirs. It wasn't supposed to be a municipal planning session."

She smiled and picked up her fork with one hand and her glass of wine with the other. Then she said, "So, Bennett, what brings a suave, urbane city fella like you to a sleepy little town like Sudbury?"

He smiled back, picking up his own fork and glass. "Well, Haven, that's an interesting story."

"I'd love to hear it. Sounds like you and I have a lot to talk about."

That, they did, Bennett agreed. But about the two of them this time, not about the house or the town or the past or the future. The present. The moment. This dinner. This night. The two of them. Whatever came later...

Well. They'd figure that out as they went.

It was nearly midnight by the time Haven and Bennett made it back to Summerlight. Dinner had lasted hours, thanks to the fact that the restaurant wasn't full, and Alice assured them she didn't mind them hanging around because she had to close anyway. They had taken her at her word and pretty much closed the place with her. And as much as Haven had carped about her plans for Summerlight before their meal arrived—her ginormous plans for Summerlight, which would take years to implement—the subject never came up again. Instead, they'd talked about the sort of things people normally did on a first date. Favorite books and movies, childhood plans that never came to fruition, how Bennett's enterprise, Greenback Directive, was making an effort to turn the corporate world environmentally friendly and how much Haven enjoyed fixing things and bringing old houses, especially, back to life.

Now as he held open the front door of Summerlight for her to precede him, she felt like the most satisfied, most mellow woman in the world. Not just from the delicious dinner and excellent wine, but from the convivial conversation, too.

And, okay, also from the realization that the house she had fallen in love with over the last month would actually be coming to life again. Bennett shared her vision now. Once it became reality—and it *would* become reality—they could tackle the town of Sudbury, too. She was confident the villagers would be as enthusiastic about the prospect of revitalization as she was. Who didn't want to live someplace that was alive and exciting after being somber and exhausted for decades?

Although it was late, and the day had been full, she was in no way ready to go to bed. Evidently, Bennett wasn't, either, because he halted at the foot of the stairs when she did. They looked at each other, and both spoke at once.

"I'm thinking it's a nice night for a fire."

"It's not that late. Maybe we could have a fire."

They laughed at their meeting of minds. Then Haven said, "If you want to start it, I'll grab us a bottle of wine and a couple glasses."

"Fair enough," he told her.

As he headed for the library, Haven headed for the kitchen, hanging her coat on a peg in the mudroom before retrieving the wine from a wooden case Bennett had brought up from the cellar—along with a dozen bottles of wine—to use as a makeshift rack. By the time she opened it, collected two glasses from the cabinet and returned to the library, the fire in the kindling was licking at the logs above and catching nicely. Bennett had kicked off his shoes and retreated to the sofa, so

Haven stepped out of hers and joined him. Although the power had been restored the day after the storm, the house was still its usual cold self, especially since she was now both bare legged and barefoot, so, after setting the wine on a side table and handing Bennett his glass, she grabbed the throw they'd wrapped over themselves the other night and brought it back to the sofa with her. It seemed crass to not share it with Bennett, even if he was better covered than she was, so she sat near him on his end and draped it over both of them.

He thanked her as she moved closer—hey, she had no choice, since it wasn't that big of a throw—then lifted his glass in a toast.

"To big plans," he said.

She raised her glass, too. "And to new beginnings."

He smiled. She smiled back. They clinked their glasses, then enjoyed a long taste. The fire crackled as the wind outside picked up, gusting down the flue and rattling a nearby window. Then everything was silent again. And Haven had no idea what to say.

Finally, she settled on, "I had a good time tonight."

"Me, too."

More silence as each seemed to wonder where to go next. It was odd coming on the heels of a meal they'd shared, during which they'd talked about everything. But then, maybe that was the point. Maybe they'd said all they needed to say for tonight.

As if compelled by an unknown force, Haven leaned forward the way Bennett had a few nights before and, after only a small hesitation, covered his mouth lightly with hers. Just as he had that first time, she skimmed her lips gingerly over his, once, twice, three times, four. She had intended to pull back the way he had, too, but the moment their lips parted, he cupped his free hand over her nape to prevent her from doing so. His gaze pinned to hers, he set his barely touched wine on the table beside him. Then he took hers from her grasp and set it beside his. Their eyes locked again for a scant second. Then she dipped her head to his once more.

This time, when their mouths met, it was with much more pressure, much more persistence, much more passion. Bennett kissed Haven as if he needed her for life itself, pulling her onto his lap and wrapping his other arm around her waist. She lifted one hand to cradle his jaw and looped the other around his neck, kissing him back as if she needed him for life, too. In that moment, she did. She needed him—wanted him—more than she'd needed or wanted anyone before.

For a long time, they kissed and clung to each other, exploring as much of each other as they could reach with their hands and mouths. Then she felt Bennett's hand at the collar of her dress, twisting free the top two buttons so he could dip his hand beneath the fabric. She gasped as he pushed aside her bra to cover her breast, thumbing the ripe peak to life. Unable to help herself, she dropped her hand to his lap, finding him hard and heavy beneath his own clothes. He groaned as she stroked her palm over him, then shifted her until she was fully on his lap, straddling him.

They were both breathing heavily, his hands on her waist, hers on his shoulders, their gazes once again locked. But, as before, she said nothing, and neither did he. No words seemed necessary. The time to talk truly had passed. So Haven lifted her hands to her dress buttons, freeing the rest of them, one by one. Bennett watched intently until she came to the last one, then moved his hands to push the garment off her shoulders. Once her arms were free, he reached behind her for her bra and released its clasp so that the straps fell off her shoulders, too. Instinctively, she lifted her hands to hold it in place. But he leaned forward and opened his mouth over her neck, dragging it down over her shoulders, curling an index finger under her bra to tug it aside and kiss the tender flesh beneath it.

She sighed at the feel of him on her breast and freed herself from the garment completely, tangling the fingers of both hands in his hair. For long moments, he tasted her, suckling first one breast, then the other before moving his hands lower and lower, and lower still, until he could dip his fingers beneath her panties and curve his hand over her naked ass. In turn, she grabbed the hem of his sweater and T-shirt, tugging both up to reveal the bumps of sinew and muscle beneath. He released her long enough that she could pull his clothing over his head, then she tossed both to the floor and kissed him again.

Somehow—she honestly didn't know how, because she was so lost in the moment—they shed the rest of their clothing and stretched out on the sofa, warmed by the flames of the now-raging fire and their even hotter need for each other. Haven lay beneath Bennett, one hand skimming along the ridges of muscle on his back, the other stroking his shaft. He laved her breasts and tangled his fingers in the damp folds of the flesh between her legs until she wasn't sure where his body ended and hers began. Then she was atop him, her legs on each side of him, rubbing herself wantonly back and forth over the long length of him until they were both slick and ready for each other. She wanted him so... Oh, so badly. But she hadn't exactly prepared herself for this moment.

Bennett, however, was more than ready. In one fluid motion, he grabbed his pants from the floor, retrieved a condom from his wallet, and rolled it on. Then he moved their bodies so that his back was against the sofa and Haven was spooned against him, facing the fire. He entered her that way, covering one breast with his hand as he sent the fingers of the other between her legs again. Over and over, he stroked her while gently rolling her nipple between his thumb and forefinger. Over and over, he pushed himself forward, thrusting in and out of her. So exquisite were the sensations rolling through her that she held in her orgasm as long as she could. But when she felt him peaking behind her, she let herself go, too, and together, they rushed over the precipice.

Then Bennett was moving them again, turning her so that she lay beneath him, his elbows braced on each side of her, her legs looped over his. He kissed her again, long and hard and deep. Then he turned to his back and pulled her atop him, dragging up the throw from the floor to drape it over them.

Not that Haven needed it. She didn't think she would ever be cold again. And judging by the smile Bennett gave her, she was pretty sure he never would be, either.

But neither spoke a word. They only nestled into each other to gaze at the fire flickering higher. There was nothing that needed to be said, as far as Haven was concerned. She had Bennett and Summerlight, and in that moment, she couldn't imagine ever wanting anything more. Because in that moment, nothing—nothing— seemed as if it could ever go wrong again. Because in that moment, everything—everything—was right.

Bennett stared at the phone he had just disconnected and did his best not to throw it through the library window. But then, that was kind of par for the course whenever he spoke to his parents. He always felt like breaking something afterward. It was why he normally relied on texts or emails to communicate with them. Because whenever he tried to talk to them, the conversation invariably turned, at best, surreal, and at worst, combative. Today's conversation had been a mix of both.

It was just reason number 273 why he had put off calling to ask them for their help in contributing to the costs of renovating Summerlight. If he could have pushed it past the week he'd already stalled, he would have. But Haven had asked him about it again this morning, and he'd run out of reasons for putting her off.

And okay, sure, the conversation started off fine, with his folks asking about the house and how it was coming along and how they'd love to visit before the weather made it impossible for them to leave the city, since who knew if they would ever get to see it again in their lifetimes, now that there was no chance they were ever going to be the ones to own it or live in it or enjoy it ever again… Oh yeah, that was another thing chatting with his parents could be—passive-aggressive. Then again, the commentary had provided him with the opening he needed to ask them about financing a good bit of the work. Unfortunately, he'd barely been able to put voice to the request before they'd begun finding reasons to shoot him down.

Why should they pay to revamp a house the family didn't even own anymore, they'd wanted to know? Now that they had to share it with the Moreaus, the Moreaus could foot the bill for maintenance on the place. The Haddens had been paying the bills for generations, and look where it had gotten them. If there were additional owners for Summerlight now, then the additional owners could take over the caretaking for a while.

It had only made matters worse when Bennett told them how much work the house needed after Aunt Aurelia had let it go for so long. The house's state of neglect was on the Haddens, he'd tried to explain, not the Moreaus. So it was up to the Haddens to foot the biggest part of the bill for improvements. Then he made an even bigger mistake by telling them how much of the work Haven would be able to do herself, thinking that might ease the pressure on them. Instead, his mother had said, and he quoted, "If the Moreau can do the work for free, all the better. Let the Moreau do it."

Let the Moreau do it, he repeated to himself now. *The Moreau*. His parents hadn't used Haven's first name once during the entire conversation, despite the fact that Bennett had made a point of using it himself as often as he could, to show them just how far along his and Haven's relationship had come without having to spell it out for them. Since spelling out the fact that he and Haven were no longer enemies—and were, in fact, lovers—would have made both his parents disown him. After they spontaneously combusted, he meant.

But even after an hour of assuring them what a good investment the renovation of Summerlight could end up being for them, he was left with nothing. Less than nothing. Because now his parents were mad that he had even asked them for help to begin with. And they knew he and Haven had moved beyond the animosity his family had spent more than a hundred years cementing, and were—gasp—cooperating with each other. His efforts to have a similar conversation with his grandfather and uncle after hanging up with his parents had yielded the same results—or lack thereof—except that in the case of those two, both had asked Bennett why he wasn't asking his parents to foot the bill. So now he'd lost two hours of his workday to an activity that had yielded nothing in return.

Great. This was just great. He hadn't expected his family to cover the costs completely—hoped, yes, expected, no—but he had thought he could count on a significant contribution, at least from his parents and possibly his grandfather. Yes, Bennett had a trust fund. Yes, it was considerable. But it wasn't as if he could just go in and take out whatever he wanted from it whenever he wanted to. He was only allowed occasional dribs and drabs at this point in his life, and he'd already used up most of the dribs this year for Greenback Directive, leaving only a few drabs for Summerlight. And there was no way a person could renovate a house this size with a few drabs.

He expelled a frustrated sigh and thumbed his phone to bring up his contact list. Thanks to his work with Greenback Directive, he knew a lot of people in the contracting fields. He knew even more who were investors and venture capitalists. Surely, someone in one or more of those groups would be interested in the potential of turning Summerlight into a hotel. Especially if he dangled the possibility of revamping the entire village of Sudbury, too, and turning it into a vacation wonderland. Hey, it could happen. In his list of *A* surnames alone, he identified three prospects. So, starting with Alicia Alvarez, Bennett began making a list.

Unfortunately, by the end of the day, after hanging up from his call with Vic Zimmerman, Bennett wasn't in much better shape than he'd been in that morning. Only a handful of the responses he'd received had been enthusiastic. Okay, maybe not enthusiastic. More like promising. Okay, maybe not promising. More like interested. Okay, maybe not interested, either. He'd spoken with a few people who thought the idea sounded doable. A couple had even said they'd be in touch.

Okay, okay, only Cal Russell had said he'd be in touch. And only, Bennett suspected, because Cal was an old college friend, and he owed Bennett a favor. The favor he owed wasn't on the scale of *Okay-I'll-invest-in-your-hotel*, though. It was more on the scale of *Here-I-bought-you-lunch-at-a-steakhouse-in-Tribeca-now-we're-even*.

He tossed his phone onto his desk in the library and

glared at it. He'd spent an entire day on this, to the exclusion of the work he should have been doing for Greenback, but he still felt like there was more he could do. There had to be. There must be some people he wasn't thinking about. He'd give himself a day to mull, then, at the end of the week, he could fly into the city for a day and meet with them in person. And he'd follow up in person with Cal Russell. Hell, he'd treat him to lunch at a steakhouse in Tribeca. And he'd try to manage a face-to-face with the couple of other people who had been polite enough to tell Bennett the idea sounded "doable." He *would* find the capital to renovate Summerlight. He would. He'd promised Haven. And he wasn't about to go back on his word. Especially not after the way she'd been treated by his family in the past, in his name.

"Hey, there," he heard her call softly from behind him.

He turned in his chair to find her leaning against the jamb in the library entrance, as if she'd been conjured from his thoughts. He didn't have to wonder how she'd spent her own day. She was wearing her usual work uniform of giant cargo pants and giant sweatshirt, both mottled with just about every color of paint Home Depot must carry. They were also blotched with bits of wallpaper and glue. Her hair was spilling out of its usual messy ponytail—all of it spattered with bits of paper, as well—and she looked as exhausted as Bennett felt. But whereas his own fatigue was due to frustration and futility, hers was clearly a good fatigue, the kind that came with a job well done.

"Hi," he said with as much spirit as he could stir. "Looks like you've had a productive day."

She strode into the room with a smile and dropped into his lap, treating him to a quick kiss in greeting. Such had become their relationship since the night they spent together after dinner at Jack's. They spent every night together now, sometimes in his bedroom, but more often in hers, since it was the more comfortable of the two, thanks to the touches she'd made to it since moving in. And although the weather had been agreeable since the night of the storm, they had retreated to a spot in front of the library fireplace a couple of times, too.

Their relationship had evolved fairly quickly, from adversarial to tentative to downright cozy. He couldn't believe it had only been a month and a half since he'd been counting the days until the two of them could turn their backs on Summerlight—and each other—for good. Now there were times when he found himself wishing their days in Sudbury would go on forever.

Times like right now, for instance. He wrapped his arms around her waist and kissed her back, putting a little more effort into it. She cupped one hand over his nape and tangled the fingers of the other into his hair, nestling into his lap more comfortably. For long moments, they settled into the kiss, until reluctantly, they ended it. They would have time for more later, they both knew. But Bennett hoped it wouldn't be too much later.

"It was a productive day," she told him. "I finished stripping the wallpaper on the main stairwell, so now it and the foyer can both be sanded and replastered, which I will get started on tomorrow."

They had put together a plan for Summerlight—
well, Haven had put together a plan for Summerlight—
starting with jobs she could do by herself during the
winter months, ones that wouldn't involve more than
cosmetic improvement. More intrusive tasks, such as
knocking down walls and installing bathrooms in the
bedrooms, could come later, when the weather was
accommodating enough to bring more workers to the
house on a regular schedule—and when they had the
funds to pay said workers.

The public rooms on the first floor, they had decided,
would remain public rooms, so there wouldn't be many
structural changes necessary there. They did want to
expand the dining room into the smoking room so that
the *breakfast* part of their bed-and-breakfast would be
able to accommodate more people than the dinner party
that could fit in there now, but that, too, could wait a bit.
Haven was confident she could take care of the majority of the jobs on that floor by spring and had hopped
right to it. And those, thankfully, wouldn't be hugely
expensive.

On that note, Bennett sobered. He had to tell Haven
about how it had gone—or, rather, not gone—with his
family. Rip off the proverbial Band-Aid and be honest with her.

"I talked to my parents about Summerlight today."
Amazingly, the words didn't come out sounding like
the death sentence they felt like.

He steeled himself to let her down gently and quickly
offer alternative solutions to hearten her. The problem
was that he didn't have any alternative solutions at the

moment. The other problem was that Haven didn't seem in any way letdown by his announcement, clearly assuming things had gone a lot better than they had.

"And?" she asked eagerly, her blue eyes sparkling. "They're going to help us out, right? I mean, how could they not? Having this house come to life again, bringing it back to its original splendor? I know my family can't help financially, but you told them about how they've already offered to do a lot of the work on the place at no charge. It's not like your family are going to be doing *everything*. Mine will help a lot, too, with hard work and elbow grease."

And they would, Bennett knew. Unlike him, Haven had contacted her family the day after their dinner in Sudbury. She'd asked if they could contribute some of the labor that would be necessary for the house, even if it was just painting or hammering or clearing brambles in the gardens. To a person, her family was on board with contributing however they could. They were all so delighted to have Summerlight even partly back in Moreau hands that they couldn't wait for spring and the opportunity to be part of their heritage in whatever way they could. Just the prospect of spending time here— free room and board in exchange for their labor—had made the other Moreaus as giddy as Haven was.

"I can't wait for the work to get underway in earnest," she continued before Bennett had a chance to tell her about his parents' disappointing response. "Summerlight is going to be so beautiful by the time we finish with it, Bennett. More beautiful than it's been in a hundred years. As exquisite as it was the day Winston

Moreau and his family first set foot in it. No, even better than that," she added with a smile. "'Cause I'll be the one doing the work this time. Hah."

He couldn't help but smile himself, in spite of the turmoil tearing him up inside. How was he going to tell her that the dream she was envisioning might never happen? She was just so animated. So happy. It felt good to see her happy after so many weeks of looking crushed at the prospect of being trapped here with him while her life in New York fell apart. What was the harm in letting her enjoy the fantasy for a few more minutes?

She sounded like a kid at Christmas talking about their favorite new toy when she told him, "I've been poking around on the internet to see what the preservation societies for some other Gilded Age mansions in the country have done with their own houses, and I think we should take Summerlight back to her roots."

"*Her* roots?" he echoed. "What? The house is a girl now?"

"Not a girl," Haven said. "She was a girl when Winston first built her. But she's aged and become wiser since then. She's much more elegant and refined than she was in her youth. Now she's a queen. She deserves to be treated like one. And she will be. Thanks to us."

Oh, he really should have stopped Haven when she first started talking. Because now he realized just how completely she'd fallen under Summerlight's spell. He strove to find a way to bring her down gently. This had gone on long enough. He had to tell her there was a good chance they weren't going to be able to make a go of this, after all.

"I found a place online, too, that replicates period wallpapers," she hurried to say. "I was originally thinking we should just paint everything a color that would be in keeping with the Gilded Age, and I still think we should do that for the bedrooms, but for the public rooms, especially the dining room and the library and such, I think we should try to find some photos of the house the way it looked a hundred years ago and do our best to stay true to what those rooms looked like then. I'm going to see if the Sudbury library or town archives might have any photos. *Oooh*, or maybe your parents or grandparents do. We should ask them."

Oh jeez. Now *she* wanted to talk to his family. His family who couldn't even refer to her by her first name.

He had to stop her now. He opened his mouth to tell her about the conversations he had with his parents and colleagues that had gone nowhere—*Tell her now!*—but what came out instead was a weak, "Sudbury has a library and town archive?"

She nodded enthusiastically. "Yep. I found them online, too."

"Wow, you really have been busy."

"I really have been."

There was a lull in their conversation while a wistful look came over Haven, and Bennett commanded himself again to tell her. But he could see she was thinking about how the house was going to look once they were done with it and how all the dreams she'd been having were going to come true.

Tell her now.

But it wasn't just Summerlight's renovation she was thinking about in that moment, he could tell.

"You know what would really be wonderful?" she asked.

Since she was still looking out at the library with her fanciful expression, and since she seemed about ready to answer her question herself—and, all right, because he was still such a chicken—Bennett stayed silent.

"What would be really wonderful," she said, "would be if this whole thing finally puts the family feud to rest, once and for all."

It was then that he realized there was no way he could tell her what his family and colleagues had said. She just looked and sounded so hopeful. So happy. There was no way he could shoot down her dream. No way he *would* shoot it down. Whatever he had to do to find funding for Summerlight, he would do it. He couldn't—he wouldn't—let her down the way she thought he had done a decade ago.

"That would be wonderful," he agreed, hoping his voice didn't reflect any of the turmoil threatening to topple him.

Haven inhaled a deep breath and released it slowly. Happily. "So tell me what your parents said. Tell me they're as excited about this project as you and I are. Tell me they can't wait to see how beautiful Summerlight is going to be again once we're through."

Bennett swallowed the bile rising in his throat and ignored the nausea rolling through his midsection. Mentally, he crossed his fingers. "You pretty much nailed

it," he lied. "Those were practically their exact words.
They said they'd help out however they can."

She smiled. Happily. "You promise?"

He mentally crossed the fingers of his other hand.
"I promise."

The lie was almost worth it when he saw the look
of pure joy that lit her features and heard her squeal of
glee. "I knew it!" she said. "I knew your family couldn't
be as bad as mine always said they were. I knew they
could be fair and kind and decent. How could they have
raised a son like you otherwise?"

How indeed? Bennett wondered. Especially since,
at the moment, he didn't feel as if he was any of those
things.

In the days that followed, Haven was happier than
she could ever remember being in her life. The revitalization of Summerlight might be getting off to a slow
start, but once winter was over, and with the help and
workers that Finn had assured her he could provide,
things would really get moving. With luck, the house
would be completely refurbished by the end of the following year. She and Bennett might even be able to
open the hotel by next Christmas. Until spring, Haven
would content herself with all the smaller projects she
could. 'Cause God knew there were plenty of those—
retiling the kitchen and what would become the public
bathrooms, refinishing the floors on the main floor, and
in the smaller rooms, cleaning, plastering, painting…

Oh yeah. She had plenty to do for now. This week,
for instance, she had decided to tackle the bedrooms and

bathroom in the attic garret. She and Bennett were planning to use them as housing for a handful of live-in staff for housekeeping, cooking, maintenance and such, as part of the compensation package for their jobs. There would be a larger room on the second floor to accommodate a general manager, too, since she and Bennett would be returning to their lives in the city once their inheritance was finalized and the work on Summerlight was completed.

At least, probably they'd both be returning to the city. Certainly Bennett would, since he'd made clear how much Greenback Directive meant to him. He'd already made it a successful venture, and there was nowhere to go with it but up. Haven, however, was beginning to think she might, maybe, possibly, perhaps, hang around Sudbury for a bit once the hotel was up and running. Maybe she'd even end up being the full-time maintenance person living in one of these garret rooms. Her business in Staten Island, although doing reasonably well for how long she'd run it, wasn't nearly the success that Bennett's was. And it was still a struggle for her to make ends meet.

She liked it here in Sudbury. She liked it a lot. The longer she stayed, the more she felt a part of it. And she had fallen completely in love with Summerlight. These last few weeks had bonded her to the house in a way that even she didn't understand. Maybe the Haddens had owned the house for generations. But it was her several-greats-grandfather who built it, and he'd built it to the specifications he knew would best accommodate his family. The Moreaus had loved Summerlight before the Haddens had, even if they'd never had the same chance to make it their own. There was still something of the Moreaus—and of Haven herself—here. And as she worked more closely with the house, she felt that relationship grow stronger and stronger.

She couldn't wait to see it all come together. Summerlight was going to be gorgeous by the time she and Bennett got through with it. She just wished he wanted to stay as involved with the place as she did.

Because that was another thing. She liked Bennett, too. She liked him a lot. Like Summerlight, she might, she had begun to admit to herself, have fallen in love with him, too. They'd spent as much time together as possible after that night at Jack's, having their coffee together in the mornings and taking turns fixing dinner to share. And their nights together… Oh, their nights. Being with Bennett, too, had made Haven happier than she could ever remember being. She wasn't sure how she was going to manage once he returned to his life in New York if she didn't return to her life there, too.

But she didn't have to think about that for now. So she wouldn't. Even so, "for now" was starting to move along at a pretty decent clip. Which was how mid-November found Haven hard at work in the fourth-floor garret, cleaning out the sole closet up there. It was attached to the sole bathroom, which was only a half bath with a sink and toilet. Her plan was to turn the closet into a bath with a shower so that any hired help living in the garret would have access to everything they needed up here. No, it wasn't ideal, asking people who worked for you to share a bathroom. But free housing came with compromises, and it was no different than the arrangements in a travel hostel. It wasn't that uncommon for people living in New York to have such living arrangements, so expensive had life in the city become. A lot of people didn't mind such accommodations if it meant saving money.

The first time Haven came up to the garret, that day when she was checking out the roof—that day when she and Bennett started realizing there was something going on between them that defied a generations-old family feud—she'd thought the closet was small and stuffed with inconsequential debris best taken to the local dump. After undertaking the work on it this week, however, she'd discovered it was nearly twice the size she first thought and was filled with three times as much stuff.

And it was stuff she never would have thought she would find tucked away in a forgotten garret closet. Lots of old clothes—some looking as if they'd been around for as long as the house had—and lots of home necessities that had grown less necessary with the advance of technology. But there were personal items, as well. A couple of boxes of baby and children's clothing, dating back decades, along with some old toys that would probably fetch a decent amount from collectors. There were travel souvenirs from all kinds of events, including a ribbon from the opening day of Disneyland and a certificate for crossing the equator in 1934, all the way back to a restaurant menu from the world's fair of 1915 in San Francisco. And jewelry. Really old, really beautiful jewelry. A whole, big box of it. Haven was certainly no expert when it came to things like that, but even she could tell that at least some of the pieces were probably genuine gems and metals.

By the time she withdrew the last few boxes from the closet, the sun had dipped low in the sky outside, and she'd had to switch on the sole overhead light in the narrow hallway. It was lined now on both sides with the boxes she'd inspected, until there was barely enough room for a path to get in or out. She heard Bennett's footfalls on the stairs, then he was poking his head through the door, looking for her.

"Down here," she said from her position seated on the floor behind one of the larger boxes midway between him and the attic window.

He found her after that, smiling at whatever picture she was creating. She couldn't imagine how she must look. Her khaki cargo pants and plaid shirt must be streaked with dirt and dust after all she'd been through. So must the rest of her. She was going to need a good, long soak to erase the centuries' worth of grime covering her.

Then she remembered she'd accessorized the filth and flannel by donning one of his great-great-great-whatever-she-was-supergreat-ancestor's tiaras and roped about three miles of someone's pearls around her neck, along with a feather boa that was, after a century in the closet, more boa than feather. No wonder he was smiling. She was surprised he wasn't bent over with laughter.

"Another busy day?" he asked with much understatement.

She started to stand up, then realized she was going to have to do some rearranging before she could manage it, so she stayed where she was, with a small box in her lap.

"You would not believe some of the stuff I've found," she said.

"Hmm, let me guess. A tiara, some pearls and…are those ostrich feathers or emu?"

She laughed. "Your ancestors had excellent taste."

"Obviously."

"They also really got around. There's some very cool travel memorabilia in all this. And there's a lot of old jewelry. You should see if your mom or your sisters want it."

He looked at her curiously. "But Aunt Aurelia left us everything in the house. It belongs to you now."

"It belongs to both of us," she clarified. "But it's not a part of my heritage." She carefully removed the tiara and set it aside. "And although I'm sure I totally rock a tiara with my rad, grunge fashion sense, I'm not really much of a jewelry person."

"They still partly belong to you," he told her.

"I'm sure the women in your family would appreciate having them more. They're Hadden heirlooms, not Moreau. If my family got a hold of them, they'd just sell them to the highest bidder. If nothing else, it can be a peace offering since your family has been kind enough to contribute so much to Summerlight's renovation."

His expression changed at that, and he almost looked… remorseful? Oh, surely not. What would he have to look sad about? She made a mental note to bring up a brighter bulb when she came back to finish tomorrow. The light in this garret was terrible.

"That's very generous of you, Haven," he said. "Thank you. I'll let my mom know."

"Besides," she told him, "I found something that's way more valuable. To me, at least."

"What's that?"

She reached into the box that held the things she wanted to take downstairs tonight and withdrew a fat, leather-bound notebook that looked nearly new, in spite of its being more than a hundred years old. Not that she was an expert at time-stamping antiques. But the minute she'd opened the notebook and read what was on the first page, she'd realized she was holding a piece of history. Her own history, at that.

She held it up for Bennett to see. "I found Lydia Moreau's journal."

Now his expression was easy to read. He was as surprised as Haven had been by the discovery. "Lydia was Winston Moreau's wife."

She nodded. "My several-greats-grandmother. It never occurred to me that there might be some of her and Winston's things left here. But I guess since they gave the place to Bertie Hadden lock, stock and barrel, it makes sense that they may have overlooked a few personal items when they moved out. Lydia must have left this in a forgotten drawer and started a new one after they got settled in their new digs."

Bennett hesitated a telling moment before quietly replying, "You just said Winston gave the place to Bertie. I thought all the Haddens thought Bertie stole Summerlight."

Haven scrunched up her shoulders and let them drop.

"Yes, everyone in my family—outside my parents, I mean—always said that. But since none of us was there, none of us can really know what the circumstances were. Maybe Bertie was a crook. Maybe Winston was a dirtbag. Or maybe they weren't those things at all. We'll never know. Whatever happened, the courts have always upheld that the transfer of the house was fair, legal and binding. It must have been a gift."

"It's still kind of weird to hear a Moreau say that."

She smiled. "All I know is that the Hadden *I've* been dealing with is a good guy. So his great-whatever-grandfather must have been a good guy, too."

Again, he looked a little pained by what she said. Seriously, she needed to change that bulb. The light it shed was in no way flattering. In fact, it made people look a little sick.

"Anyway, I can't wait to read it," she said, flipping carefully through the gilt-edged pages. "Not that I expect to find much but accounts of tea parties and the latest fabric for dresses and handing over the baby to the nanny whenever he had a dirty nappy." She closed the journal and cradled it in her lap. "But who knows? Maybe Lydia was a suffragist or labor union activist. That would be cool to read about."

"Suffragist, possibly," Bennett said. "Pro-union? With a robber-baron husband? Unlikely."

Haven chuckled at that. "You take care of your family history. I'll take care of mine."

He smiled. "I just put dinner in the oven," he told her. "Should be ready in about half an hour."

"What are we having?"

"I found ground lamb at the grocery store, so I figured it's a good night for shepherd's pie."

He was putting her tuna noodle bakes and Tater Tot casseroles to shame. As it was, she'd had to google to find those recipes when she realized she wasn't going to be able to rely on frozen lasagna and potpies all winter. Maybe she could find something interesting to do with ramen next time. Ramen was, after all, the staff of life.

"That sounds delicious," she told him, even though she had no idea what shepherd's pie was and was pretty sure she'd never eaten lamb. "Just let me tidy my mess and clean up. I'll be right down."

He nodded. "Okay. See you in a few."

After he left, it occurred to Haven just how comfortable the two of them had become over the last couple of weeks. Sometimes, like right now, it felt as if they'd been together for years and were living every day the way they would live for the rest of their lives. She really couldn't imagine what was going to happen at the end of their year here at Summerlight. Even if they both decided to return to New York, their lives there would have little reason to overlap. He lived in Manhattan, where the bulk of his work also took place. She lived on Staten Island, where the entirety of her own work was located. There was no reason for him to ever come to her borough. And, really, there was no reason for her to visit his. Not unless the simple pleasure of each other's company compelled them to make the trip. A trip that would be more than a little inconvenient for them both.

It just felt so good, living here at Summerlight the way they were now. But there was little chance they would both stay here at Summerlight beyond the end of Aurelia's required year. Even if they did, it wouldn't be like this, with just the two of them. They'd be sharing the house with other people. Their time together alone was finite. Every day brought them closer to its end. And then...

And then.

Haven didn't want to think about "and then" right now. And she told herself she didn't have to. She had a shower to take, fresh clothes to change into, and a beautiful, wonderful, lovable man to eat dinner with. Later, there would be a fire and soft conversation in the library, since they pretty much always had a fire and soft conversation in the library, followed by a night of exquisite lovemaking—since there was pretty much always that, too. Truly, what more did she need for the foreseeable future? She had the house and the man and the life of her dreams right now. Things were only going to get better from here on out.

Bennett had promised, after all.

Chapter Nine

Haven was looking for her several-greats-grandmother Lydia's journal when she remembered the last place she'd been reading it—two nights ago in Bennett's room while she was waiting for him to come to bed. So far, the journal had been pretty much what she had thought it would be, a record of everyday life for a prominent patrician of her time. Which meant it had been fascinating. Lydia Moreau's life was so far removed from her own, so full of wealth and glamour and excess, that Haven had felt as if she was reading the novelization of a movie. The last passage had been an account of a dinner party at the Fifth Avenue mansion of none other than Caroline Schermerhorn Astor herself—or, as Lydia had referred to her, The Mrs. Astor, with *The* underlined twice—where two of the husbands had nearly come to fisticuffs over a slur about New Money. As with any good novel or movie, Haven couldn't wait to see what happened next. And since she was breaking for lunch, she had time to read another few pages.

She hesitated before entering Bennett's bedroom, however, telling herself she shouldn't poke around in there when he wasn't home. Or, at the very least, without his permission. But he'd driven to Syracuse for the day again, and this time it was to meet with a couple of people he'd told her might be interested in investing in Summerlight. He could, at that very minute, be *this close* to securing some major funding, and no way was she going to risk bringing everyone out of the moment by texting him. Especially since she knew he'd changed her text notification sound on his phone to the Noir option, which was a supersexy sounding tone choice, and everyone would know it was his girlfriend texting.

Not that she was his girlfriend, she hastily reminded herself. No more than he was her boyfriend, anyway, which he also wasn't. At least, she didn't think they were boyfriend and girlfriend. "Boyfriend and girlfriend" suggested a lifestyle that included a lot more than shacking up together at a remote, charming-if-dilapidated house because they'd been forced to by circumstances—not that there was anything wrong with that—and almost never going anywhere else because either the weather prohibited it or one of them was in a Zoom meeting or waist deep in drywall mud or…

She expelled an errant sound. Anyway, they didn't seem like boyfriend and girlfriend. What they did seem like was… Gah. She wasn't sure of that, either. Whatever the two of them were, though, she needed to go into his room to see she had left Lydia's journal in there. And it wasn't as if Haven hadn't already been in his bedroom a million times. She practically spent as much time in here as she did her own room. If she wanted to get technical, she owned half of this room anyway, the same way he owned half of hers. So maybe if she just stayed on one side of it, everything would be okay.

But the journal wasn't on the nightstand on her side of the bed, where she'd thought it would be. Then she grew a little warm inside thinking that Bennett's bed had a "her side" of it, just as her bed had a "his side." The two of them really had come a long way.

She made her way to the dresser, giving it a perfunctory search. Not there, either. Bookcase? Nothing. She looked around the room again, and her gaze lit on a chair in the corner beside a full-length mirror. There were two dress shirts draped over the back, along with an assortment of neckties. She smiled. He must have changed his clothes a few times that morning. He'd dressed to impress. Whoever his potential investors were, he must have hoped they would open their wallets as wide as possible.

There was a small stack of folders on the chair, too. The navy blue kind, very much like the ones Sterling Crittenden had passed to her and Bennett that morning in his office almost two months ago, which felt like a lifetime ago. The kind of folders people used for business. Her curiosity got the better of her, and she walked over to investigate. The folders were all the same, each bearing a sticker on front that contained the name of the house and its address in Sudbury followed by a two-sentence pitch for how attractive a project involving it would be for investors.

She smiled. Wow. He'd put together a whole prospectus. He really did want to impress.

She opened the folder on top and found a photo of Summerlight gazing back at her. Here, she was surprised to see, he maybe hadn't done as good a job as he could have. Because the house didn't look all that great. Where she would have included one that depicted the house in its prime—and if Bennett had asked for her help, she could have provided one, because she'd found a few during her garret-closet clean out—the photo he'd used had clearly been taken recently, with a gray sky behind it and the fall foliage, which had been so bright and beautiful when they arrived, mostly stripped away from the surrounding trees.

It wasn't the kind of first impression she would have liked any potential investors to see for themselves. But Bennett knew about this kind of thing better than she did, so maybe he was going for the bad-news-first, good-news-later approach. She turned to the next page, expecting to find a brief history of the house or maybe the floor plans Mr. Crittenden had given them that first day. But instead of more information about the house, she found a plat of the property and its boundaries. Turning more pages, she found even less about the house itself and more about the land surrounding it, including a page that turned it into individual plots that could be used for the development of projects ranging from tourism businesses to residential development.

Her stomach pitched at the implications. Surely, she

was looking at this the wrong way. Surely, she was misunderstanding. He couldn't possibly be trying to attract people to invest in the land instead of the house. But on the last page of the prospectus, she found a definitive answer. The plat here was a reimagining of the Summerlight grounds that didn't include Summerlight at all. In its place was something called Hilltop Resort.

Turning the page again, she saw a rendering of what Hilltop Resort might look like when it was completed. Not a gorgeous Gilded Age mansion, bursting with vibrant gardens and a shaded veranda, but a sleek, glass-and-chrome behemoth that was as cold and colorless as an ice cube.

Nausea rolled through her belly again. Bennett had lied to her. He'd been lying to her for weeks. He had no intention of restoring Summerlight to its previous charm and grandeur. He was proposing to tear the place down. All the work she'd been doing, all the work *he'd known* she'd been doing, would be for nothing if he got his way. Everything he'd promised her—

She shoved the other folders from the chair and collapsed into it. Promised. Right. Like any promise from a Hadden was worth the air carrying it. Hadn't she been told all her life that they were liars and thieves? Hadn't she known better than to trust one? Hell, he'd probably lied to her about that day in Central Park ten years ago, too. It probably *had* been him texting her that summer— he'd just lied about it to keep the tenuous peace they'd managed to win by that point.

She opened the prospectus again and began reading from page 1. She wanted to be fully informed about his deceit before he returned tonight. And she needed to get her emotional armor in place. Because Bennett had just managed to reignite their family's feud. With a flamethrower. Lying to her the way he had, endangering Summerlight's very existence…

Well. That went beyond feud. That meant war.

Bennett knew something was wrong the minute he stepped through the front door. The house felt even more oppressive this evening than it had the first night he arrived. And it seemed darker, even though the foyer light was on, and it was a hell of a lot cleaner now than it had been then, thanks to Haven's efforts. Somehow, he knew something terrible had happened while he was in Syracuse that day, and immediately, his thoughts went to the worst-case scenario. Was she hurt? Had she gotten up on the roof again? Or, hell, even a ladder, which was another thing he'd made her promise to never do when he wasn't there? Was she, at this very minute, lying unconscious in some dark corner of the house where it would take him hours to find her?

"Haven?" he called into the silence. When he didn't receive an answer, he tried again, louder this time. "Haven? Are you home?"

The question was met by more silence. His stomach roiled, and he suddenly felt more alone than he'd ever felt in his life.

He dropped his leather briefcase on the floor and, without even shrugging off his coat, went to look for her, calling her name as he went. But she was nowhere on the first floor. He hurried up the stairs, still yelling her name, knowing he sounded like someone in a state of panic. There was a reason for that. He was panicking.

"Haven, where are you?" he cried as he headed down the hall toward her bedroom. Where he didn't find her. Something that made him panic even more.

He searched the other rooms in that wing, then backtracked toward his own room. All the while, he called out her name. All the while, he received no answer. So he was both massively surprised and massively relieved when he found her in his bedroom, sitting in the chair where he'd left his cast-off wardrobe selections that morning. Until he realized what she was holding in her lap.

Had he thought he was panicking before? Wow. What he'd felt in those minutes, fearing Haven was lost to him, were nothing compared to the terror welling in him now. Because if she had read the prospectus she was holding, then he no longer had to fear she was lost to him. If she had read that, she was well and truly gone from his life.

"Uh, hi," he said, hoping he was wrong about everything. Knowing by the look on her face that his worst fear was about to become reality.

"What the hell is this?" she demanded in return, holding up the folder as if it were something heinous.

Which, to her, it was. But that was only because Bennett hadn't had a chance to explain it to her yet. Well, okay, he'd had a chance. He'd had several chances, actually, because he'd created that prospectus days ago, and they'd seen each other every day since. He just hadn't quite had the, ah, dexterity—yeah, that was it—to explain it to her yet. Or the words. Or the guts.

He didn't have any of that now, either, he was dismayed to realize. There was no way he would be able to explain it to her the way he needed to explain. Not with her looking at him the way she was now. And not with him having absolutely no idea how to explain it. Things had just been going so badly where finding funding for Summerlight was concerned. Everyone he'd spoken to had shot him down before he could even finish his spiel. Even the people who owed him favors—and a couple of them owed him more than dinner at a steakhouse in Tribeca, that was for damned sure—had told him his and Haven's plans weren't the sort of thing *any*one would be interested in investing in these days. No one wanted to go back in time that way. The future was where it was at.

He'd be much better served, he'd heard time and time again, if he wanted to pitch something forward-thinking. A more modern approach to an area that was already filled with old-timey attractions. "Maybe a lifestyle center," one of his prospective investors had told him, "with housing and retail, right on the lake."

"Or what about an all-inclusive resort?" another had suggested. "With power boats and jet skis and wave runners?" One with all the modern amenities travelers wanted to have these days. All the comforts of home, but taken to a level where home was the last thing a visitor was thinking about.

And even though Bennett knew none of those things would work with the quiet, serene, pastoral setting of Sudbury, he'd become just desperate enough to entertain such ideas. Maybe they could work. Maybe he and

Haven had been going about Summerlight all wrong. Maybe what Sudbury needed to inject new life into its small-town vibe was a taste of big city life here in the country. Something that would set it apart from the other villages in the area. Something that would make it an exciting getaway full of fast-paced activities.

Yeah, he'd thought frantically—and, okay, looking at Haven now, also stupidly—maybe that was it. It could work. It could.

In his desperation, Bennett had mulled everything and developed the project Haven now held in her hands. The proposal was so new, he hadn't even had the chance to pitch it to anyone until today. And the response he'd received from his contacts in Syracuse this afternoon had been the first ones in weeks that had been halfway enthusiastic.

In spite of just thinking otherwise, he told her, "Haven, I can explain everything."

"No, you can't," she immediately countered. "You promised me we would return Summerlight to her former beautiful self, not raze her to the ground and throw up some awful modern eyesore to replace her."

He knew he had to tell her the truth. Finally. It was the only way he'd be able to make her see sense. "Haven, no one wants to put money behind the restoration of Summerlight the way you want it to be." She opened her mouth to object, but he cut her off. "No one. Not one single person I spoke to was interested in contributing so much as a dime. And trust me—I spoke to every person I could think of to speak to."

"But your parents said they'd—"

"My parents," he interrupted, "think your family should be the ones to provide the funding."

"What? No. Nobody in my family has money like that. You know that. You said your parents would totally be on board."

"I lied, all right?" he admitted. He was already the villain here. He might as well come clean about all of it. "I'm sorry," he said hastily. "I should have told you they refused right after my first conversation with them. They won't contribute anything."

She looked so stricken by his confession that Bennett felt physically sick. But what could he do?

"Why didn't you tell me?" she asked softly.

"I thought they'd eventually come around," he said. And for a while, he really had thought they would. "I tried talking to them three times." Every time, though, his parents had said the same thing. Let the Moreau do it. Not that he was going to tell her that part and just add insult to injury. "They refuse to help us out. Neither will my grandfather. Or my aunt and uncle."

She shook her head, as if doing that would negate everything he had said and done. If only it were that easy.

"I'm sorry, Haven," he said again. "I should have told you. But you were so happy that day after I spoke with them the first time, with all your plans for the house. I loved seeing you so happy. I couldn't stand the thought of disappointing you. I was so sure they'd change their minds. Or that I'd be able to get funding from somewhere else. I didn't think we'd need my family's money. I didn't think you'd ever have to know the Haddens had let you down. Again."

He knew the explanation was lame. But he didn't know what else to say. Especially when he saw her looking at him with such desolation. Such injury. Such—*dammit*—betrayal. He had betrayed her. He knew that. He hadn't meant to. Betraying Haven was the last thing he'd wanted to do. He just hadn't known how else to handle a situation that was fast going from bad to worse. He'd never been in a position where things didn't go the way he'd planned. Then he'd begun to think that even if they couldn't save Summerlight, they could still save Sudbury if they built some kind of resort here. He'd thought maybe, once Haven got over her disappointment about losing the house, she would at least find some comfort in knowing how much they'd done to bring back the village.

Sadly, he summed it up as gently as he could. "We just can't save Summerlight, Haven. It's going to be too expensive. The house needs too much work before it can meet the standards necessary to turn it into a hotel. And no one is interested in seeing it become a hotel anyway."

She looked at him in silence for a long time, her brows arrowed downward, her mouth flat, her eyes filled with so much anguish, Bennett could hardly bear it.

Then, very quietly, she said, "I can fix it. Maybe it will take a lot longer to finish the work, but I can fix Summerlight myself."

He expelled a soft sigh. If only that were true. "No, you can't," he told her bluntly. "Especially not when you're considering turning it into a public place of business. There's not a government agency out there, state or municipal, that will issue us the permits or licenses we need unless the entire place is up to code. And forget about getting any kind of insurance. Hell, you do this for a living. You know I'm right. The whole place will have to be gutted, rewired, replumbed, re-everything. You doing it alone will take years. And you'll have no income in the meantime. You need funding. *We* need funding," he hastily amended. "And no one will give it to us."

"What about a bank loan?" she asked halfheartedly.

He shook his head. "I looked into that, too. Only a handful of places would even consider us, and only with interest rates that were obscene. Without knowing for sure this place would be a huge success—and we have no way of knowing that—we might not ever be able to repay a loan. And then we'd lose everything. And after the bank foreclosed and sold the place, the new owners would do what all my prospective investors told me to do before they'd be interested anyway—tear down the house and open a more progressive money-maker instead."

Haven went quiet again, but her gaze never left his. Bennett wished with all his heart and soul that he could do something, anything, that would make this all okay. Not just so they could rehab Summerlight and turn it into the inn she envisioned, then go to work on making over Sudbury, too. But he wished he could go back to that first day he spoke to his parents and tell Haven the truth immediately after they declined to help out.

It had been a stupid thing to do, lying to her the way he had. But he'd been caught unprepared and hadn't wanted to hurt her. He really had thought his family would change their minds once they had time to reflect

on Summerlight's fate. Worst-case scenario, he'd figured they could attract investors little by little, through
each stage of Summerlight's renewal. Not once had it
occurred to him that they wouldn't be able to secure
enough funding to even get started, let alone see the
project through to completion.

"I'm sorry, Haven," he said for a third time. Not
that the third time would be any kind of charm that put
things to rights. But maybe if he kept saying it, she'd
realize just how bad he felt about the whole thing.

She stood and tossed the prospectus onto the floor to
join the others she must have placed there to sit down.
"I'm sorry, too," she said, her voice even more quiet
now than it had been before.

Her expression was more somber, too. More dejected.
More heartbroken. It broke Bennett's heart, too, to see
her this way.

He didn't know what else to say, so he waited for her
to say more. Instead, she picked up what he'd come to
recognize as her several-greats-grandmother Lydia's
journal, which she must have been reading when he
came home, and she started to make her way to the door.
In spite of the topic and tone of their exchange, her reaction surprised him. He'd thought she would want to stay
and talk about what their next step should be. Even if
it came in the form of arguing. At least they'd be com-
municating on some level. Her silence, though… Her
silence was more than a little ominous.

"Haven?" he asked as she reached the door.

She turned to look at him, but said nothing.

He hesitated only a moment. "Don't you want to talk more?"

"What could you and I possibly have to talk about?"

"What we're going to do about Summerlight's future."

She shook her head. "There is no *we* when it comes to talking about Summerlight's future," she told him.

"But—"

"*You've* made clear what *you* think we should do," she said. "Turn it into some soulless, cookie-cutter vacation site that will be as out of place in Sudbury as a skyscraper would be." When he said nothing to deny it, she added, "*I'm* not going to let that happen. So there is no *we* when it comes to Summerlight. There is no *we* at all, Hadden."

He winced at her use of his last name. Surely, she was only using it to make a point. Surely, she wasn't suggesting they'd reverted back to their adversarial relationship. Okay, he shouldn't have lied to her. But he'd explained why he had. And he'd apologized. Once she realized he hadn't meant to hurt her, and once she realized he was right about Summerlight, she'd come around. Wouldn't she?

"You lied to me," she reminded him. As if he needed that reminder. "You've been lying to me about Summerlight for weeks. You're a liar. For all I know, you lied about that summer at Bow Bridge, too."

"I didn't lie about that," he quickly assured her. He could assure her about the other things later. Except for this one, admittedly major lapse, he'd been nothing but honest with her since their arrival. Especially where his feelings for her were concerned.

"What happened to you that day at Bow Bridge was horrible, Haven, but I had nothing to do with it. I promise."

She laughed at that, a sad, hollow sound. "You promise? Yeah, we know how much water your promises hold. What happened today was horrible, too," she added. "And you had everything to do with that. You're a liar, Hadden. And I've had my fill of those."

"But, Haven—"

"Don't speak to me again," she told him. "I can't trust a word that comes out of your mouth."

"But—"

"Not one word. I just have two things left to say to you, and then we're done."

He opened his mouth to object, but she cut him off.

"We're done. Number one," she hurried on, "That Thanksgiving dinner we were going to cook together next week? Yeah, that's canceled, since there is nothing to be thankful for."

"But—"

"Number two," she interrupted him again, "I'm telling you because if I didn't, I'd be an even bigger jerk than you are."

He started to speak again, but her expression made him reconsider. They could talk later, he told himself. She was angry right now—and he didn't blame her—but once she'd had time to think about everything he said, she would understand and be more open to discussion. Surely, she would be. Surely. So he only crossed his arms defensively in front of himself and waited to see what she had to say.

She lifted her grandmother's journal in front of herself with both hands, as if she might use the book as a shield. Obviously, he wasn't the only one feeling defensive.

"I finished Lydia's journal while I was waiting for you to come home," she said. "And I know now what really happened and why Winston gave Summerlight to Bertie."

Although Bennett was still reeling from her assurance that they were done—they couldn't be done, he assured himself again, not after everything they'd come to mean to each other—he was amazed at what she had uncovered. No one in either family had ever been able to produce unequivocal proof about Winston's or Bertie's motives. If Lydia Moreau had actually recorded what happened, it could put a rest to the feud even better than Aurelia Hadden's bequest had.

Haven closed her eyes and swallowed hard, as if she were having trouble maintaining her composure but was determined to finish what she needed to say. When she opened them again, they seemed darker somehow. He understood why when a single tear began to tumble from one before she quickly wiped it away.

"Winston and Lydia threw a picnic on Cayuga Lake the summer of 1884," she began, "for their servants and anyone in town who had done work for them, to thank them for everything they did for the Moreau family. At one point, their three-year-old son, Thomas, wandered off and somehow fell into the lake. He would have drowned if the Moreaus' chauffeur, Bertie, hadn't run into the lake after him, then pulled him out and resuscitated him. Bertie saved Thomas's life. Winston and Lydia were so ecstatic that they rewarded him with Summerlight, lock, stock and barrel. Winston had just finished building a new summer house for them in Rhode Island, so he said Summerlight was Bertie's now, and he signed the deed over to him with everything in the house included.

"That's what our families have been feuding over for five generations, Hadden. We've all hated each other because your grandfather saved the life of a little boy, and my grandfather was grateful to him for it. Bertie was a hero. Winston was a decent guy. And both their families have been horrible about it ever since."

As last words went, hers were pretty powerful, Bennett had to admit. But before he could even consider everything she'd said, before he could utter another word himself, Haven spun on her heel and left him alone.

Alone with nothing but the bitter irony that had brought them to this place. And the silence of a lonely room. And an emptiness inside him that went all the way down to his soul.

An emptiness, he couldn't help but think, that felt as if it would go on forever.

Chapter Ten

When Haven heard Bennett coming out of the library for lunch three weeks after she outed him as the double-crossing crook he was, she was in what used to be the smoking room but was now the breakfast room, because the first thing she had done after he double-crossed her was knock down the wall joining the smoking room to the dining room—and wow, had wielding that sledgehammer felt *good*—to show him how much she'd meant it when she said she could and would revamp Summerlight all by herself if she had to. And it was going to stay the breakfast room, dammit, since there was no way she would sign off on anything that turned the house into anything but the stately beauty she used to be, and Haven had worked too hard on this place to have some scumbag, developer carpetbaggers raze it to the ground, and…and…and…

Well, anyway, she was in the new breakfast room, which still needed wallpapering, something she would get to as soon as the rolls she'd ordered from a historical society she'd found online could deliver them. That would show Bennett. *Hmpf.*

He glanced into the room as he strode by but said nothing, because he knew better than to greet her. They'd gone as no-contact as they could, living under the same roof, despite his efforts to try to make amends following their breakup. He'd even brought home a small, pre-lit Christmas tree and set it up in the library in an effort to bring her around to the spirit of the upcoming holiday season.

There would be no holiday season with things being the way they were between them. And there would be no amends, either. Haven wasn't about to set herself up for that again. Even if she did miss terribly the closeness they had fostered before he lied to her. And even if she did feel a hole inside herself without him that she feared would never go away.

He wasn't the man she'd thought she loved, she reminded herself. Again. That man didn't exist. She was just going to have to forget about him. Even if she didn't think she'd ever be able to forget about him, no matter how hard she tried.

She'd gone back to her early-morning rising and enjoying her morning coffee alone—well, as much as she could enjoy anything, now that her life and she were both in a shambles. Bennett, in turn, always waited until she was buried somewhere in the house working before he left his bedroom. In between, he stayed in his library office, and she worked elsewhere in the house. The only words they'd spoken to each other had been along the lines of "Do we need anything besides coffee and eggs from Wegmans?" and "Don't touch the circuit breaker unless you want to turn into a charcoal briquette."

Today, however, after his passing glimpse into the room, Bennett backtracked a few steps and peered in in earnest. Probably because he realized Haven wasn't in here alone. For a moment, he said nothing, as if he were waiting for her to explain what the guy sitting in the chair next to her was doing. The young, good-looking guy with the trendy tortoiseshell glasses and neatly trimmed black hair and beard. The guy who was so wrapped up in what he was doing on the MacBook in his lap that he hadn't even noticed Bennett standing in the doorway. In response, Haven said nothing and just gazed back at him defiantly.

So, after glaring at her one more time, Bennett demanded, "Who's this guy?"

The guy—Pax Lightfoot by name, Cornell PhD candidate in information science by game—looked up at that. "Oh, hi," he said. He smiled. "You must be the backstabbing SOB Haven told me about."

Bennett glared at her harder, then looked back at Pax. "No, I'm the co-owner of this house. Bennett Hadden." To his credit, he strode into the room and extended his hand. "And you are...?" he asked again.

Pax shook his hand amiably and released it. "Pax Lightfoot. Haven hired me a few weeks ago to do some work on the house."

Bennett looked from Pax to Haven. Who still said

nothing. Why should she? She wasn't speaking to Bennett unless she had to. And Pax could speak just fine for himself. It would be good practice for his dissertation defense, which would be coming up after the holidays.

When Haven offered no explanation, Bennett said, "I haven't seen you around the house for the last few weeks."

"That's because I've been working for her at Cornell," Pax told him. "I came to the house today because I wanted to show her, in person, the fruits of our labors. And also to see Summerlight up close, since I've heard so much about it. Man, the photos didn't do it justice. I didn't know places like this even existed anymore. And I've been living less than an hour away for the past ten years."

Now Bennett looked really confused. Not that Haven blamed him. Half the stuff Pax had been doing confused her, too, and he'd been keeping her apprised of his actions every step of the way. Not to mention, she was the one who'd been paying him for his work. She'd used up nearly every penny left in her emergency fund to make sure he had whatever he needed. After all, saving Summerlight was the biggest emergency she could imagine.

Bennett opened his mouth to say something, then seemed to need a minute to think. After a moment, he asked, "What could you have been doing at Cornell that would involve Summerlight?"

"Crowdfunding," Pax told him.

Bennett looked even more bewildered. "Crowdfunding? For what?"

Now Pax looked at Haven, thinking she would want

to join in. Okay, fine. She'd made her point with Bennett. Now she could give him an education.

"With bringing Summerlight back to life," she said. "It's going to happen, Hadden. Thanks to Pax—and me," she added pointedly, since the whole thing was her idea. "We're going to raise the money we need to do everything that needs doing to turn the house into a B and B, right down to a shiny new Hobart for the kitchen. That's an industrial dishwasher," she added, since she was reasonably sure no Hadden had ever gotten near manual labor in their life, because they were too busy backstabbing people.

He frowned at her use of his last name. She didn't care. He was a Hadden through and through. He'd proved that more than once.

"I know what a Hobart is," he told her. "I volunteered at a food center when I was at Colgate, working in the kitchen."

Oh. Okay. How could she have not known that? Why hadn't he told her? Most self-centered jerks would jump at the chance to paint themselves as a do-gooder.

She shoved the thought aside. "Pax set up a page at HelpMeOut.com called 'Save Summerlight.'"

She didn't add that she'd really wanted to call it "Save Summerlight from a Backstabbing Traitor Whose Name Rhymes with Hennett Badden," but Pax talked her out of it, suggesting it might be too long for people to remember and brevity was key in these sorts of things.

She continued, "Then he created a Save Summerlight hashtag and set up pages on every social media site out there—including some I didn't even know existed—

and emailed every preservation and historical society he could find about it, and…" They would honestly be here all day if she told Bennett everything Pax had done. Suffice to say, the guy had been incredible when it came to all things techy. "Long story short," she finally concluded, "it went viral among all the history buffs and old house lovers out there, and we've raised a ton of money."

"Money that's still rolling in," Pax told them both. "Here, Haven, look at this."

He turned his laptop toward her to show her the current balance in their HelpMeOut account. It was jaw-dropping. Literally. Her mouth fell open when she saw the amount. She'd been checking the page nightly and had been awed by watching the contributions scroll in. But something must have happened in the last twenty-four hours to boost it *a lot*, because there were more numbers to the left of the decimal point than she could have ever imagined.

"Yeah, I know," Pax said with a chuckle when he saw her response. "I messaged a particularly hot preservationist on TikTok about it the other day. She linked to the HelpMeOut page last night, and her followers went right to town. *And* she paid for the deluxe package herself, so you can expect her to stay at Summerlight for a week once the place is up and running."

"Whoa, whoa, whoa," Bennett said. "Putting aside for now the fact that *hot* and *preservationist* are two words I never thought I'd hear used together, what's a 'deluxe package?'"

Haven quickly explained to him how, depending on the amount of a person's donation to the HelpMeOut fund, they received something in return. Everything from T-shirts and coffee mugs bearing a pen-and-ink rendition of Summerlight Pax had commissioned from a Cornell art student to weekend getaways at Summerlight once the inn opened. There had only been three deluxe packages offered—a full week's stay with every amenity she envisioned them being able to offer at the B and B—at a price Haven never thought anyone would pay since it far exceeded the return, but as Pax had said, *What the hey, why not try?* Now at least, one of them had been claimed. In a word, *cha-ching*.

Bennett looked from Haven to Pax, then back again. "So then...just how much have you raised?"

Pax turned his laptop to show him. Bennett's jaw dropped, too. He leaned in closer to double-check the figure. Which was still climbing as they watched.

"That much?" he asked in an awed whisper. "I could never have gotten close to that amount, even if everyone I asked invested what I asked them to invest."

"*Vive la* viral content," Pax said with a satisfied grin.

"And also *vive les* hot preservationists and history buffs and old house lovers," Haven added. And because she couldn't quite help herself, she added, "See, Hadden? I told you so. There are *lots* of people out there who would *love* to visit a house like this and spend time in a place like Sudbury. And if we can do this for Summerlight, we can do it for the town, too."

Because that was another thing she'd done in the last few weeks—met with both the town council and the chamber of commerce of Sudbury to explore the possibility of injecting new life into the community. To a person, she'd been met with nothing but enthusiasm. Sudbury was totally on board and eager to see its own renewal once things panned out with Summerlight. She told Bennett about that, too.

"Okay," he said softly. "I surrender. You were right, and I was wrong. I guess you can start making your vision a reality as soon as the funds from the campaign become available to you. You win, Haven."

His words should have delighted and vindicated her. Instead, she felt lousy. Some victory. Yes, Summerlight would be saved and returned to her former glory. But the price had been higher than Haven could have imagined. Because she'd lost so much in the process. The man she had thought she loved—oh, hell, the man she had indeed loved—was lost to her. The Bennett she'd loved didn't exist. He was just like every other Hadden who had come before him. A lousy, crooked liar.

Except that that wasn't true of all Haddens, she reminded herself. Bertie Hadden had been a selfless hero who'd risked his own life to save that of a little boy. Clearly, not every Hadden was a lousy, crooked liar. Clearly, there was a rogue gene somewhere in the Hadden DNA that allowed for kindness, compassion and decency.

Then she realized how Bennett hadn't included himself in any of his statements. You *were right*, he'd said. You *can start making* your *vision a reality as soon as the funds from the campaign become available to* you. He'd removed himself from the Summerlight equation entirely.

Well, yeah, she immediately reminded herself. Because she'd assured him there was no "we" when it came to the future of Summerlight. That the two of them were through.

Except there was still a "we" when it came to Summerlight, and the two of them couldn't be through for months. They both still owned the house, and they would be living in it together until next fall. And even if Bennett had just conceded that Haven won their disagreement, she couldn't move forward with anything that had to do with the house without his explicit permission. There was no way she could remove herself from him, literally or figuratively, at least, not for a while.

Then again, if she were honest with herself, she would make herself admit that it wasn't just the house that was still clinging to the concept of *we*. Parts of Haven were still clinging to it, too. Even while she'd been tearing down the wall between the dining and smoking rooms last week to spite Bennett, she'd found herself thinking about what color scheme the two of them should consider for it, before remembering to make the decision on her own. And, after having her second cup of coffee in the morning, she invariably set up the coffee maker again for Bennett, before remembering that, oh, yeah, the two of them weren't together anymore, so she didn't have to be considerate. And there had been nights when, after she finished brushing her teeth, she automatically bypassed her bedroom to start heading for his, before recalling that there would be no sharing of bedrooms—or anything else—anymore.

Like the house, her brain still seemed to need for her and Bennett to be together.

Or maybe it wasn't her brain doing that. Maybe it was a different body part. Maybe it was her heart that didn't want to let him go.

She pushed the thoughts away. Breaking up was hard to do, nobody said it was easy, they had run their course, and all those other things people sang about after a breakup. Even if what had happened with her and Bennett still didn't quite feel like a breakup. Even if, for the two of them, like Summerlight, it felt as if there was still a lot of work to do.

"So when are you going to tell your investors about the new plan?" Haven asked him, trying to put the conversation—and herself—back on track. "Will there be any problem, dropping them from the project?"

He shook his head. "I already called them. I told them three weeks ago my prospectus was off the table because the project was going in a different direction. That Summerlight would be rehabbed instead of replaced."

He'd done that three weeks ago? That meant he'd done it right after their fight. But before she'd even spoken to Pax.

"How did you think we were going to pay for it?" she asked him.

He shrugged. "I had no idea. But you said you could do it. You said you would do it. I had faith in you, Haven. I trusted you to know what you're doing. In that, at least, I was obviously right."

He trusted her, she echoed to herself. He had faith in her. Even after she'd chewed him out, called him a liar and told him the two of them were through. He'd called his investors and told them to shove off. Because he trusted her. Which was more than she'd done for him.

She looked at Pax, who had gone back to his work on the laptop, thoroughly engrossed. Then she looked at Bennett again. "Can we talk?" she asked softly.

His expression changed drastically, from the defeated fatigue she'd seen on him every day since their breakup to a wary sort of hopefulness that made something inside her spark a little brighter.

"Hell, yes, we can talk. I've been wanting to talk for three weeks."

And she'd been determined for three weeks to never speak to him again. Now that they were talking, however, even if their exchange hadn't been the warmest... Well, she had to admit it felt good to be this close to him again, sharing anything at all.

Still looking at Bennett, she said over her shoulder, "Pax, will you be okay without me for a few minutes?"

"Sure," he said with much distraction. "I need to respond to this email we just got from HGTV anyway. They want to talk to us about the possibility of making Summerlight's rehab part of an ongoing series they're doing. We gotta jump on this while the iron is hot."

A little while ago, a comment like that would have sent Haven's heart racing. And although her heart was indeed racing at the moment, it had little to do with Summerlight and a lot to do with her partner in Summerlight. With her partner, period. Because as angry as Bennett had made her in the past, he was still her partner in the present—with more than just the house, she made herself admit. Was he going to be her partner in the future? And would that be with more than the house, too? All Haven knew in that moment was that, over the last three weeks, she'd felt lousier than she'd ever felt in her life. Even worse than the summer she'd been betrayed on Bow Bridge. A betrayal Bennett had assured her he'd had nothing to do with. A betrayal he'd promised he had nothing to do with.

She realized then that she believed him about that. He'd come clean right away about his attempted sabotage of Summerlight. Once she'd made clear that she knew what he'd done, he'd been honest with her about it. And, looking back, she supposed, in his mind, it hadn't been the sabotage she'd considered it to be. He'd been doing what he thought he had to do to keep as much of her vision alive as possible. He'd done his best to keep his promise to her that they would make Summerlight viable. The fact that it would have been viable as something other than Summerlight, though...

She sighed inwardly as she led him into the library. *He'd been desperate*, she told herself. That's what he'd said that night. And she knew desperation could make someone do things that weren't necessarily in the best interest of themselves or their loved ones. Haven had been desperate when she graduated from Barnaby. Desperate to free herself from the taunting and bullying of her classmates. She'd done that by refusing full-ride scholarships to some of the best universities in the country and staying home to attend college in Staten Island instead, much to her family's disappointment. Had she not succumbed to her panic and broadened her horizons by going someplace else, who knew where she would be? Better off? Maybe. Maybe not. The point was, she had no idea, because she'd reacted impulsively without thinking through the consequences and maybe hadn't made the best decision.

The point was that Bennett had done the same thing when it came to Summerlight. But whereas Haven had made peace with her own rash actions, she was punishing Bennett for his. Her life had worked out just fine, with her coming home and attending college locally, in spite of decisions she'd made in a cloud of fear and hopelessness. Summerlight, too, was going to work out just fine, in spite of Bennett's decisions made in the same frame of mind. Haven had cut herself some slack after her own decisions. Maybe she should do the same for Bennett.

He'd promised her they would make a go of Summerlight. And she supposed, in his own way, he'd done his best to make good on that promise. Maybe, like the Moreaus and the Haddens, her and Bennett's feud was based on a misunderstanding. And maybe, like that feud, theirs should be put to rest, too.

She made her way to the library sofa, where their lifelong tensions had first begun to ease that night when the power was out and they'd shared their first kiss. It was also where their affection for each other had been made complete that night after dinner at Jack's. It was the perfect place for their—she hoped—reconciliation, too. Bennett joined her there, but, like that first night, he situated himself at the far end of the sofa, as if he wanted to give her room for whatever it was she wanted to say.

It was he, though, who actually spoke first. "What did you want to talk about?"

"I'm sorry," she said without preamble.

His dark brows shot up in surprise. "You're sorry? For what? You don't have anything to be sorry about. You're the one who got everything to fall into place for Summerlight. I'm the one who's sorry. I nearly ruined everything."

"I know you're sorry," she assured him. "And you didn't ruin everything. I'm the one who nearly did that. I should have accepted your apology three weeks ago. I was just…" She inhaled a deep breath and released it slowly. "I reacted badly that night, Bennett. When I realized what you had done without telling me, I felt like I was sixteen years old again, surrounded by Haddens in Central Park who were making fun of how naive and stupid I was, and I—I just… I wanted to…"

When her voice trailed off, he said, softly, "You weren't naive or stupid that day, Haven. You were trusting and happy. And my family took that away from you. You were trusting and happy about my plans for Summerlight, too. And I took that away from you all over again. I don't blame you for hating me."

"I don't hate you," she told him before she could stop herself. Probably because, on some level, she didn't want to stop herself. Probably because, on some level, she wanted to tell him she felt so much more.

He smiled sadly at that. "I'm glad. I just wish you could find it in yourself to forgive me, too."

"I do forgive you."

Now his brows arrowed downward. "Thank you." He

hesitated a telling moment before adding, "Any chance you might find it in yourself to trust me again at some point, too? I mean, I know that's asking a lot," he hurried on before she could reply, "and I know I probably don't deserve it, but I truly didn't mean to lie to you, Haven. I really was trying to do my best to make everything work out, the way I promised I would. I just didn't think it all through the way I should have."

"I know," she told him. "And I understand that now. That's why I'm apologizing to you, too. Because I didn't give you a chance to explain. Or to try to make things better. And although you don't have to explain—believe it or not, I do understand now why you did what you did—I would like for us both to be able to make amends."

Now he smiled. It wasn't a big smile, but it wasn't bad. It made something inside Haven ripple with happiness, a feeling she hadn't experienced in weeks. She'd missed happiness. She'd missed it a lot. As much as she'd missed Bennett. Which wasn't surprising, now that she was beginning to understand that her happiness and Bennett were irretrievably linked.

"I know we still have a lot of work to do," she told him. "Not just with Summerlight, but with us, too. I just hope, now that Summerlight's work can well and truly begin, that maybe you and I could start to work on us, too."

His smile broadened. "On us?" he echoed. "I thought you said there was no 'us.'"

"No, I said there was no 'we.'"

"And the difference in that is…?"

She tried to remember what she'd learned in elementary school English about objects and subjects and grammar and usage, but all she could think about was how much happier Bennett looked than he'd been for the last few weeks, and how she had been the one to make him happy. Looked like she and his happiness were permanently linked, too.

"You know, I'm not entirely sure," she finally said. "That's probably something that should be up for discussion, too."

"*We* need to talk about *us*, you mean?"

She nodded. "Yeah. We do. And there are probably some practical ways to do that that would help us."

He smiled. Lasciviously. "You mean, like…activities?"

She smiled back. Salaciously. "I'm sure there are one or two things *we* could do together that would help *us* work things out."

He smiled again, and this time all lingering traces of fear and worry were gone. "I like how much you and I are saying *we* and *us*. It means you and I are thinking less like 'you and I' and more like 'we and us.'"

"We are an 'us,'" she told him. Because the more they had said it over the last few minutes, the more certain she had become that it was true. They were a "they," too. And a "them." And a "their." And maybe, someday, if they were very lucky and showed them how to do it, their families might come around to being more united, too.

"Then, we should look into those things that will help us right away," Bennett told her.

Haven studied him in silence for a moment, letting what was left of her tension and unease roll off her.

Smiling softly this time, she scooted herself a little closer to the center of the sofa. He smiled gently back. And scooted himself a little closer to the center, too. Haven pushed herself closer still. So did Bennett. Then, with one last, simultaneous, little scooch from each of them, they found themselves perfectly centered on the sofa. Meeting halfway. Compromising. Cooperating. Unifying. The way people who cared about each other did.

The way people who loved each other did.

Before she could say it to him, Bennett told her, "I love you, Haven. And I'm sorry for not saying or showing you that sooner."

"I love you, too, Bennett," she told him. "And I'm sorry for not saying or showing you that sooner, too."

He expelled the kind of sigh people did when they suddenly realized everything was going to be all right. Haven knew that, because she released the same kind at the same time.

"Just goes to show it's never too late to make things right," he said.

She nodded. "I hope wherever Winston and Bertie are, they can finally stop shaking their heads in frustration at their descendants."

"Well, at least two of us," Bennett said. "We can work on the rest of them once we've gotten everything worked out ourselves."

"We should get right on that," she told him. "The 'working things out ourselves,' I mean."

"We should."

With another smile, they each leaned in, Haven tilting her head one way while Bennett tilted his the other. The kiss they shared was as brief as their first one, but no less significant. It was a kiss of beginnings. A kiss of love. A kiss of promise.

A promise, Haven knew, that each of them would keep to the other. Forever.

* * * * *

Chapter One

There was one box of Frosted Flakes on the shelf.

Which shouldn't have mattered in the least to Sierra Hart, because she already had cereal in her cart.

The spoon-size shredded wheat (tucked between the loaf of twelve-grain bread and a package of low-fat, low-sodium crackers) was undoubtedly a healthier choice, and she was trying to make healthier choices. Over the past few weeks, she'd willingly reduced her intake of sodium and fat (*goodbye* convenient microwavable meals) and completely cut out alcohol (*au revoir* cabernet sauvignon), but her sweet tooth continued to protest the lack of brownies and cookies and ice cream.

And now, apparently sugary cereals that reminded her of her childhood, too.

Frosted Flakes had been her breakfast of choice while she was growing up in Summerlin South, a suburb of

Las Vegas—or at least after her fourteenth birthday. Prior to that, her favorite morning meal had been home-made breakfast burritos: scrambled eggs and crumbled bacon wrapped up with shredded cheese and tangy salsa inside a warm tortilla. Whenever Sierra had a test at school or a basketball game after, her mom insisted that she start her day with a home-cooked breakfast to fuel her brain and her body.

She shrugged off the memories. It wasn't so easy to shrug off the ache in her heart that, sixteen years later, had faded but not disappeared.

It was when her brother had come home that she'd started eating cold cereal in the mornings before rush-ing out of the house to catch the bus for school. Week-ends usually meant toaster waffles, and sometimes Nick sat at the table with her, always with a textbook of some kind at his elbow despite having taken a hiatus from college.

He'd grumbled only a little about buying the sugary cereal for her when she was a teen, but she imagined he'd have a lot more to say if he knew she still craved it now.

But why should she feel guilty about the occasional indulgence when the other items in her cart were healthy?

When she'd lived in Las Vegas—and been on a part-nership track at Bane & Associates—she hadn't had the time to cook. And with countless take-out options available, there had been little incentive to bother. But her new job in the Haven District Attorney's Office had, so far, afforded her a more regular schedule, and so she'd started to prepare her own meals.

At first, she'd been more resigned than enthused about tackling that particular chore, but she didn't really have much of a choice as dining options in town were severely limited. There was the Sunnyside Diner, famous for its all-day breakfast and not much else; Jo's Pizza, which offered wings and some simple pasta dishes alongside its namesake specialty; Diggers' Bar & Grill, a popular choice for those wanting standard roadhouse fare; and The Home Station, whose menu boasted creative and upscale cuisine.

Of course, even in Vegas there had been times when she wasn't in the mood for takeout and opted to pour herself a bowl of cereal instead. And quite often it was Frosted Flakes.

She started to reach for the box—

"Never go shopping on an empty stomach."

She drew her hand back and turned to the shopper who'd drawn her cart up alongside Sierra's. The other woman had long dark hair tied in a ponytail, pretty blue-gray eyes and a warm smile.

"That's what my sister tells me, anyway," the stranger confided. "But since I got pregnant, I'm constantly hungry, which makes it impossible to follow her advice."

"Um...congratulations?" Sierra finally ventured.

The expectant mother laughed. "And now you're wondering why you ever decided to move to this town where people overshare personal information in the breakfast foods aisle at the local grocery store," she guessed.

"I don't think it's just the breakfast foods aisle," Sierra said. "The guy working behind the deli counter told me all about his upcoming knee replacement surgery while he was slicing my oven-roasted turkey."

"That would've been Dustin Hobbs," the other woman said, reaching for a container of steel-cut oats and dropping it into her cart. "He's been grumbling about his bad knee for years."

"Since 2010—the year he carried three passes over the goal line for the state champion football team?" Sierra guessed.

"Sounds about right." A box of Corn Pops joined the oats. "You're Sierra Hart, aren't you?"

"Have we met?" Sierra was certain they hadn't, though the other woman did look vaguely familiar to her.

"Not formally, but our paths sort of crossed at April's House last weekend. I'm Sky Gilmore—Sky *Kelly*," she quickly amended, offering a smile along with her hand.

Though Sierra had only been in town two weeks, that was long enough to have heard about the Gilmores. In addition to being one of the founding families of Haven, they were owners and operators of the Circle G, one of the most successful cattle ranches in all of Nevada.

She'd also heard about the historic feud between the Gilmores and the Blakes, the gist of which was that both families had come to Nevada to settle the same parcel of land more than a hundred and fifty years earlier. Rather than admit that they'd been duped, they agreed to split the property. Everett Gilmore, having arrived first, took the prime grazing land for his cattle, leaving Samuel Blake with the less hospitable terrain. As a result, Crooked Creek Ranch—and the Blakes— struggled for a lot of years before gold and silver were discovered in their hills.

Although both families had ended up ridiculously wealthy, the animosity between them had remained for a long time. It was only in recent years—and as a result of a handful of reunions and romances—that the Gilmores and Blakes had finally managed to bury the hatchet.

"Do you work at April's House?" Sierra asked, shaking the woman's proffered hand.

"I'm a volunteer counselor," Sky responded.

"Tough job," she noted. And because Sierra had some experience of her own working with abused women and their children, she felt an immediate kinship with—and a lot of respect for—the other woman.

"I'm sure being an ADA isn't a walk in the park."

"It's just a temporary gig," Sierra told her.

"And your stay in Haven?"

"Also temporary."

Sky's smile was knowing. "That's what my husband said, too, when he came to Haven. Three years ago."

"What did I say?" a masculine voice asked from behind her.

Sky's smile was quick and warm as she turned her head. "That your stay in Haven was only temporary."

Obviously this was the aforementioned husband, and Sierra couldn't help but think that the counselor had lucked out when she fell in love with the six-foot-tall, dark-haired, hazel-eyed man standing beside her now.

"How was I to know that I would fall in love—with Haven almost as much as you?" he said.

Spoken by another guy, the response might have made Sierra want to gag, but not only did Sky's husband sound absolutely sincere, the way he looked at his wife when he said the words made her heart sigh.

"Well, I have no intention of falling in love with the town—or with you," Sierra said lightly.

Sky laughed. "Jake, this is Sierra Hart—the new ADA. Sierra, my husband—Jake Kelly."

"*Temporary* ADA," Sierra clarified.

Now Jake grinned. "And what do you think of Haven so far?"

"It has its charms," she noted.

"But being able to make a quick stop at the grocery store isn't one of them," he warned.

"So I've discovered."

"For the first few months that Jake was in town, he went to Battle Mountain to buy his groceries so that he wouldn't have to make small talk with the locals," Sky told her.

"Something to consider," Sierra said, only half joking.

"Which completely backfired on him," the other woman continued. "Because that's how he happened upon me, stranded on the side of the road one day."

"And while I don't mind strolling down memory lane now and again, I'm sure the ADA is more interested in finishing her grocery shopping," Jake said.

"You're right," his wife acknowledged. Then to Sierra she said, "I'll bore you with the story over coffee sometime."

"I'll look forward to it," Sierra said, a little surprised to realize that she meant it.

"It was nice to meet you," Jake said, nudging his wife along.

"And both of you."

Sierra watched them make their way down the aisle, walking side by side, so close that their shoulders were almost touching. They seemed completely in sync with one another, like her brother and sister-in-law, and Sierra's heart sighed again, more than a little wistfully, as they disappeared from sight.

Maybe one day she'd be lucky enough to meet someone who looked at her the way Jake looked at Sky and Nick looked at Whitney, but that was a dream she'd put on the back burner for at least the next seven and a half months. The move, the job and swearing off romantic entanglements had all been her choices, and while she didn't have any regrets, she couldn't deny that she yearned for something more.

"Excuse me," a deep voice said, at the same time an arm reached past Sierra to pluck a box of cereal from the shelf.

Not just *any* box but the *last* box of Frosted Flakes.

The very same one that she'd been eyeing.

"Hey," she protested.

The cereal-stealer turned his head. His dark blue gaze locked with hers, and Sierra felt a frisson of awareness shiver down her spine.

Well, *damn*. She certainly hadn't expected *that*.

"Is there a problem?" he asked, sounding completely unconcerned about the possibility there might be.

She swallowed and tightened her grip on the handle of her cart. "Yes, there's a problem," she told him. "You took my Frosted Flakes."

Of course, the bigger problem was that Sierra seemed to be attracted to men who inevitably ended up trampling her heart, and she already knew that this was one she should walk away from—as far and as fast as her legs could carry her.

Unfortunately, her feet seemed glued to the floor and her brain stubbornly determined to battle over a box of breakfast cereal, even as her eyes enjoyed a leisurely perusal of the hottest guy she'd crossed paths with in the fourteen days she'd been in Haven. He had slightly tousled dark blond hair and a squarish jaw covered with golden stubble that, on another man, might have looked scruffy, but definitely worked for this one. He wore a dark brown bomber-style leather jacket, unzipped, over a blue sweatshirt, faded Levi's and brown cowboy boots. His shoulders were broad, his hips narrow, his legs long.

"*Your* Frosted Flakes?" he echoed, clearly amused by her declaration.

She yanked her errant gaze back to his mouthwateringly handsome face. "I was just about to reach for that box of cereal."

"Were you really?" he challenged. "Because you stood in front of it for at least three minutes without making a move to pick it up."

"I doubt it was three minutes," she said indignantly.

"*At least* three minutes," he said again.

"Which still doesn't give you the right to elbow your way past me to take it."

"I said *excuse me*," he reminded her.

As if being polite justified his actions.

"A gentleman would give up the box of cereal," she said, her tone both piqued and prim.

He grinned, and her knees turned to jelly. *Dammit.*

"You're definitely new in town," he decided. "No one from around here would mistake me for a gentleman."

She could see it now, in the devilish glint in those blue eyes. He was a bad boy. The kind a mother warned her daughters about. Not just dangerous but dangerously tempting.

Sierra knew that she should walk away—it was just a box of cereal!—but she decided to give it one last shot.

"You're really not going to give me the cereal?"

"I can't," he said, sounding almost regretful as he shook his head. "But I can give you some advice—add a couple tablespoons of sugar to a bowl of cornflakes."

"Why can't *you* add sugar to a bowl of cornflakes?" she challenged.

"I don't have to." He grinned and held up the box in his hand. "I've got Frosted Flakes."

She scowled, annoyed that his smug arrogance somehow added to his appeal. "I hope your milk is sour."

"That's harsh," he chided. "But the truth is, the cereal isn't for me. I've got company coming tonight and they have very specific breakfast demands."

"*They?*"

She didn't realize she'd spoken aloud until she saw his lips twitch, as if he was fighting against a smile.

"Twins," he said, with a wink.

She shouldn't have been surprised. Men like this one always had women clamoring for their attention, and he was obviously willing to give it—and to more than one at a time.

Rather than continue this pointless conversation, she decided to relinquish her claim to the cereal and move on.

He deliberately stepped into her path as she started to push her cart past him.

"I'd be happy to share the cereal, if you wanted to come over for breakfast. Better yet," he said, with another wink, "you could *stay* for breakfast."

Her gaze narrowed in response to the blatant innuendo even as her hormones stirred with interest. "Aren't you going to be busy with the twins?"

"Tonight and tomorrow, yes," he agreed. "But my schedule's wide open next weekend."

A not-at-all tempting offer, because as much as she had a weakness for bad boys, she had more important things to focus on while she was in Haven. "In your dreams, cowboy."

"I'm not a cowboy," he said, refusing to take the hint. "I'm a lawyer."

"Let me guess—" she zeroed in on the logo emblazoned on the front of his sweatshirt "—Columbia Law?"

"That's right." He pulled a business card out of his pocket and offered it to her.

Deacon Parrish
Attorney at Law
Katelyn Davidson & Associates
355 Page Street
Haven, NV

"In case you ever need a lawyer—" he flashed that devastating smile again "—or breakfast."

"That's not going to happen," she said, ignoring the card in his outstretched hand and steering around him.

"Legal troubles or breakfast?"

He called out the question as she walked away.

Sierra forced herself not to look back.

"Neither."

Chapter Two

Deacon Parrish was a man on a mission—and a very tight schedule. He didn't have time to waste flirting with an attractive stranger in The Trading Post, but there had been something about the stunning brunette in the cereal aisle that had piqued his immediate interest and encouraged him to linger.

Haven wasn't such a small town that everyone knew everyone else, but it was a safe bet that he'd crossed paths with all the other residents at one point or another in his almost twenty-eight years. Which meant that this woman was either a visitor or newcomer, because he'd never seen her before. Maybe it was cliché, but he was certain he would have remembered.

He guessed that she was average height for a woman—but that was the only ordinary thing about her. In deference to the frigid January weather, she'd been wearing a long coat—black wool—and black knee-high boots with a modest heel. Beneath the coat, she wore a slim-fitting skirt the color of ripe cranberries and a matching jacket buttoned over a snowy-white blouse with a deep V neckline.

She was overdressed for grocery shopping, which suggested to Deacon that she'd come from work and led him to speculate as to what profession would require her to work on a Saturday. Real estate was the first thing that came to mind, and he'd heard that The Ruby Realty Team had recently hired a new agent. Perhaps she'd had an open house earlier that afternoon and was now picking up a few essentials on her way home. Or maybe she had a list of ingredients to cook a meal for someone special.

His gaze had automatically gone to the fingers curled around the handle of her shopping cart then. She wore what looked like a college ring on her right hand, but her left hand was bare. There was no sparkling diamond to herald an engagement and no wedding band to indicate a more permanent commitment.

He'd exhaled a grateful sigh of relief. Because Deacon didn't have any particular type when it came to the women he dated—blondes, brunettes, redheads, short, tall, skinny, curvy—but he did have two hard and fast rules when it came to dating. The first was to never make a move on another man's woman.

Once that concern had been alleviated, he'd shifted his attention back to her face, admiring the flawless skin, dark eyes fringed by darker lashes, high cheekbones and glossy pink lips. She was focused on the shelves as if choosing a breakfast cereal was a matter of great internal debate.

Deacon experienced no such indecision. He'd gone into The Trading Post knowing exactly what he was after, but when he reached past her for the familiar blue box with the tiger mascot on the front, he'd somehow started an unexpectedly provocative conversation that seemed to be about a lot more than Frosted Flakes.

Until she'd abruptly shut him down.

Perhaps she would have been more amenable to his flirtation if he'd relinquished the cereal, but that wasn't an option.

Not if he wanted peace in the morning.

And while he knew why *he* needed the cereal, as he made his way toward home, he found himself wondering why *she'd* been after the perennial kids' favorite and acknowledging that the absence of a ring didn't mean the absence of a family. Maybe she had kids at home who would kick and scream when she returned home empty-handed.

And if she had kids, she was off-limits to him. Because that was his second dating rule: no women with children.

It wasn't that he didn't like kids. In fact, he was crazy about his brother's two little girls. But aside from the fact that kids were an inevitable complication in any relationship—and potential collateral damage when a romance didn't work out—he simply wasn't dad material.

Maybe he sometimes wished it wasn't true, but there was simply too much of his own father in him to ever let himself believe otherwise. And yeah, it sucked that he still carried some emotional scars from the man who'd walked out on his family two decades earlier, but he couldn't deny that he did. And he knew that the only way to ensure that his kid never hated him the way he'd hated Dwayne Parrish was to never have a kid—or pretend to be a dad to someone else's.

Because Deacon wasn't the only one who'd been scarred by his dad's "parenting." His half brother Connor had suffered even more, being the preferred target of Dwayne's drunken fury—and deliberately putting himself in front of Deacon on the rare occasions that the man lashed out at his own son.

It was a testament to his brother's character that Connor had managed to turn his life around and not only let go of the past but embrace his future. Or maybe it was a testament to his feelings for the woman he'd married. Whatever the reason, Connor had been able to fall in love and have a family, and perhaps that example should have given Deacon hope that he might someday do the same. But while the brothers had both suffered at the hands of Dwayne Parrish, there was one crucial difference between them—only Deacon carried the man's blood in his veins.

It was a fact he tried not to think about too often, and he pushed it out of his mind now as he turned onto Sherwood Park Drive. As he drew closer to home, he saw the deputy sheriff's personal vehicle parked in his driveway.

Damn, he was late.

He'd no sooner pulled up alongside the curb and

shifted his Jeep into Park when the back door of his brother's truck flew open and two little girls spilled out.

"Unca Dunca! Unca Dunca!" They raced toward him, blue eyes sparkling and wide smiles on their faces.

He set the bag from the grocery store on the hood of his SUV and crouched to catch the twins in his arms.

"Can we build a snowman?" Piper asked.

"Can we have hot choc'ate?" Poppy wanted to know.

"Can we watch a movie?"

"Can we have p'za?"

"Can we—"

"Can you give Uncle Deacon a minute to catch his breath?" the girls' dad interjected to suggest dryly.

"I'm good," Deacon said, rising to his feet with a smile on his face and a child propped on each hip—a more cumbersome task than usual as both girls were bundled up in snowsuits and winter boots.

"You're late," his brother admonished.

"Three minutes," he guesstimated.

The same amount of time he'd stood watching the stranger contemplate her cereal options.

Piper and Poppy lavished him with hugs and kisses then wriggled to be set down again. Deacon obliged, and they immediately threw themselves onto the snow-covered ground and began making snow angels.

"Two more minutes and I might not have had time to come in for a cup of the hot chocolate that you're going to make for the girls," Connor remarked.

"I don't know that Regan would approve of them having hot chocolate before dinner," Deacon said, picking up the grocery bag again and fishing his keys out of his jacket pocket.

"Which is why they love coming to Uncle Deacon's house—because he doesn't follow Mommy's rules."

"I follow some of them," he protested. "But not so many that I risk losing my 'Fun Uncle' title."

"It's not as if you've got a lot of competition," Connor noted. "Both of Regan's brothers have kids of their own, so they understand the importance of rules."

Deacon unlocked the door and called for Piper and Poppy to come inside as he exchanged keys with his brother. He helped out with the girls often enough that he and Connor had long ago discovered it was easier to swap vehicles than transfer car seats.

"But we're makin' snow angels, Unca Dunca," Piper said.

"Well, I'm going to be making hot chocolate," he said.

Apparently those were the magic words, because both girls jumped to their feet and hurried—as much as they could hurry in their heavy boots and bulky outerwear—toward the door.

"With whipped cweam?"

"An' spwin-kohs?"

"Snowsuits and boots off right here," Connor reminded his daughters as they pushed into the foyer.

They dutifully started yanking on zippers and tugging at Velcro fastenings to reveal fuzzy sweaters and printed leggings.

"Then can we watch *Fwozen*?" Piper asked, kicking off her boots.

"I wanna watch *'canto*," Poppy said.

"How about *Frozen* today and *Encanto* tomorrow?" Deacon suggested as a compromise.

"Okay," Piper said.

"'Kay," Poppy agreed.

"That's a lot of screen time," Connor noted, as the girls scampered off to the living room.

"Don't worry," Deacon said. "I've also got sharp knives and matches to keep them busy."

His brother slid him a look.

"Okay, we'll stick with coloring pages, building blocks and modeling clay."

"They've got some toys and books in their backpacks, too," Connor said, as he followed Deacon to the kitchen. "Which reminds me—Regan asked me to remind you to make sure they brush their teeth *before* story time, in case they fall asleep while you're reading."

"I know the drill," he assured his brother.

"And bedtime is eight o'clock. Actually, it's seven o'clock at home, but eight o'clock is okay for a sleepover. But no later than eight," Connor cautioned, "or they'll be cranky all day tomorrow."

Deacon set a pot on the stove, filled it with milk. "This isn't my first sleepover—or theirs."

"I know, but Regan likes to remind me to remind you."

"And what are your plans for tonight?" he asked.

"I've got a table booked at The Home Station for dinner and dessert at home from Sweet Caroline's for after."

"What's the occasion?" Deacon asked curiously.

"Does there need to be an occasion for me to take my wife out for a romantic meal?" his brother challenged.

"Maybe not," he allowed. "But I'm getting the feeling there's something you're not telling me."

"Regan and I are thinking about having another baby," Connor finally confided.

"Because Piper and Poppy don't keep you busy enough?"

"Because we love our life with the girls and we've got a lot more love to go around."

"Do you really work in law enforcement?" Deacon wondered aloud. "Because it should be illegal for someone who carries a gun in his job to say something so sappy."

Connor shrugged, clearly unoffended by his remark. "Talk to me after you've had a child with the woman you love."

"That will be...never," Deacon said, reaching into the cupboard above the stove for the hot chocolate mix.

"Never say never," his brother warned.

Then Connor's gaze zeroed in on the old-fashioned glass canister, with the hand-printed label that identified it as *Hot Chocolate* in a decidedly feminine script, as if it was evidence at a crime scene.

"What kind of hot chocolate is that?"

Deacon measured out the mix in accordance with the (also hand-printed) directions on the back of the container and whisked it into the milk. "The same kind you get at Sweet Caroline's."

His brother's jaw dropped. "Who gave you the recipe?"

"No one gave me the recipe. According to Annalise, it's a proprietary mixture. But I did sweet-talk her into letting me buy some of it."

"You mean you slept with the Sweet Caroline's barista?" Connor guessed.

Deacon couldn't prevent the smile that curved his lips. "Not for the hot chocolate."

"How long has this been going on?"

"It's not going on," he said. "We went out for a few weeks and then things fizzled out."

"Have you ever gone out with a woman longer than a few weeks?" his brother wondered.

"Sure." He poured cold milk into two plastic mugs, filling them halfway, then topped them off with the hot chocolate.

"Have you ever thought that any of those women was the one?"

"Every one of them was the one—at least in the moment," he said easily.

"Are you trying to be an ass or does it come naturally?" Connor wondered aloud.

"It comes naturally," Deacon said, with a grin. "But if you're asking if I ever thought one of them might be someone with whom I want to spend the rest of my life, I'd have to say *no*, because I don't see my future following the same path as yours."

"You don't want to get married and have a family?"

"I don't see it happening," Deacon said again.

"Which isn't actually what I asked," his brother noted.

Deacon popped his head into the living room. "Who wants whipped cream on their hot cocoa?"

"I do!"

"I do!"

Two pairs of feet pounded as his excited nieces dashed into the kitchen, clamoring for their treat.

"I'm glad you're going to be dealing with the sugar rush and not me," Connor muttered.

"Is that your way of saying you don't want whipped cream?"

"Of course I want whipped cream."

He grinned and filled two ceramic mugs with the steaming liquid, then topped all four drinks with a generous heap of whipped cream and a sprinkle of chocolate shavings.

"You make the best hot choc'ate, Unca Dunca."

His heart melted like the cream on top of his hot drink.

Still, he felt compelled to remind her, "It's Deacon, Pop. Uncle *Deacon*."

She wrinkled her nose. "But that does'n rhyme."

Connor chuckled.

Deacon sighed. "I'm going to be Unca Dunca forever, aren't I?"

"Probably not forever," his brother said. "But at least another few years."

Chapter Three

Living in northern Nevada was taking some getting used to, Sierra acknowledged, as she tugged the fleece-lined hat over her ears and stuffed her hands into matching gloves. Then she opened the door to step outside and sucked in a shocked breath.

When she'd told her brother that she was taking a job in Haven for six months—starting in January—he'd warned her that it would be cold. Sierra hadn't been concerned. No one had ever accused her of being a shrinking violet.

But right now, she felt like a frozen violet—and she'd only been outside for fifteen seconds.

A quiet whimper escaped her as she thought longingly of the twenty-four-hour gym in the basement of her apartment building in Las Vegas.

Former apartment building, she reminded herself.

She'd vacated the premises at the same time she'd walked away from her eighteen-month relationship with Eric Stikeman. She still missed the spacious two bedroom with the floor-to-ceiling windows and mountain view. Eric…not so much.

In any event, when she'd agreed to take the job in the Haven DA's office, she'd been hopeful that she might find similar accommodations here. Those hopes had quickly been dashed.

The good news was that she'd found a fully furnished townhouse in a newer development. Unfortunately, the furnishings hadn't included a treadmill.

The real estate agent had told her that there was a gym at the community center, but Sierra was reluctant to commit to a membership, not knowing how often she'd use it when her only goal was "moderate" daily physical activity. But the gym also offered yoga classes, and her friend Aubrey had frequently remarked that Sierra should take up yoga to help her relax.

Former friend, she amended.

And a reason for some of her current tension, as well as more evidence that she was a lousy judge of character—at least when it came to her personal interactions.

So for now, Sierra had decided that morning walks would provide not only exercise but also the opportunity to explore the area and maybe even meet some of her neighbors.

Apparently the locals were a hearty breed, as she crossed paths with more than a few residents out walking their dogs, spotted a couple others up on ladders taking down holiday decorations and observed several children playing in the snow.

But if she was going to continue walking in frigid weather, she was going to need a warmer pair of boots. And a thicker coat. And probably some thermal underwear, too.

On second thought, a gym membership might be cheaper.

She exchanged greetings with a man holding a leash attached to an Old English sheepdog and considered the benefits of a canine companion. It would be nice to have company, she mused, not only on her daily walks but at home.

But as appealing as the idea was for now, she was only going to be in Haven for six months. After her contract with the DA's office was finished, she'd be going back to Las Vegas, where she no longer had an apartment. Which meant that she'd be staying with her brother and sister-in-law until she could find a place of her own—which she wouldn't be able to do until she found a new job—and Whitney was allergic to dogs.

She paused on the sidewalk near where two little girls were building a snowman—or trying to with the limited amount of snow on the ground. Because the air might be frigid, but it was still desert, and snow was as scarce in the winter as rain was in the summer. Still, they'd managed to put one modest-sized ball of snow on top of a slightly bigger ball of snow.

Sierra didn't have a lot of experience with kids, but one of the partners at Bane had a four-year-old grandson who sometimes came into the office and these girls looked to be a similar age. One was dressed in a pink snowsuit with blue boots, the other wore a purple snowsuit and orange boots.

Twins, she guessed, and shuddered at the possibility of heightened nausea and vomiting, which she'd read could be experienced by women carrying multiple babies.

The girl in pink took the knitted hat off her own head to set it on the snowman.

"Now your scarf," she said to her sister.

The girl in purple dutifully began to tug at the knot by her throat.

"That's a nice snowman you've got there," Sierra said.

Both girls beamed with pleasure.

"He needs a scarf," Pink said.

"Can you help me wif it?" Purple asked, still tugging on her scarf.

"I don't know that your mom would want you dressing up your snowman in your accessories," Sierra said.

"It's okay," Pink told her. "Mommy's not here."

Sierra wasn't sure how to respond to that and was relieved when the front door opened and a man walked out.

Relieved, that is, until she recognized him as the thief of her Frosted Flakes.

"Here we are," Deacon said, his attention on the two girls. "Mini Oreos for the eyes and mouth and a baby carrot for the nose."

Then he spotted Sierra on the sidewalk. Their gazes locked.

"Oh," he said, obviously as surprised to see her as she was to see him. "Hi."

"Hi," she said back.

"She wikes our snowman," Pink chimed in.

"Well, of course she likes your snowman," Deacon agreed. "He's very handsome. Or he will be when you give him a face."

The girls took the proffered items and returned to their snowman-in-progress.

"Did you change your mind about needing a lawyer?" he asked Sierra.

She shook her head. "I was just out for a walk."

"You live around here?" he asked.

"A couple blocks over."

"I guess that makes us neighbors, sort of."

"Sort of," she agreed, before shifting her attention back to the little girls who were now stuffing mini Oreos in their mouths. "Your daughters are adorable."

"They're not mine," he said, shaking his head to emphasize the point. "They're my brother's kids."

"So...your nieces?"

Now he nodded.

She looked from one child to the other, noting their similar heights and features.

"Twins?" she guessed.

He nodded again. "Double Trouble, I call them."

The girls giggled at the obviously familiar nickname.

"We need mo' cookies," Purple said.

He glanced over, sighed. "You were supposed to use them to make the snowman's mouth, not put them in *your* mouths."

That remark earned another round of giggles.

"You know where the cookies are," Deacon told them. "You can go get one more package, but that's all."

They raced toward the door.

"I get the carrot," she said. "But why mini Oreos?"

"Because I'm all out of lumps of coal."

"None left in your Christmas stocking?"

His lips twitched at the corners. "Is it so hard to believe that I might have been on Santa's 'nice' list?"

"Were you?"

"I can be naughty or nice, depending on the situation," he told her.

And suddenly their conversation was inching toward potentially dangerous territory again, the air between them charged with electricity.

Deciding that a change of topic was in order, she asked, "Did your nieces enjoy their Frosted Flakes for breakfast?"

"They always do," he said.

She should have left it at that, but she felt the teensiest bit uneasy thinking that she might have judged him not only too quickly but also unfairly.

"So why did you let me think that you would be spending the night with two women?" she asked him.

"Is that what you were thinking?"

She narrowed her gaze. "You know it was. You *winked*."

"And somehow you interpreted that as code for a threesome?"

She huffed out a breath. "I don't even know why we're having this conversation. It doesn't matter."

"Maybe it does," he countered. "Maybe I want to know why you'd assume a casual mention of breakfast with twins meant a night with two women."

"It was the wink," she said again.

"Or was it the fact that you looked at me and wanted me and guessed that most other women do, too?"

"What I guessed is that you'd be as obnoxious as you are arrogant—and I was right."

"Here's an idea," he said, seemingly unfazed by her retort. "Why don't we talk about my character flaws over dinner?"

"Because I don't date players."

"And, after two very brief conversations, you think you've got me all figured out, don't you?" he challenged.

She shrugged. "Some people aren't very complicated."

"Are you always so quick to rush to judgment?"

No, she wasn't. But she was apparently quick to judge *him*, and that was something she'd have to give some consideration to on her own time.

For now, she simply said, "Goodbye, Mr. Columbia Law."

"It's Deacon," he reminded her. "And you haven't given me your number. Or even your name."

"Not an oversight," she told him.

She was right.

He'd acted like a dick, and she'd called him on it.

Well, she'd accused him of being arrogant and obnoxious, which was essentially the same thing. And not a completely inaccurate characterization of his behavior, Deacon acknowledged, if only to himself.

He was usually much smoother in his interactions with the opposite sex. But there was something about the cool reserve of the woman—who still hadn't even told him her name—that made him want to elicit a reaction.

He'd at least succeeded in that, even if the reaction wasn't quite what he'd hoped for. But as his high school baseball coach used to say, if you're going to go down, go down swinging.

"We got the cookies," Piper announced, running toward him, her sister close on her heels.

He imagined the snow they'd tracked inside melting on his hardwood floors but decided that he'd wipe it up later. Now he helped the girls put the finishing touches on their creation, took some pictures of them posing beside it and sent the photos to his brother and sister-in-law.

They both immediately responded to his text with heart emojis, then Regan sent another message:

We'll be there to pick them up in about an hour.

Make it 2 hours, he suggested. We haven't watched *Encanto* yet.

2 hours, she confirmed. And thank you again. xo.

"Okay, girls—take your hat and scarf off the snowman now so we don't forget them out here," he instructed.

"But he'll get cold," Poppy protested.

"He's a snowman," Deacon said. "If he wasn't cold, he'd melt."

"Like Fwosty," Piper said, nodding sagely.

"I don't want him to melt," Poppy said worriedly.

"I don't think you have to worry about him melting anytime soon," Deacon said.

It was far more likely that the snowman would meet his end courtesy of the seven-year-old bully who lived three doors down and already had a reputation for kicking over and stomping on the neighborhood snow people. Not that he was going to tell his nieces that.

"And even when he does eventually melt, it just means that you can look forward to building him again when the snow comes back," he said instead.

"Can we watch *'canto* now?" Poppy asked.

"First, we need to pack up your stuff, so you're ready to go when your mom and dad come to get you, then we can watch *Encanto*."

"Can we have popco'n with the movie?" Piper wanted to know.

"An' Wed Vines?"

"You ate all my Red Vines last night," he reminded them. "But yes, we can have popcorn."

While the girls hung up their snowsuits, he wiped up the melted snow on the floor, then together they gathered up pj's, toothbrushes, books and toys before carrying their backpacks downstairs and settling in front of the television to watch the movie.

He adored the two little girls and was always happy to spend time with him. Of course, he would have been even happier if his brother hadn't confided that his babysitting services were being utilized so that the twins' parents could focus on making another baby.

Not that Deacon objected to his brother having an intimate relationship with his wife—because wasn't

that supposed to be one of the benefits of marriage?—
he just didn't want to hear about it. Especially when he
was achingly aware that it had been far too long since
he'd enjoyed any action between the sheets.

His own fault, Deacon knew. He'd had a good thing
going with Mariah Traynor for almost six months—
or they'd had some pretty good chemistry, anyway.
But it turned out that they didn't have much in com-
mon beyond that. He was a Dodgers fan; she couldn't
stand baseball. He cheered for the 49ers; she abhorred
football. He enjoyed watching the Golden Knights; she
didn't even know that Vegas had a hockey team.

Now, of course, he was kicking himself for ruining a
good thing—or at least a sure thing. Because since then,
he'd discovered that one really was the loneliest number.

And if Mariah wasn't the type of woman that he
could envision spending the rest of his life with, maybe
that was because he couldn't envision spending the rest
of his life with any one woman.

Never say never.

The problem was, Haven wasn't exactly overflow-
ing with single women.

Or maybe the real problem was that he'd already
dated most of them—way back in high school when he'd
been looking for love (or at least sex) in all the wrong
places. And if he hadn't found love, he'd at least discovered the pleasures of physical intimacy. There had
been plenty of girls willing to share those pleasures
with him—and others who'd looked at him with obvious disdain, who'd snickered in the hallways when he

walked by and whispered (not very quietly) about Faith-less Faith Parrish's youngest son.

With his brother's words still echoing in his head, and Piper and Poppy singing about not talking about Bruno, Deacon went into the kitchen to make the kids' snack.

He tossed some mini marshmallows and M&M's in with the hot corn when it was popped, and Piper and Poppy immediately declared it was "the best popco'n ev-uh."

Of course, they weren't quite four, so he didn't put much stock in their use of the superlative. Case in point, they also claimed that he read "the best sto-wees," gave "the best hugs" and was, overall, "the best unca."

While he appreciated their enthusiastic endorsement, he was painfully aware of his own shortcomings. And he was definitely not looking forward to the day that they learned the truth about him.

Because he wasn't the best anything—he'd found that out long ago. But he was determined to be better than his beginnings.

Chapter Four

Sierra bought a pair of waterproof boots with a minus-forty-degree cold rating and a down-filled hooded coat so that she could continue to walk every morning, no matter the weather. She continued to explore the neighborhood in various directions, and if she avoided Sherwood Park Drive—where she now knew Deacon Parrish lived—that was simply because she wanted to discover new paths.

Unfortunately, not seeing him didn't stop her from thinking about him—and then she ended up annoyed with herself for thinking about him.

Damn hormones.

At least at work her mind was too busy to wander in his direction. And by the end of her third week on the job, Sierra felt more and more confident that the move to Haven—albeit temporary—had been the right move for her. Even if her brother and sister-in-law remained unconvinced.

Of course, they didn't know all the reasons that she'd chosen to leave Bane & Associates, and she had no intention of telling them. As a result, Nick worried that she was being impulsive, and while Whitney tried to be supportive, her sister-in-law wasn't happy that Sierra had decided to move so far away, especially now.

She understood why they wanted to keep her close, but she'd needed some distance from the mistakes she'd made. And while she knew she'd miss her family—and she did—Haven wasn't so far from Vegas that she couldn't go back to visit during the six months of her contract. She was also hopeful that Nick and Whitney would come to see her, when their schedules allowed, as her townhouse had plenty of room for guests.

For now though, she refocused her attention on proofreading the pretrial memo she'd drafted for her boss, then clicked the print icon on the screen and leaned back in her chair.

Her lips curved a little as she glanced around at the four walls that comprised her office. It was a small thing, the fact that she had an office—and it was a small office—but it was a big step up from the cubicle that she'd spent sixty hours a week in for the past three years. Not only four walls but also a door that closed, to afford her privacy for confidential phone calls or meetings with colleagues, and even a trio of windows with a view of the courthouse across the street.

A sharp rap of knuckles on the open door drew her

attention back to the present as her boss stepped into the room carrying a file box.

She retrieved the pages she'd printed and stapled them together as Brett dropped the box on her desk. "What's that?"

"The Dornan file."

Sierra had taken careful notes when he'd briefed his staff on upcoming cases, so she immediately recognized the name. "The fraud case?"

He nodded.

"You want me to write up a sentencing memo?" she guessed, recalling that he'd mentioned he was working on a plea deal with Rhonda Dornan's defense attorney.

Now he shook his head. "She turned down the deal her counsel negotiated and got a new lawyer. She wants to go to trial."

"So what is it that you want me to do?" Sierra wondered aloud.

"Prep for the trial."

She felt a frisson of excitement shimmer through her. She'd been one of the most junior associates at Bane, hired right out of law school, so she wasn't surprised that she had to start out researching case law and drafting arguments for other lawyers to present in court. But almost three years later, she'd been inside a courtroom only a handful of times, and most often only to deliver documents to one of the partners.

"You want me to assist?" she asked cautiously, unwilling to get her hopes up.

"No," Brett said. "I want you to take the lead on this one."

She swallowed. "The lead?"

"Trial starts on Monday," he told her. "And I'm on vacation next week."

She remembered him mentioning that, too, but she hadn't expected the vacation to actually happen. At Bane, she'd known several colleagues who'd booked holidays only to cancel them when something came up at the office that required their attention. Because the work always came first, and any associate who wanted to move up the ranks had to demonstrate that nothing was more important than the job.

Sierra had never had to cancel a trip, because she hadn't been foolish enough to make plans to go away. But she'd bailed on outings with her friends more times than she liked to admit and had even stood up the occasional date when one of the partners dropped something on her desk at the eleventh hour.

"Disneyland," Brett said now, returning to the topic of his vacation with a shake of his head. "What was I thinking?"

Sierra smiled. "You were probably thinking that your kids will love it."

He had three sons, ages ten, seven and five, with his wife of almost fifteen years. A photo taken at their wedding was prominently displayed on his desk alongside another of Jenny and the boys, and he wore a chunky band on the third finger of his left hand. Brett Ryckell was a man devoted to his family and proud to let everyone know it.

"Have you been to Disneyland?" he asked her now.

"Once," she said. "A long time ago."

Before her parents had died and her life had been turned completely upside down.

"Any words of advice?" he asked.

"Take lots of pictures."

"I can do that," he said, as he started for the door.

She lifted the lid of the box, eager to dig into the files.

He turned and gave her a gently admonishing look. "It's almost six o'clock, Sierra."

"Yes, sir," she said, not sure what point her boss was trying to make in mentioning the time.

"Go home," he said.

"But…it's not even six o'clock."

"The contents of the box aren't going to change overnight," he pointed out. "You'll have plenty of time to familiarize yourself with the case before Monday."

"Yes, sir," she said again, reluctantly replacing the lid.

"Don't misunderstand me," Brett said. "I appreciate your enthusiasm, but I don't want you to burn yourself out before you've been on the job a month."

"I don't think there's any danger of that."

"Still, you should take some time for yourself, go out with friends."

"I haven't been here long enough to make friends," she said, even as she thought fleetingly of the woman she'd met in the grocery store the previous weekend. But despite Sky's suggestion that they should get together for coffee sometime, Sierra had yet to hear from her.

"Then you should go out and make some."

She managed a smile. "I'll work on it."

Truthfully, though, she didn't see the point in making friends when she was only going to be in town for six months. That was the length of the contract she'd been offered, temporarily filling in for ADA Jade Scott who was on maternity leave for the same period of time. And even if Jade decided that she wasn't ready to come back at the end of six months, Sierra wasn't in any position to stay in Haven beyond that.

She left the office with the file box and made her way to Jo's Pizza.

She'd heard nothing but good things about the place since her arrival in town, and she figured it was time to try the infamous pie for herself.

Jo's had a front entrance with a sign over the door that said Restaurant and a side entrance designated as Takeout. Sierra opened the Takeout door and stepped inside, her stomach growling hungrily as she breathed in the scents of garlic, oregano and tomato sauce. If the pizza tasted half as good as the restaurant smelled, then Jo's would undoubtedly live up to its lofty reputation.

She turned toward the take-out counter and stopped mid-stride, because wasn't it just her luck that Deacon Parrish was there, flirting with a pretty blonde working on the other side of the counter?

Deacon needed to get a life.

Instead, it was six thirty on a Friday night and he was picking up pizza.

A single medium pizza that he would take home to eat by himself.

Even Lucy, daughter of the infamous Jo, had teased him about his lack of plans as she'd taken his order.

And she was right—he was an old man at twenty-eight.

Well, almost twenty-eight, but that clarification didn't make him feel much better about the fact that it was a Friday night and he had no plans.

Worse, he didn't want any plans.

He sincerely wanted nothing more than to go home, put his feet up on the coffee table—because it was his house and his coffee table, and there was no one to tell him to get his feet off the table—and eat his dinner while watching the hockey game on TV.

Well, there was maybe one thing that he wanted more—and wasn't it a happy coincidence that she'd walked through the door just as his pizza came out from the kitchen?

"Who's that?" Lucy asked curiously, having followed the direction of his gaze.

"I was hoping you could tell me."

She shook her head. "I can't say that I've ever seen her before."

"But you're about to get her name and number," he mused. "And if you happened to leave her order slip right here on the counter for your ninth grade lab partner to take a peek at—"

"No," Lucy said bluntly. "You want someone to help you get a date? Join match-dot-com."

"Come on, Luce."

"No," she said again.

The phone rang just as his not-quite-neighbor approached the counter.

"I'll be right with you," Lucy told her, before snatching up the receiver.

"Hello, again," Deacon said, grinning.

"Hi," she replied, with a distinct lack of enthusiasm.

"Long day for you?" he asked.

She shrugged. "No longer than usual."

"I thought winter was generally slow season in the real estate market," he said, determined to engage her in conversation and at least learn her name.

"Sorry," she said, sounding more dismissive than regretful. "I don't know anything about the real estate market."

"You don't work at Ruby Realty?"

She seemed taken aback by the question. "What made you think that I did?"

He gestured to her attire. "The red jacket is part of their signature outfit."

"My jacket isn't red, it's cranberry."

Which is exactly what he'd thought the first time he saw her wearing it. "Isn't cranberry just a more specific shade of red?"

"I have a question for you," she said, declining to answer his. "If I was wearing a green jacket, would you assume I'd won it at the Masters?"

"Probably not, as women don't currently compete at the Masters."

"Touché."

"So you don't work in real estate, but you are new in town," he mused.

"Is that a statement or a question?"

"A statement."

"Because you know everyone in town?" she guessed.

"Maybe not by name," he acknowledged. "But I'm sure if I'd ever met you and known yours, I would have remembered."

She narrowed her gaze on him. "Are you capable of having a conversation with a woman without flirting with her?"

"I am," he assured her with a wink. "But flirting is so much more fun than regular conversation."

"Can I give you a word of advice?"

"I'm all ears."

"Save your flirtatious charm for someone who might be interested, because I'm not."

"Ouch," he said.

"You don't look particularly wounded," she noted.

"Because I know you're lying."

"I'm not lying," she said.

"You don't want to be interested," he said. "But the flush of color in your cheeks suggests that you are."

"Which can also be a physiological response to irritation."

"Can be," he agreed. "But in this case, I'd bet that it's indicative of attraction."

She rolled her eyes. "Apparently you're someone who likes throwing his money away."

"Okay, let's forget any kind of wager and instead grab a table so that we can share our pizzas and conversation," he suggested as an alternative.

"No, thanks."

"You've got that down to a fine art, don't you?"

"What?" she asked, with obvious reluctance.

"The affected disinterest and casual brush-off."

"I'm not trying to hurt your feelings," she said. "But I'm really not looking for any kind of romantic entanglement."

"What kind of entanglement are you looking for?"

"None," she told him.

But there had been a slight hesitation before her response—as if she regretted turning down the offer.

Interesting.

Lucy finally finished on the phone and returned to the counter. "Sorry about that," she said to his neighbor. "Are you here to order or pick up?"

Deacon effected a casual pose against the counter, as if he wasn't listening for her to give her name.

"Pick up," she said. "Medium pizza for—"

"Deacon Parrish!"

The excited squeal drowned out the rest of what she said, and he barely had a chance to turn his head to identify the source before a woman threw herself at him—so hard she nearly cracked his ribs. Soft breasts pressed against his chest and teased blond hair tickled his nose, but it was the cloud of Viva La Juicy perfume that took him back to tenth grade, which was, coincidentally, when he'd lost his virginity with Liberty Mosley.

"Oh. My. God." Liberty drew back a little to smile at him. "I can't believe it's you." She pressed her red-painted lips to his. "I haven't seen you in…forever."

"It's been a few years," he acknowledged, sliding a cautious glance at his neighbor.

"Last time I saw you, you were just heading off to law school," Liberty recalled, oblivious to the fact— or maybe not caring—that she might have interrupted something. "And now you're a big shot lawyer."

"Well, the lawyer part is right, anyway," he acknowledged.

"Where was it you went? Somewhere in New York, right? Harvard?"

"Harvard's in Massachusetts," he told her.

Her brows drew together. "I was sure your brother said you'd gone to New York City."

"I did," he confirmed. "Columbia."

"Wouldn't want to miss an opportunity to slip *that* into the conversation," he heard his neighbor mutter under her breath.

Before Deacon could respond, Liberty linked her arm through his and tipped her head against his shoulder. "Obviously we've got a lot to catch up on—why don't we order a pizza and take it up to Lookout Point?"

"For starters, because it's about ten degrees outside."

"I'm sure we can figure out a way to stay warm." The statement was accompanied by a smile that promised a lot more than conversation.

"Also, because your husband would likely object to that plan."

"I'm not married yet," she pointed out. "And anyway, Travis is out of town this weekend with his buddies— his last weekend of freedom, he called it, so I figure it should be my last weekend of freedom, too."

"And finally, because I've already got a pizza—"

Deacon continued, gesturing to the box on the counter "—and other plans for tonight."

And while Deacon had some very fond memories of Liberty, he wasn't interested in revisiting their history—and even less interested in hooking up with a woman who would be exchanging vows with another man in the near future.

She pouted prettily, but Deacon's attention was on the sexy brunette who was staring at the screen of her phone, pretending not to eavesdrop on his conversation.

Or maybe she really wasn't.

"How about tomorrow, then?" Liberty suggested hopefully, toying with the zipper of his jacket.

Out of the corner of his eye, Deacon saw Lucy return from the back with another pizza box. She set it on the counter and rang up the order. His neighbor paid for her food, picked up the box and headed for the door.

"No." His tone was firm and final. "It was nice to see you, Liberty. And congrats on your upcoming wedding, but I have to run."

"Deacon—wait!"

It was Lucy who called to him this time, and he turned with his hand on the door.

She gestured to the box on the counter. "Don't you want your pizza?"

Of course he wanted his pizza.

And by the time he raced back to the counter to grab the box and rush out the door again, his neighbor was already gone.

#2995 A MAVERICK REBORN
Montana Mavericks: Lassoing Love • by Melissa Senate
Handsome loner cowboy Bobby Stone has his issues—from faking his own death three years ago to discovering a twin brother he never knew. But headstrong rodeo queen Tori Hawkins is just the woman to break through his tough facade. First with a rambunctious fling...and later with the healing love Bobby's always needed...

#2996 RANCHER TO THE RESCUE
Men of the West • by Stella Bagwell
Mack Barlow may have broken Dr. Grace Hollister's heart in high school, but sparks still fly when the now-single father walks into her medical clinic. His young daughter is adorable. And he's...too dang sexy by far! Can a very busy divorced mom take a second chance on loving the man who once left her behind?

#2997 OLD DOGS, NEW TRUTHS
Sierra's Web • by Tara Taylor Quinn
When heiress Lindsay Warren-Smythe assumes a false identity to meet her biological father, she's not expecting to develop a connection with her new coworker, Cole Bennet, and his lovable dog. Cole has learned the hard way not to trust beautiful liars with his heart, so when he lets his guard down with Lindsay, will her lies tear them apart?

#2998 MATCHMAKER ON THE RANCH
Forever, Texas • by Marie Ferrarella
Rancher Chris Parnell has known Rosemary Robinson all his life. But working side by side with the beautiful vet to diagnose the sickness affecting his cattle kicks him completely out of his friend zone! Roe can't deny the attraction sizzling between them. But will her friend with benefits stick around once the cattle mystery is solved?

#2999 HER YOUNGER MAN
Sutton's Place • by Shannon Stacey
Widow Laura Thompson falling for a younger man? Not on your life! Except Riley Thompson is so dang charming. And handsome. And everything Laura's missing in her life. The town seems to be against their romance. Including Riley's boss...who's Laura's son! Are Riley and Laura strong enough to take a stand for love?

#3000 IN TOO DEEP
Love at Hideaway Wharf • by Laurel Greer
Chef Kellan Murphy is determined to fulfill his sister's dying wish. But placing an ocean-fearing man in a scuba diving class is ridiculous! Instructor Sam Walker can't resist helping the handsome wannabe diver overcome his fears. And their unexpected connection is the perfect remedy for Sam's own hidden pain...

Get 3 FREE REWARDS!

We'll send you 2 FREE Books plus a FREE Mystery Gift.

FREE Value Over $20

Both the **Harlequin® Special Edition** and **Harlequin® Heartwarming™** series feature compelling novels filled with stories of love and strength where the bonds of friendship, family and community unite.

YES! Please send me 2 FREE novels from the Harlequin Special Edition or Harlequin Heartwarming series and my FREE Gift (gift is worth about $10 retail). After receiving them, if I don't wish to receive any more books, I can return the shipping statement marked "cancel." If I don't cancel, I will receive 6 brand-new Harlequin Special Edition books every month and be billed just $5.49 each in the U.S. or $6.24 each in Canada, a savings of at least 12% off the cover price, or 4 brand-new Harlequin Heartwarming Larger-Print books every month and be billed just $6.24 each in the U.S. or $6.74 each in Canada, a savings of at least 19% off the cover price. It's quite a bargain! Shipping and handling is just 50¢ per book in the U.S. and $1.25 per book in Canada.* I understand that accepting the 2 free books and gift places me under no obligation to buy anything. I can always return a shipment and cancel at any time by calling the number below. The free books and gift are mine to keep no matter what I decide.

Choose one: ☐ **Harlequin Special Edition** (235/335 BPA GRMK)   ☐ **Harlequin Heartwarming Larger-Print** (161/361 BPA GRMK)   ☐ **Or Try Both!** (235/335 & 161/361 BPA GRPZ)

Name (please print)

Address   Apt. #

City   State/Province   Zip/Postal Code

Email: Please check this box ☐ if you would like to receive newsletters and promotional emails from Harlequin Enterprises ULC and its affiliates. You can unsubscribe anytime.

Mail to the **Harlequin Reader Service:**
IN U.S.A.: P.O. Box 1341, Buffalo, NY 14240-8531
IN CANADA: P.O. Box 603, Fort Erie, Ontario L2A 5X3

Want to try 2 free books from another series? Call 1-800-873-8635 or visit www.ReaderService.com.

---

*Terms and prices subject to change without notice. Prices do not include sales taxes, which will be charged (if applicable) based on your state or country of residence. Canadian residents will be charged applicable taxes. Offer not valid in Quebec. This offer is limited to one order per household. Books received may not be as shown. Not valid for current subscribers to the Harlequin Special Edition or Harlequin Heartwarming series. All orders subject to approval. Credit or debit balances in a customer's account(s) may be offset by any other outstanding balance owed by or to the customer. Please allow 4 to 6 weeks for delivery. Offer available while quantities last.

Your Privacy—Your information is being collected by Harlequin Enterprises ULC, operating as Harlequin Reader Service. For a complete summary of the information we collect, how we use this information and to whom it is disclosed, please visit our privacy notice located at corporate.harlequin.com/privacy-notice. From time to time we may also exchange your personal information with reputable third parties. If you wish to opt out of this sharing of your personal information, please visit readerservice.com/consumerchoice or call 1-800-873-8635. **Notice to California Residents**—Under California law, you have specific rights to control and access your data. For more information on these rights and how to exercise them, visit corporate.harlequin.com/california-privacy.

HSEHW23

HARLEQUIN
PLUS

Try the best multimedia
subscription service for romance
readers like you!

Read, Watch and Play.

Experience the easiest way to get
the romance content you crave.

Start your **FREE TRIAL** at
<u>www.harlequinplus.com/freetrial</u>.